The ART of
PERSUASION

Susan Midalia grew up in the Western Australian wheatbelt and has lived in Perth for most of her adult life. She is the author of three collections of short stories, all shortlisted for major literary awards: *A History of the Beanbag, An Unknown Sky,* and *Feet to the Stars.* She retired from teaching in 2007 to become a full-time writer and freelance editor. *The Art of Persuasion* is her first novel.

The ART of PERSUASION

SUSAN MIDALIA

 FREMANTLE PRESS

To Dan, again,
of course.

Passing the time

Hazel peered through the window of their flat, watching out for Beth. She'd be easy to spot in her striped yellow dress and pink floppy hat, the one she always wore to protect her very fair skin. *Alabaster*, she insisted, her only compensation for having curly red hair. But there was nothing to see except masses of cars and hulking trucks clogging up the four-lane highway. There'd been talk of turning it into six—or was it eight?—to accommodate all the commuters, who were not so much attached to their cars as riveted to the metal. More roads would mean even more noise, congestion and toxic fumes: an evil incantation for her hometown city. Perth. It might have more cars per capita than most other cities in the world, but it was a great place to bring up children, according to her mother: lots of sunshine, beautiful beaches, a relatively low crime rate. Which was great if you wanted to bring up children. Hazel turned to face the room, tried to feel grateful for the glossy jarrah floorboards, high ceilings and art deco cornices that almost made up for the dodgy plumbing, peeling paint and cockroach visitations. Tried to give thanks for a landlord who wasn't lordly and had even changed a light bulb at the last inspection.

Hazel remembered the riddle: How many Marxists does it take to change a light bulb?

None. The light bulb contains the seeds of its own revolution.

She checked her watch. Five pm. Beth should have been home by now, her first day of relief teaching at a private boys school. It was hard to imagine Beth in a place like that, trying to look buttoned up and decorous. Hazel had tried to dissuade her — *the school's named after a saint, think about that* — but it was only a couple of weeks, Beth said, plus she needed the money, and after a month of waiting tables in a café that served a coffee called ristretto and another called doppio and where the barista was even wankier than the coffee, even the smallest stab at teaching would make her feel professional again. *Professional?* Hazel had held her tongue. What other profession was held in such contempt by the general population — well, apart from politics, the law, journalism, banking and the arts? In what other profession did nearly fifty percent of new recruits leave within five years? No mentoring, unruly classes, the burden of useless bureaucracy, and no time to go to the toilet some days, what with lunch duty, bus duty, playground duty. Not that the students had ever *played*, as such; more like pushed and elbowed and hung out in gangs and tried not to think of their future.

Hazel padded to the kitchen, poured milk into a saucepan and put it on a hot plate. Milo, her comfort drink since childhood, although you had to stop the milk from coming to the boil so it didn't form that horrible skin on top. Another first-world problem, she knew, like the fact that her favourite shampoo had gone up two dollars and she hadn't had sex for seven months, and the even worse fact that she'd never been in love. But her most pressing problem right now was being out of work. Seventeen months since she'd quit her teaching job, then failed to complete another uni course, failed at serving beef empanadas at corporate conventions, bailed out of an online program about selling real estate. She heaped in three spoons of sugar and stirred. Wasn't there a reason that sugar lifted the spirits? Something about boosting serotonin levels? Or was it an evolutionary thing, how sweet things in the wild could soothe the savage beast? Or was it the savage breast? Probably breast, because *savage beast* was a tautology. Or was it a redundancy? All these pointless questions, when the only question worth asking, apparently, was *to be or not to be*. He'd be a gloomy bastard to wake up to in the morning, old Hamlet, moaning that life was *weary, stale and flat*, then barking *get thee to a nunnery*. A nunnery also meant a whorehouse, her lit. teacher had explained, insisting that the play, like life as a whole, was full of double meanings. Life was a hole, alright: Hazel knew she'd fallen right into it, after thinking it would be cool to be a teacher, pointing out double meanings to her students, encouraging reflection on being and not being.

She finished making her Milo and trudged to the living room, which had barely enough room for two beanbags and a mini coffee table. She put down her mug, eased her way into the purple beanbag, tried not to think about her latest debacle in the chatting-up routine. Last week, in the pub. *I'm Pilar,* she'd said, hoping to sound breathily alluring (while forced to shout above the clamour). She'd always loved the sound of Pilar: it conjured a dark-eyed señorita leaning over a balcony, an importunate lover calling from below, violins melting in the background. The guy in the pub had dark brown eyes, a kissable mouth, and not a hint of macho in his voice. So what had she been hoping for? Escape from her humdrum self, a smudge of warmth, a hint of affirmation? Whatever else might be on offer when you took off your clothes, took a deep breath and tried to make yourself known?

He'd asked if Pilar was *a wog's name*.

The door opened onto an angry face.

'I got the sack,' said Beth. 'After one fucking day.' She stepped inside, slammed the door, put her hands on her hips. 'A mother complained cos I told her year nine brat to pull his head in. I wish I'd told him to shove it up his arse instead.' She made a loud harrumphing noise. 'I did lunch duty today, and all these boys were swaggering round saying the c word, which I really,

really hate because it's so degrading to women. So I went over and gave them a serve, didn't I, but all they did was laugh cos I'm only the relief. Which is exactly what that year nine brat said when I told him to stop being so disruptive. And then he gets on his phone and squeals to mummy, the little shit.'

'They don't know what they're missing,' said Hazel. 'Having you for their teacher.'

She struggled out of the beanbag and gave her friend a wish-I-could-help-you-beat-the-system kind of hug, which was tighter than a normal hug but didn't last very long.

'Well, all is not completely lost,' said Beth, chirpy again. 'The social science teacher asked me to a party on Saturday night. He said to bring as many people as I like.'

'I'm not in the mood for a party,' said Hazel. 'And in any case, I'm busy. I want to keep working on my project.' Because everyone needed a project, and she knew she'd be hopeless at knitting scarves or making jewellery out of beads. 'I'm reading the less famous works of famous writers,' she said. 'I've started with A for Jane Austen.'

'What, her entire oeuvre?'

'It's just oeuvre, Beth. You don't need *entire*.'

'OK, smart-arse. So why do you want to do that, anyway?'

'Because I've only read *Pride and Prejudice*.'

'Which always makes the top ten when they do those best-of lists,' said Beth.

'Along with *To Kill a Mockingbird*,' added Hazel. 'Plus *All Quiet on the Western Front* and *Cloudstreet*.'

God, hadn't anyone read anything since they'd left high school? Her friends only read online these days, good stuff admittedly, about the environment and marriage equality and politics in general, but an awful lot of garbage as well. Like the compelling fact that one of the Kardashians had just given birth or was about to give birth or was keen to regain her pre-birth body by working out with a personal trainer for ten hours every day.

'*Persuasion* is Austen's last completed novel,' said Hazel. 'I think the title's intriguing. And when I've finished that, I'll try *Mansfield Park* and *Emma*. I've forgotten the names of the other two. Anyway, it will give me a structure. A goal.'

'So it's not for fun, then?'

Hazel screwed up her face. 'I have to admit, I'm not exactly enraptured by *Persuasion*.'

'Then come to the party instead. You might get enraptured by a man like Mr Darcy.'

'Who isn't in *Persuasion*.'

'But remember that scene when Darcy walks out of the lake in those tight, wet breeches? Talk about hot!'

'But that scene's not in the novel.'

'Who cares?'

'I do. Those wet breeches. The blatant sexual display. It's not in keeping with nineteenth-century sexual morés.'

'Oh, *morés*, is it?' said Beth, and laughed. 'Do you know how Colin Firth managed to play Mr Darcy all haughty and stiff? He said he kept imagining a poker up his arse.'

'You waste too much time reading celebrity magazines.'

Beth shot her a look. 'It was in a serious article about adapting the novel into a TV series. And you spend way too much time in your room.' Her voice softened. 'Come to the party, hey? It might even be fun. Remember fun?'

Hazel shrugged. 'My novel might pick up,' she said. 'Captain Wentworth's back in town after seven years away and he's meant to be a bit of a charmer. Seductive, in Austen's read-between-the-lines kind of way.'

'So you'll settle for sex in the head, then. That's no fun at all.'

She gave Hazel a pleading look. The girl who'd sidled up to her on their first day of school and told her she looked good. *Good?* Beth had gone on to explain: *You look like you won't hurt anyone.* And then she'd asked if they could be friends. *Best friends, if I really like you and you really like me.* Eighteen years ago, and still they loved each other fiercely.

There were days, sometimes weeks, when Beth was the only person who touched her.

***

Hazel had been right after all, because according to Beth, the party was a disaster. Not that you should judge a decision by its outcome: Philosophy 101. Still, the only guy who'd talked to Beth was a happy clappy who carried on about resurrection, and the only girl who talked to her thought Taylor Swift was a musical genius. Beth said she was ready to shoot them both and was home by ten o'clock. Would have been home by nine except for all the stupid roadworks.

They managed to survive Easter Sunday by rationing their chocolate eggs. Hazel's mother had given them a gigantic Cadbury's rabbit apiece; Beth's mother had given Beth a lecture about getting a decent job. Then the two friends survived Monday by going to Rikki's flat and watching old DVDs of *Seinfeld*, whose unspeakably narcissistic characters made them all feel better about themselves. The following morning, after Beth had made pancakes and then mooched back to bed, Hazel took a walk to Bay View Terrace. The street was bristling with gym-fit mothers and their sylph-like daughters in their designer jeans ripped across the knees, silky black tops sliding off tanned shoulders. Hazel felt invisible among these glamorous women, as she walked past the funky boutiques and the trendy hair salon, the restaurant with windows so dark that people on the outside couldn't possibly see in. Talk about symbolic. Next up was an exclusive bed-and-bath shop selling towels big enough to dry the corpulent participants in an ancient Roman orgy. She looked at the entrance to Claremont Quarter, with more high-end clothes shops inside: Alannah Hill, Gorman, Tiger Lily, and a huge glossy sign for Calvin Klein, promising *Deep Euphoria*. As opposed to shallow euphoria, Hazel thought.

All this gloss and style, so different, her mother had told her, from the shop that used to nestle at the bottom of Bay View Terrace. A homely space, run by two sweet old ladies and crammed with cotton reels, buttons, zips, hooks and eyes. A haberdashery, that was the word, devoted to the small things in life, now superseded by obscenely pricey off-the-peg clothes made in third-world sweatshops. And near the corner there'd once been a family-run bakery selling homemade pies and sloppy vanilla slices and doughnuts as big as saucepans. Hazel would have killed for a doughnut right now, especially one dripping with artificial strawberry jam. But this part of town offered only really fancy stuff like iced chai frappes and turmeric lattes, or earnest muffins stuffed with bran and completely devoid of taste.

Still, she'd had to come here to check out *the dress*. Again. The one she'd seen in the window a few weeks back, when she'd dared to slink inside and sneak a look at the price. Two hundred dollars: an absolute steal for Claremont Quarter but roughly one hundred and fifty dollars more than she could spare. And yet here she was, taking another look at the black lacy number with its low-scooped neckline, classy and sexy at the same unaffordable time. Not that she'd have an occasion to wear such a dress, or anyone to wear it for. Still, it couldn't hurt, could it, to saunter into the shop and try it on? Just to feel, for a moment, like the person she imagined she could be.

And then something else came into her head. The angry guy at a party last week, telling some other guy to stop complaining about his *brand new majorly disappointing* video game. *Quit fucking moaning, you dick,* the angry guy had railed. *Try walking twenty kilometres for a bucket of clean drinking water.*

Parties

Another invitation arrived from out of the blue, this time from an old friend: *Huge announcement for me and Dora my place Saturday at 8*. Smart, big-hearted Todd, who told Hazel way back in school about *the restorative power of language* in William Wordsworth's poetry. *Restorative*. She'd nearly swooned.

William Wordsworth, Captain Wentworth, Todd Liu. All the good guys were either dead, fictional or taken.

'Do you reckon they're moving in together?' said Beth. 'After all these years?'

'Five.'

'Maybe they're getting engaged,' said Beth. 'Dora's been hinting for ages about putting a big sparkly thing on her finger.' She shook her head. 'Think of what you could buy instead. You could donate to a worthy cause. You know, buy a well for a village. Plus a goat and a pig. And a trip to Paris with what's left over.'

'Still, he's devoted to Dora.'

'Another one of life's great mysteries.'

'She's very sweet, Beth. She never says a bad word about anyone.'

Beth laughed. 'Yawn, yawn,' she said.

***

'Hazel! It's SO FABULOUS to SEE YOU!!'

Dora was one of those people who, no matter what the subject, always spoke in capital letters and exclamation marks. She would tell you that the weather was MILD!!!! Or the movie was OK!!!! The first time Hazel met her, she thought Dora was INCREDIBLY ENTHUSIASTIC about life, but now she was convinced that she wasn't VERY BRIGHT!!!!, because in five mildly envious years of knowing her, Hazel had never heard her say one vaguely interesting thing.

'Where did you get that DRESS!! And your HAIR!! You look so GLAMOROUS!!!'

The dress was, in truth, killing her. It was not so much nipped in at the waist as digging great chunks into her flesh. Snug when she bought it two years ago and even tighter now, but Beth insisted it looked amazing. She'd insisted on dyeing Hazel's hair as well: the colour on the packet was a subtle golden-brown but had turned out a lurid kind of copper instead. Hazel gave Dora a peck on the cheek and wandered off, spotted the usual crowd of old uni friends, plus a couple of lugubrious teachers. They reminded Hazel why she'd rather not be here, in her tight dress and with her outrageous hair. She'd much rather be invisible.

Beth handed her a glass and filled it to the brim with wine.

'You're going to have fun tonight,' she said, 'whether you like it or not.' Emphatically, like a former teacher. Then she was gone, offering wine, dispensing good cheer. Hazel chatted to some friends who were going camping down south, lying under the stars and getting stoned, and did she want some of it now because they had some really good stuff. She had to say no because the last time she was stoned she'd felt like a lettuce being nibbled by angry rabbits. Next she talked to Gav, who was dropping out of law and switching to music because he liked to sing in the shower. She figured he must be stoned. Then she bumped into Will and James, who'd broken up so many times that no one knew for sure if they were on again or off again. They debated the relative merits of *Please Like Me* and *Arrested Development*, until Ed charged up with the latest medical gossip. *A really gross story*, he said—everyone gathering round now—about some student who got chucked out of the faculty after a female patient lodged a furious complaint. The student thought he'd share a laugh while the woman was lying on the bed, legs wide open, and asked her a simple question. *Do you know why they call it a pap smear? No. Because ladies wouldn't have one if they call it a cunt scrape.*

Everyone looked horrified, then tried not to laugh.

Next up, Hazel commiserated with Chloe, who'd just thrown in her PhD in cultural anthropology because she'd looked down from her doctoral mountain and knew she was going to fall. Then more commiserations with Sarah who'd lost her job as a graphic designer because the company had gone bust. *Last hired, first fired*, she said, and shrugged. And what's more, she was so damned fed up with horrible men.

'Like, this morning, I'm standing at the bus stop and a car slows down and guess what? A couple of meatheads lean out the window and shout disgusting things at me, mostly involving my vagina.'

'Well, get this,' said Chloe. 'I'm getting ready for the party, right? And this guy I used to date, Craig. Remember Craig?'

Hazel and Sarah shuddered.

'Well, he phones me out of nowhere, about some argument we had way back when. He starts shouting at me, tells me women don't have the monopoly on victimhood because dickhead is just as offensive as the c word. And then he called me the c word.'

'What a dickhead,' said Sarah.

'Even worse,' said Chloe. 'Yesterday, I'm standing in the supermarket queue and some middle-aged corporate in a suit rubs himself up against me. And you know how you're so gobsmacked you just can't believe it's happening? Well, by the time I reacted he'd already taken off.'

Hazel tried hard to remember what they'd learned in gender studies: that masculinity was a social construct that could always be deconstructed and then reconstructed for benefit of both genders, for society as a whole. But hearing those nasty stories, it was hard to forget the morons hanging out of their cars, the bullying creep on the phone, the guy who'd treated Chloe like a lamppost or a fence.

And then they spotted Simon. Three unattached women looking his way. Blond, blue-eyed Simon, with his boyish face and sun-gold hair that kept falling into his eyes.

'Simon's going places in the Greens,' said Chloe. 'I see his name all over the place. I heard he might contest the next election.'

Hazel was surprised. Simon was only twenty-five, like her.

'He cornered me last year,' she said, 'and talked me into handing out how-to-vote cards.'

She'd been hoping to see him at the polling booth, but instead she'd seen a lot of grumpy voters moaning about being forced to vote. Even more who'd rolled their eyes at her borrowed T-shirt: 'Standing Up for What Matters'.

Chloe nudged her in the side. 'You should think about it, too, Hazel.'

'What? Simon?'

'No, standing for the Greens. You're smart and really artic-ulate and—'

'Shall I laugh now, or save it for later? I'm not even a member.'

'Well, it's about time you joined,' said Sarah. 'The issues are important. Plus you get to meet a superior brand of male. Clever and caring and sometimes really hot.'

'Hazel!'

A pair of arms grabbed her round the waist, spun her round. Todd. As beautiful as ever: Malaysian-Chinese, fine-boned, smooth-skinned, with a newly shaven head that added to his sexy, sculptured look. He told Hazel, in lower case letters, that she looked gorgeous, and as Chloe and Sarah drifted away, she asked him for a hint about the big announcement. Todd lowered his head, told her quietly that they were *having a baby. Well, Dora is, anyway.* Hazel was startled, but kissed him on the cheek, said what people usually say: 'Congratulations! Any wedding plans?'

'I've bought the ring,' he said, flatly. 'The diamond. But it's being re-sized, so Dora has to wait til she can wear it.'

'Oh, a diamond. That's, well—'

'Yeah, I know, but it's what she wanted. And her mum and dad wanted. I had to borrow the money from mine to pay for the stupid thing. And I don't even have a job, do I?'

'But, well, you'll have the baby,' Hazel said, carefully. 'That's the important thing, isn't it? And each other.'

Todd kept his voice low. 'Do you think someone can really forget to take the pill?' he said. 'After five years?'

Hazel couldn't help looking round the room to see what might be written on his girlfriend's pretty face. But Dora was surrounded by a bunch of girls Hazel didn't know, all of them oohing and aahing over something, maybe the prospect of a diamond or one of those puffy white wedding gowns that in a high, swirling wind might lift you into the sky. She turned back to Todd. Disconcerted. Wary.

'I know it's none of my business,' she said, 'but, well, there has to be—'

'Trust, yeah, I know. But see, the thing is, I love her and we've been together for a lifetime and so I can't—you know—accuse her. I just can't.' He fixed Hazel with a look. 'She's a very good person,' he said, as though Hazel might object. 'She's loyal and kind and, well, we fit together really well.'

So there it was: fantastic sex as the key to enduring couple-dom. She was sick of hearing about sex, however obliquely. Sick of thinking about it and trying not to, of wanting it and trying not to. It dismayed and sometimes distressed her.

She saw Dora rushing up, putting her arms around Todd's waist, telling him it was time for their announcement, while Hazel stood there passing the time, hoping for a better time, because it was always about time, wasn't it? No time and show time and time for you and time for me, a time for every purpose under heaven. Was that T.S. Eliot quoting the Bible? One of those saints he was always on about?

'Hazel, are you OK?' said Dora. 'You look REALLY WEIRD!'

'I'm fine, thanks. Just hearing things in my head.'

'You could see a DOCTOR!! If the VOICES get REALLY BAD!!!'

How long will this take, thought Hazel. How many more hours until she could go home and stick a pillow over her head? Not to do herself in, though, because she was only mildly, not clinically, depressed, and you had to cling to the crucial difference.

Still, here was Simon, standing right in front of her and smiling.

'Hazel, great to see you,' he said. 'We haven't caught up for ages.'

'Months.' Nearly eight, to be precise. 'Since the federal election, remember?'

'And what a bummer that—' Simon stopped. 'Are you OK, Hazel? You look a bit down. Has something happened?'

God. Not tears. A few sensitive words and she was in danger of blubbering. So she pulled back her shoulders, told him she just needed a good night's sleep. Or was it a night's good sleep? And why should the world care anyway?

'How's law going?' she said.

'Boring as bat shit. But I'm volunteering at Legal Aid so that helps relieve the boredom.'

'Well, it's great that you're helping.'

She remembered another reason she liked Simon: he was a really caring guy, committed to changing the world. But not the kind of person who threw their caring in your face so you had to wipe it off with a tissue.

'I wish I could help get more votes,' he said. 'You know the Greens had a swing against them? Over three percent.'

She did. And she knew she'd been useless as well. She'd handed out—what?—maybe twenty how-to-vote cards in two long hours? Simon was beginning to fire now, about people getting *so pissed off* with the two major parties. 'All their lies and broken promises,' he said. 'And not listening to the people. There's going to be more and more people voting for the minor parties. For independents.'

'You mean the independents who hate minor parties like the Greens,' said Hazel. 'Who hate asylum seekers and women and gays, just about any victimised group you care to name.' She remembered the obnoxious guy at the polling booth. 'So get this, Simon,' she said. 'There was a guy handing out cards for the Lib Dems, carrying on about women getting *special treatment* while poor old men like him get nothing. So, I was thinking, would that be the special treatment women get at the hands of their abusers? Or less money going into their pay packets? More women living in poverty than men? Then he started bleating about needing massive cuts to health and education to bring down the deficit. And don't get him started on foreign aid. *What have foreigners ever done for us,* that kind of thing. But I didn't say a word because he was pretty massive himself, with a face like a demented pugilist.'

'Well, I had a guy from Family First next to me,' said Simon. 'A guy in a pure white shirt and a phony grin, like he's flogging used cars. Anyway, this woman's walking in to vote and the Family First guy shoves a leaflet in her hands and she checks it out, screws up her face like she's thinking really hard. *Family, that sounds nice,* she says, *I think I might vote for you.* She didn't have a clue that his idea of family is exclusively nuclear and exclusively straight.'

'And don't forget xenophobic and fiercely Right to Life,' said Hazel. 'Never trust a party with the word *family* in it. Or *democratic.* Or *freedom.* They'll all be tyrannical or bigoted.'

She could see Simon's eyes widening.

'You know, Hazel, the Greens could use some volunteers right now,' he said. 'We're spreading the word about our policies. Another grassroots campaign.'

'But there's no election for ages, Simon. Federal *or* state.'

'Sure, except we need to keep people aware of the big issues. Asylum seekers. Climate change. Get this: I had one guy at the booth who said he wasn't fussed about climate change cos he wouldn't be around when it happened. People in this joint, they just don't seem to care.'

Hazel laughed. 'My dad said we used to have a number plate with the slogan *State of Excitement*, but he reckoned we should call it *State of Couldn't Give a Damn.* I suggested *Vegetative State.*'

Simon didn't laugh with her. He was looking kind of stern.

'You know, Hazel, you'd be really good at doorknocking,' he said.

'You're kidding me, right? I'd rather poke my eye out with a burnt stick. Which is another thing my dad likes to say. Seriously, I could do without doors being slammed in my face or people abusing me. I'm way too much of a coward.'

'It's actually not that hard,' said Simon, and took a step closer. 'You focus on the issues instead of your fear. And you listen. That's the most important thing, because people always want to be listened to. It makes them feel empowered.'

His eyes were so bright, fixed on her. Only her. 'You'd be great, Hazel, honestly. You're smart and articulate, believe in social justice, and we can get you up to speed on policy.'

He moved even closer. 'You can be very persuasive,' he said.

Was there something in his voice as well?

She looked into his eyes, at the point of no return. Told him she'd do it. He called her an angel and gave her a mighty hug. Most definitely not an embrace. Because words had important shades of meaning, which was why you should never use a thesaurus, and she'd done it again, hadn't she? Misread the sexual cues. Then Simon drew away, said he'd text her details of some training meeting coming up soon. Grinning broadly, pleased with himself.

'You'll be fine, honestly,' he said. 'I can't thank you enough.'

Hazel could think of other ways for him to thank her, but the moment—if there'd ever been one—had already passed her by. And now she was stuck with a commitment. Really soon. A terrifying one. Serves me right, she thought: it's a punishment for my impure motives.

Simon dug her in the ribs. She really wished people wouldn't do that.

'Hey, come and meet my new girlfriend,' he said. 'Felicia. She's a maths student from Italy, she's only been here for a couple of months. She's really clever and crazy beautiful, and she has a great big heart.'

Well, who would have thought?

'We met at the beach. We were both body surfing and accidentally collided.'

'Accidentally? You're not fooling anyone, Simon.'

'But it's true. It was just one of those crazy things, a stroke of good luck.'

So that's what it came down to in the end, Hazel thought. None of that complex, heady stuff about free will versus determinism. You just needed to be involved in a non-fatal accident to find that person of your waking, sleeping dreams.

Simon dug her in the side. Again. 'What do you think of the big news?' he said. 'The baby.'

The whole bloody room must know by now, Hazel thought. Maybe she should just have a baby and be done with it. Women always had that to fall back on, didn't they? Because what else could she do, she sighed, feeling her body slump: with her B.A., majoring in English, plus a dash of gender studies, philosophy, ancient history and French. A mercifully brief Dip. Ed.

Well, pretty much what she was doing right now: standing around at a party, leaden with disappointment, and waiting to go home.

She heard a male voice behind her *checking out the talent*, turned to see a really lanky guy looking round the room, staring telescopically. *Checking out the talent indeed*: as though women were merrily tap dancing on *Australian* fucking *Idol*.

The man who loved children

The last day of April. Sitting on the train at Perth Station, Hazel remembered her Shakespeare: *Men are April when they woo, December when they wed. As You Like It.* Feisty Rosalind speaking her mind about the deceptiveness of men. Still, Hazel thought, she wouldn't have minded a bit of wooing, even the deceptive kind; anything to boost her flagging ego and blot out the memory of another humiliating job interview, this time in the city: cutting up fish in an upmarket market for pernickety affluent foodies. This is what she was reduced to. She looked around the compartment, saw everyone with eyes down checking their phones, as usual, or eyes closed listening to their iPods. Not one other person reading a book. Although every now and then she'd spy someone with a book in hand and, if they were close enough, she'd take a look to see what they were reading. Imagine a life for the reader. Like the young guy sitting next to her a couple of weeks ago, wearing a leather jacket and reading Sartre's *Huis Clos.* He could have been a student of French literature, or maybe a French tourist missing his sophisticated culture, because anyone reading *Huis Clos* had to be sophisticated, or just plain masochistic.

Another time, on her way to Freo to check out the second-hand bookshops, she'd seen a middle-aged woman with a sagging face reading *Torn by Desire.* No prizes for guessing that one: a woman escaping from her passionless life, or trying to revive it. Then again, maybe she'd been planning to write a steamy romance and make a whole pile of money. Hazel had tried it herself last year, assuming it would be dead easy: *Torn* by this, *Shredded* by that, *Undone by the Sultan*, *Captured by the Sheik*. But when the publishers sent her *the kit*, she hadn't been able to stop laughing: mandatory kiss by page fourteen, partial disrobing by page thirty, definitely no orgasm until at least page seventy-three, when the hero's imposing organ would be on full display. So she just couldn't do it in the end, couldn't even make a start. And besides, she had enough deferred gratification in her own life without trying to imagine it in the life of a woman called Rebel or Flame.

Hazel felt the train begin to move and opened her book. *Persuasion*: a romance of the higher-order variety, the kind that encouraged you to think. But so far it was all long-winded backstories and tedious character sketches, with not a hint of an erotic subtext. Like Elizabeth and Darcy, talking about playing the piano: *We neither of us perform to strangers*. So damned sexy, their talk, much more subtle than *imposing organs*. Maybe she wouldn't like *Persuasion* after all. Maybe there was a reason it wasn't in the top ten or even the top one hundred, with its melancholy story of love thwarted, hearts wounded, time running out for the heroine. Anne Elliot: she'd been pining for the Captain for seven dreary years and too many listless pages.

The train sped through a tunnel and out again, past the high-rise buildings and concrete walls of Northbridge. Hazel thought about her destination: Claremont Quarter. *That dress* again. She could always put it on her credit card, couldn't she, if she ever managed to find a job.

Compensation, she thought, is my stupid middle name. Or Sublimation.

Simon's new girlfriend wouldn't have to compensate or sublimate. Felicia. She'd been just as Simon had described her: smart and warm, and since English was her second language, speaking like a charming translation. Like calling her slightly sunburnt face *caught by the sunfire*. And she certainly was beautiful, exquisitely beautiful, with long black hair, high cheekbones. Sultry. Hazel looked down at her book again, wondered how life might have been if she'd been exquisitely beautiful and/or sultry.

The train was pulling in to City West. Scitech, and shops for people furnishing their suburban houses, hoping to make their lives complete. As if my own life is complete, she thought. It wasn't even semi-complete. Not that you could have degrees of completeness; like perfection or uniqueness or pregnancy, it had to be all or nothing. People were streaming out of the train now, a whole lot more streaming in. A muscly guy with tattoos of dragons all over his arms. Half the population had a tatt these days, yesterday's revolutionary gesture today's dull-and-boring. A woman struggling with a screaming child, a teenage girl with skeletal limbs, and a lot of overweight people. She returned to her book, to the soothing movement of the train and then on to West Leederville, with the antique bookshop that must have been there for decades. Serendipity, it was called, the favourite haunt of one of her old tutors, a collector of first editions. The kind of teacher who liked to ramble and digress and leave you to learn for yourself. He'd told the class that 'serendipity' meant *fortunate happenstance*, that the word was coined by Horace Walpole, a member of parliament in the eighteenth century and a man of indeterminate sexuality. All this meandering stuff, as though the tutor was talking to himself. He took months to return their essays.

Suddenly they were plunged into another tunnel, then out into Subiaco Station, with its gleaming mass of steel and glass. More people pouring in, jostling and pushing, a guy plonking down next to her. A middle-aged guy with a solid build, reaching into his satchel and—well, there you go—pulling out a book. Shuffling in his seat, ready to begin.

Hazel couldn't help glancing at his profile: a slightly hooked nose, grey stubble, full mouth. Maybe forty, forty-five. The train was moving again and she craned her neck slightly, took a surreptitious peek: *The Man Who Loved Children*. She'd never heard of it.

'The title's ironic,' he said, out of the side of his mouth.

He turned to look at her, gave her a wry kind of smile. He had striking, pale blue eyes, rimmed with black.

'Do you know this novel?' he said. 'It's Australian.'

Hazel shook her head.

'Not that I'm chastising you,' he said.

No one she knew said *chastising*.

'For being—you know—unpatriotic.'

She nodded blankly, saw him gesture towards her book.

'*Persuasion*,' he said.

She nodded again.

'Who wrote that?' he said, peering more closely. 'Ah. Jane Austen. I only know *Pride and Prejudice*. Not that I've read it, but everyone's heard of it, haven't they?'

She nodded again, superfluously.

'So.' He gave her a different kind of smile this time. More open. 'Are you reading this for study?'

She shook her head. Nod nod nod, shake shake shake: like one of those toy dogs that people dumbly put on their dashboards.

'Just for pleasure, then?'

He was nothing if not persistent. But still, he'd asked her, was trying to engage her, and he didn't seem sleazy, not at all. He was—well—attractive. For an older man.

Hazel cleared her throat. 'I can't say I'm really *enjoying* it,' she said. 'It's, well, autumnal in tone. You know. The sense of things dying, coming to an end.'

'Autumnal? But didn't Jane Austen write comedies?'

Hazel gathered her thoughts. She wanted to sound intelligent, after all her fluffing about. So she explained that *comedy* as a literary term didn't mean funny ha-ha, it meant that everything turned out well in the end: the good were rewarded, the bad were punished and the heroine found Mr Right. In romantic comedies, anyway, like Jane Austen's. It was a structural definition, she blathered, and an optimistic way of looking at the world. Hoping she didn't sound like a know-all, when she didn't know much at all.

'So that's basically the appeal of comedy, then?' he said. 'The happy ending.'

'Sure. But it's also discovering *how* things happen, and why. And who does the telling is important, too. The technical name for that is point of view. Which always slants the way you see the world created in a book.'

He nodded. She rattled on.

'Mind you, a story is slanted even when it uses an omniscient point of view. Omniscient means all-knowing, you know. Because there's no such thing as objectivity, is there? Philosophically speaking.'

Was she being a gasbag now? Would he switch off, return politely to his book? But no, he was nodding again and smiling now, full-on.

'That's all very interesting,' he said. 'Thanks for the instruction.'

She found herself feeling pleased. That he was pleased.

Maybe she could ask him—this stranger who knew that Jane Austen wrote comedies—if he'd ever been to Serendipity in search of a worthy tome. Or whether he knew the meaning of the word *serendipity*. Knew about Horace Walpole. And now the train was pulling up at Daglish. Would he stand and leave? No, he was still there. Very present. She rummaged in her brain for something else to say.

'So you're not a fan of comic novels, then?'

'I don't read much fiction of any kind, really. This novel... well, a friend passed it on to me. She's keen to educate me, I guess.'

Hazel found herself leaning in, just a little closer.

'You can tell that your title's ironic,' she said.

'Really? How so?'

'*The Man Who Loved Children*. I mean, love doesn't have to proclaim itself, does it? Love just is.'

He looked at her as though he'd just slid open a drawer and seen a curious object inside. Which was hardly surprising, since she didn't know what to make of herself right now, sitting next to this man, who was big and craggy in a Ted Hughes kind of way. Ted Hughes. The first time he met Sylvia Plath, he'd bitten her mouth so hard that he'd drawn blood. Or was it her neck he'd plunged his teeth into? Or had Plath taken the first bite? Whatever the truth of the story, it was pretty damned tempestuous.

Hazel felt the train coming to a stop, in between stations. Probably making way for another train, although they never told you the reason for delays, or when you might start moving again. Or maybe it was because of a leaf stuck on the railway track, which had actually happened to one of Beth's old colleagues. He'd sent her a postcard from London with the heading *Leaf causes major delay*, then went on to denounce shabby British Rail, crappy British food and dough-faced British girls. *Nothing like travel*, Beth had quipped, *to narrow the mind*. Not like the man beside me, Hazel thought, who was settling back in his seat, relaxed, turning to look at her again. He really did have the most dazzling eyes.

'I wonder how long we'll be stuck,' he said.

She was beginning to feel un-stuck. Positively serendipitous.

'So, what about *your* title, then?' he said. '*Persuasion*.'

'Oh. Right.' She could feel the heat of his face now and it was really quite unsettling. 'Well, persuasion is at the heart of the novel. Well, of course it's at the heart, that's what titles are about. Like *A Journal of the Plague Year*. There's no mucking about there.'

Had she really just said that?

'So, in *Persuasion*...' she battled on. 'There's an older woman, a mentor, who thinks she knows what's best for the young heroine, Anne. And so the mentor, Lady Russell — you can tell by the name, can't you, that she has a bit of clout — well, Lady Russell persuades Anne to give up the man she loves.'

'Because he's a cad and a bounder?'

'No, no, not at all. Captain Wentworth's thoughtful, kind, sensitive. A good man, you know. But his prospects aren't the brightest.'

'No money, you mean?'

'In a nutshell, yes. But Lady Russell isn't mercenary. She's acting in the young woman's best interests, because back then — two hundred years ago — most women were completely dependent on men for an income, and if they didn't marry they became a burden on their family. So a woman literally couldn't afford to marry for love.'

Had she used *literally* correctly?

'I'm glad I wasn't born back then,' she said, stupidly. 'Not that it's a picnic for women today.' Sounding even stupider. 'I used to tell my female students to marry a very old man with a terminal illness who was also incredibly rich. Which was meant to be joke, of course.'

She was approaching rock bottom.

'Only they didn't laugh,' she said. 'They probably weren't even listening.'

She'd just crashed.

'So you were a teacher?' he said.

'For two long years. I was a bit of a disaster.'

'I'm sure that's not true,' he said, quietly. 'It's the nature of teaching, isn't it? It can take years for students to see the value of what you've given them.'

The train was starting up again, and she knew she had to speak, keep him engaged for however long they had.

'You sound like a teacher yourself,' she said.

'History. I quit a few years ago.' He laughed. 'The world's

full of us, isn't it? Someone should start a support group.'

She liked his laugh. It wasn't overdone, but not underdone either. They were rocking side by side now as the train gathered speed, began to hurtle in fact, as though the engine was conspiring against her. Rushing her brutally through time and back to her usual place. Next stop: Shenton Station; she could see Shenton College on top of the hill. An Independent Public School with cream-of-the-crop teachers. Not like the one she'd taught in, which was more like sour milk.

She turned to face the unknown man again. 'I could have used a support group before I quit,' she said. 'I left after a girl spat in my face. I know she must have been very unhappy to do that but it didn't change the way I felt. Humiliated. Angry. I wish I could have, you know, risen above it.'

'You're being hard on yourself,' he said. 'It's difficult to rise above feelings you know are unworthy. To be the person you wish to be.' He stopped, cleared his throat. 'Don't listen to me,' he said. 'I can hear myself sounding like a—'

'Tosser?'

'I was about to say a pompous prat, but tosser will do very nicely.'

They laughed.

The train was moving again and they gave a little shuffle in their seats, both of them silent as the train rocketed along, slowed down, pulled into another station.

'Is this your stop?' he said.

'No, I'm going to Claremont. Only I don't live there.'

'Are you doing something interesting in Claremont?'

Hazel swallowed. 'Not really. Nothing important. And you?'

'Me?'

'Your stop.'

'Oh. Swanbourne. Just after yours.'

She felt the train pulling out of the station. Felt his thighs perilously close.

'So, how's life after teaching, then?' he said.

Hazel held back a sigh. That question again: *And what do you do for a living?*

'A bit up and down, really,' she said. 'I started a diploma in arts management but I couldn't manage something arcane called the creative economy. Then I had a miserable job serving hors-d'oeuvres to people in suits, capped off by a few months learning to sell real estate. I still haven't forgiven myself.'

'Selling your soul, hey?'

'Well, I'm sure I wouldn't have sold any properties. But now' — she didn't want to sound too mopey — 'I'm looking to do something kind of useful.'

She glanced down at his hands. No wedding ring. Which didn't tell her anything, really. He had graceful hands, with long, fine fingers.

He nodded. 'It's the important question, isn't it?' he said. 'How should we live?'

She found herself glancing at his hands again, wondering what it would feel like to trace those long, fine fingers. Thread them through hers.

He leaned in a fraction closer. 'I'm Adam, by the way,' he said.

She thought for one whole second. 'I'm Hazel.'

'That's an old-fashioned name. It's rather quaint.'

Quaint? Was that meant to be a compliment?

'You certainly fit the old-fashioned bill,' he said. 'Reading a good book. And you haven't once checked your phone, or used the f word.'

He'd been paying attention. Figuring her out. She felt her heart do that little flip thing.

'Oh, I say the f word a lot,' she said, casually. 'But I try to keep it in my head.'

And still he was looking and smiling and she felt a rush of desire: for his thoughtful words and his listening, and for those striking, pale blue eyes. For his full mouth as well, wondering how it might feel, how it might taste.

'So why did *you* leave teaching?' she said.

'Oh. Well. Because it felt empty. History matters to me but I couldn't make it matter to the students.'

'Now who's being hard on himself?'

He shrugged. 'Of course there are always a few who make it worthwhile,' he said. 'But to be honest, I didn't have an ounce of classroom control, even after years in the job. I left after a boy punched me in the face.' Then his own face suddenly tightened. 'Not that I'm trying to outdo you,' he said.

'Of course not. You don't seem like an outdoing kind of person.'

He blushed. She'd never known a man who blushed, or even thought he needed to.

'So what do you do now?' she said. 'For work, I mean.'

'I'm retired, actually.'

'Retired? Did you win Lotto or something?'

'Nothing quite so lucky,' he said. 'But I've paid off the mortgage, and I manage because...well, I live very simply.'

'You mean you don't buy a lot of stuff?'

'Exactly. I have everything I need, really.'

He kept saying *I*. Not *we*.

'But don't you want to—I don't know—go travelling?' she said. 'Buy a grand piano or something, and take lessons.'

He laughed. 'My mother put me off piano lessons for life. She and Miss Onions.'

'Onions?'

'Yes, my teacher, Clarissa Onions. On that basis alone I should have felt sorry for her, but she kept rapping me over the knuckles with a steel ruler every time I made a mistake. She belonged to what's called the old-fashioned style of teaching.'

'Sadism, you mean.' She was looking at him closely but trying not to stare. Was she staring? Was she being too obvious? 'So what do you do with your time, then?' she said. 'Now that you've retired.'

'Well, that's very simple too. I do a bit of volunteer work. And I like to go swimming in the ocean. Out in the deep, far away from the noise of things. But most importantly, I'm raising a son.'

'Oh. So you're a single parent, then? Divorced?' Out before she knew it.

'My wife is dead.'

Hazel swallowed. Because he hadn't said *passed away*.

'It's alright,' he said, quietly. 'Honestly. It was a while ago now.'

'But still' — feeling the need to say something — 'I've never lost someone I love. I couldn't begin to imagine it.'

'It was actually a relief in the end,' he said. 'For her, for all of us. She had cancer, and it took a long time until she died.'

'So she tried to battle on?'

His mouth suddenly hardened. '*Battle*,' he said, decisively. 'That's an injunction to put up a fight and so if you lose, it's your own damned fault.' He was looking her straight in the eye now, unflinching. 'You see, cancer's not about winning or losing, it's just terrible, rotten bad luck. All those people cheering her on, urging her not to give up, making her feel like she'd failed. She already had so much to deal with.'

Hazel sat blankly. Everything had changed in an instant, as if she'd blundered into a crime scene and didn't know how to get out. She heard him mumble an apology for something she couldn't quite catch but his tone was clear enough: flat, resigned, as though he'd given up on her, or just given up. She kept her eyes on the opposite window, feeling flustered, embarrassed, then saw that the next stop was hers. She'd passed two stations in between and hadn't even noticed, hadn't even felt the movement of the train. All she felt now was regret, for the sharpness of his voice and the shame in her heart; for this bungled, gloomy ending.

She stood up quickly, almost took a tumble, turned to look at him at last. His face was impossible to read.

'It was good to talk to you,' he said. 'Autumnal Hazel.'

She hitched up her bag, thanked him for the conversation.

She was a callow, useless girl stepping off a train. A girl sprouting a cliché about terminal illness in order to impress a man. A man who'd lost a woman he loved. What did she know about such suffering, after all? What did she know about loss, and what you might hope to save? She tried to think of what she could do, now that she'd ruined things again. Stuffing up an interview, offending a man she'd warmed to, a man she really liked. Maybe she'd buy a bottle of rotgut wine and ask some friends to come over. Or she could take a bubble bath in her very small bathtub, which was the best you could do in a very small bathroom. But most of all she was hoping to rub it from her mind: her showing off, the harshness in his voice. Just scrub it all away.

Then she heard a shout: her name. Turned to see him running. Adam.

'Your book,' he said, puffing. 'You left it on the train.'

His hair was messy in the wind and there he was with his arresting blue eyes and strong nose and stubble on his face and all of this was beautiful to her. He handed her the book, ran his fingers through his hair as she gushed out her thanks... *library book... so lucky you saw it...*

He pulled at the collar of his shirt.

'I just wanted to say—properly this time—that I'm so sorry,' he said. 'I must have sounded insufferable. So damned self-righteous.'

'But it was my fault. I shouldn't have been so—'

'No, no, of course it wasn't your fault. How could you possibly have known?'

'Well, I know now. I'll know what not to say next time. I don't mean...I don't mean with you next time, I mean if the subject should ever arise. You know, in conversation.'

She shuffled her feet, feeling nervous and gauche, not wanting him to walk away. Not for a moment.

'Please don't feel bad,' he said. 'I feel bad about making you feel bad, so you'll make me feel better if...'

They were tangled up in words in the nicest possible way.

'May I buy you a coffee?' he said. 'By way of atonement.'

Hazel took a tiny leap. 'I'd rather have a glass of wine,' she said. 'If you don't think it's too much. Too early, I mean.'

His eyes were bright, searching. He had a sprinkle of freckles across the bridge of his nose.

'Wine it is, then,' he said. 'Do you have a favourite place round here?'

She wanted to say that she'd go anywhere with him, that he could take her to his bed and do anything he liked. But she knew she needed to be sensible: calm and temperate and rational. She didn't want to be empty-headed Rebel, the star attraction of *Torn by Desire*. Because she was Hazel. Who told him calmly — she couldn't believe how calmly — that she knew a wine bar just down the road.

'Perfect,' he said.

And it was. It really was. It was all she could do not to reach out her hand and twine her fingers through his.

'So. Lead the way, Hazel,' he said.

Happenstance

What did they discuss as they walked to the wine bar? Well, more like Adam asking questions and Hazel rattling on about growing up in Perth but hating the summer heat and the hedonistic worship of the sun. So glad it was autumn, she chattered, nervous now, gabbling on about how she loved the yellow leaves and the cooler weather and did he know they'd just had one of the longest stretches without any rain? A whole heap of days, she couldn't remember how many but it was very long. It was even more embarrassing when Adam opened the door to the wine bar: *doof doof* atavistic music, crowds of beautiful people shouting to be heard, heaps of stick-insect girls with pneumatic breasts who made Hazel want to hide in the shadows. How could she admit that she'd never been inside this look-at-me place? Then more agitation, with Adam offering to buy her a drink and she insisting not, even though he'd offered before. Finally: *two reds it is*, pointing to an empty table in the distance. Hazel made her way over and sat down, swatting back a potted palm that threatened to swipe her face. Already beginning to wonder if her feeble shot at courage had been a big mistake.

But at least it was quieter in the corner, and she could watch him from a distance. He was wearing a pair of scruffy jeans, a long, baggy white shirt. He had a mop of greying hair in need of brushing. If he was the answer to fashion, he clearly hadn't heard the question. And she liked it, this lack of vanity and fuss, and the way he waited at the counter, not taking up too much space despite his solid build, not trying to muscle others out of the way.

He might be old enough to be her father. Did this matter? Why should it matter, if your father was one of life's good men? And watching Adam now, his broad back and rounded bum, the curve of his neck, she felt her nipples tingling, tried to settle as he walked towards her, drinks in hand, looking a bit shaky. He put the glasses on the table, sat down, gave her a sheepish glance. It was different now, sitting in this pretentious place, as he loosened the collar of his already loose white shirt. And while she didn't want him saying *cheers* or anything in the least bit prosaic, she did want him to speak, to help break the rising tension.

Then she remembered what he'd told her. About his child.

'So tell me about your son.'

Adam looked taken aback. 'My son?'

'You said he was the most important thing of all.'

He took a sip of wine, set down his glass. 'So I did. Yes. Jessie.'

'So tell me about him.'

'Well, he's four years old. Nearly five. But, well, are you sure you want to know?'

Hazel raised an eyebrow. 'I asked, didn't I? About Jamie.'

'Jessie.'

Now it was her turn to blush. And why did this have to be so difficult?

'So tell me about Jessie who's nearly five.'

He nodded. 'OK. Sure. Well, he's a wonderful companion, the most engaging little boy. Who can also be a gigantic pain in the arse.'

'So it's tough then? Bringing him up on your own.'

'Women do it all the time,' he said, a little sharply, and then his face fell. 'I'm sorry, I didn't mean to snap at you. It's just that, well, I don't usually come to places like this. And I must be the only person here over forty.'

So that was it. The key to his shaking hands. The edginess.

'You didn't snap at me,' she said. 'And if you feel out of place—well, to be honest, I've never been here before either. It's got narcissism written all over it.' She took a sip of wine, plucked up some more courage. 'Besides which, I'm sitting here with you, and as far as I'm concerned, you're in exactly the right place.'

She couldn't get more obvious, could she? But he didn't say a word.

'And so what if you're over forty?' she bumbled on. 'You make yourself sound *antediluvian*.'

What if he didn't know the meaning of antediluvian?

But he was smiling now and his eyes were bright, and again she felt that sweet rush of desire.

'I bet you were one of those children who read the dictionary just for fun,' he said.

'I used to flip though the pages sometimes, but it doesn't help if you don't know the context. Although I do know a funny joke about the dictionary. How *lumpy jaw* comes just before *lunacy*, but in life there are no such clues. That's by one of my favourite writers.'

'So tell me, why do you like reading so much?'

What could she say? That didn't sound like an undergrad essay?

'It's partly the pleasure of words,' she said. 'You know, the shapes they make, the stories they tell. It's an aesthetic thing, the making. You admire the skill, the textures and rhythms. That kind of thing.' She swallowed, because she was sounding like an undergrad essay. Except if he hadn't studied literature, maybe he wouldn't notice. And he wasn't going to give her a mark, was he? B minus: *get beyond the clichés, extend your argument, watch use of semi-colons*. The usual comments from her tutors.

'But what about ideas?' he said. 'You must get ideas from reading.'

'Well, yes, of course. Certainly.' Was he implying she was one of those belles lettres types, infatuated with style? 'Reading can be dangerous,' she pronounced, 'because it can make you think.' Then she laughed, remembering. 'I said that in a tutorial once and the tutor told me that writers can't make you do anything. *They don't have a gun to your head, Hazel.* And he said it in bright red ink.'

'The condescending school of pedagogy,' said Adam.

'Absolutely. Another time he told me there were no wrong answers in literature, but if there was one, mine would be it.'

'And that didn't turn you off reading?' he said. 'All the put-downs?'

She waved her hand, airily. 'Oh, I tried not to take it personally. And I did say some dumb things every now and then. Only not as bad as Jemma Hawkins in high school. She asked the teacher once if Euripides had another name, and when he said *Euripides You-buy-me-new-pair*, she actually wrote it down.'

Adam laughed. 'Poor Jemma Hawkins,' he said.

'I'll never forget Euripides' play *Medea*,' said Hazel. 'Have you read it?'

'Isn't it about a woman who kills her children?'

'That's right. But the worst part is the murder of the princess. She's the one Medea's husband runs off with, so Medea gets her kids to poison the poor woman, and the details are horrific. Not that you see it, thank goodness, it's reported, because violence always occurs offstage in ancient Greek tragedy. *Abskene*, it's called, *offstage*. Which is where we get the word obscene. You know, something that's too shocking or sickening to see.'

'Is that right?'

He was watching her closely, studying her, it seemed.

'But most of all,' she said, 'I read to know I'm not alone. A famous writer said that. I don't mean about me, personally, he was talking about all of us. I've always liked that idea. It's comforting. Consoling.'

Still he was watching her carefully, as though waiting for her to say more. Was she sounding too obvious again, about loneliness? When she wanted to say that the famous writer whose name she couldn't remember right now and maybe she should whip out her phone and google the quote, she wanted to say that the writer meant something much deeper, more profound. Existential loneliness, she wanted to say, but that would have sounded so phony. Like those private school nobs in her tutorial, proclaiming that choosing to give life meaning in the face of the void was courageous, heroic, before they jumped into their sports cars and roared off to the pub. One of those nobs had even worn a beret.

She tried again.

'I don't mean to say I'm alone. Not in the ordinary sense, that is. Because I'm blessed with some wonderful friends and I have two great parents. Well, of course I have two. Well, no, not of course, one of them could be dead. Which would make me an orphan. Because you only have to lose one parent to be an orphan.' She swallowed. She was showing off again.

'I didn't know that,' said Adam. Indulgently, she thought, as though he was listening to a chatterbox child. 'So what do they do, your parents?' he asked. 'Apart from being great.'

And now he was definitely making fun of her. Wasn't he?

'My dad's a carpenter and my mother does his books and they're both good people.'

Was *good* any better than *great*?

'Not good in the namby-pamby sense. I mean, they're not churchy people. I just mean, well, we're all atheists, actually, the three of us. The unholy trinity, my grandparents used to call it. Before they died.' She heard herself sounding more and more like Beth. 'Anyway, we all believe in reason,' she said.

Adam began tapping his glass. 'So you think believers are irrational?' he said.

Oops. What if he trotted off to church on Sundays and helped out in soup kitchens in the name of the Lord?

'I didn't mean that either,' she said. 'Non-rational isn't the same as irrational. But what about that bunch of Christians who reckoned the Boxing Day tsunami was god's punishment on gays? That's not only irrational, it's appallingly cruel.'

'But what about the other kind of Christians who believe in a god of compassion?'

'You mean the hateful kind who'll forgive gay people as long as they don't have sex?'

Adam folded his hands on the table. 'Of course there are religious extremists,' he said. 'We've got some in the government right now. But what about the church's position on asylum seekers? Anglicans, Catholics, the Uniting Church. They've all been very vocal, very active, trying to shut down the offshore detention centres. Do you know about them?'

Hazel drew herself up. 'Of course I know about Nauru and Manus Island,' she said. 'I'm not one those young people who only cares about the Kardashians.'

'What's a Kardashian?' he said, straight-faced. 'Someone from a newly formed Balkan State?'

Hazel had to laugh. 'You're joking, right?'

'I am. I saw them on TV once. There were three of them, and they all looked like nothing on earth. Entirely artificial.'

'So you like your women natural, then?'

'I don't like women as a group,' he said. 'I mean, well, I don't mean I'm gay. Not that there's anything wrong with that.' He looked down at the table, up again at her. 'I like particular women and I don't like others,' he said. 'It's a matter of their values, their character. It's very simple.'

'Your guiding principle. Simplicity.'

He took in a breath, seemed to relax. 'I know a famous saying too,' he said. 'About simplicity. *All evil stems from our inability to sit quietly alone in a room.*'

'That's Pascal. And it's not *evil*, actually, it's *problems*. You must have read a bad translation.'

Adam banged his head, playfully. 'You mean all this time,

I've been living a virtuous and noble life because I don't know any French?'

'Quite possibly.'

She wished she could say that two in a room would be much better. Companionable. Possibly exciting. But maybe he was only assessing her character. Just being friendly. Returning a book, making amends.

'So what takes you out of your room, Hazel?' he said.

She remembered her doomed attempt of — what was it — a matter of an hour ago?

'I attend interviews for jobs I don't get.'

He gave her a look, like a warning. 'Tell me something hopeful,' he said.

How to explain her more-or-less aimless life? 'I meet up with friends and we talk about work, study, relationships,' she said. 'The usual stuff. And sometimes I go to parties, although I think I'm getting too old for parties, they're mostly very superficial. Except' — she would be a woman of character if it killed her — 'the last party I went to, someone persuaded me to volunteer for the Greens. You know, the political party?'

'Yes.'

'Not that I haven't helped them before,' she said, warming to her theme. 'I persuaded my parents to vote for them, when they've been rusted-on Labor supporters all their lives. Asylum seekers and climate change, I told them, the two big issues. The Greens are the only party with moral vision and evidence-based policies, I said. Plus I handed out how-to-vote cards at the last election.'

'And how was that?'

'Oh, I thought it might be a bit scary, that people would be aggressive or rude because they think the Greens are loony.' She flinched. 'Do you think the Greens are loony?'

'Not at all.'

'Good. It's just that some people — obviously not you — they think the Greens will ruin the economy and flood us with refugees, that kind of thing. But I have to say it wasn't too bad in the end, handing out the cards. I was in conservative heartland but the worst thing that happened was people turning up their well-bred noses at me. All those women wearing un-creased linen shirts. I mean, how do they do that? Linen always creases the second I put it on. And all those men with meaty faces and yachty kinds of shoes and probably a house by the ocean that I hope will be engulfed by massive, vengeful waves.'

He laughed, said she'd got it just right.

'And now I'm going doorknocking,' she said, trying not to sound too smug. Now that she'd proved her point, several times over. 'You know, raising awareness about what matters. I don't think the Greens have much money because they don't take dodgy donations. You know, from fossil fuel companies, property developers, organisations like that. So doorknocking can make a lot of difference. It's important to do your bit.'

'That's very commendable,' he said.

'And I'm supposed to be doing some training soon.'

'So am I. I'm one of the trainers, in fact.'

'A trainer? You mean, you —'

'It's what I do. I volunteer for the Greens. I've been doing it for years.'

'And you let me gabble on.' She could feel her cheeks burning. 'You just sat there and let me make an idiot of myself.'

'No, no, not at all. I was enjoying listening. You're very funny.'

She stiffened. 'Well, I'm glad you found me so amusing,' she said. 'If I believed in reincarnation I'd come back as a stand-up comedian.' She saw his face drop, heard him rush to apologise, as she toyed with her glass, churned up inside by all her silly talk. 'I didn't mean to be prickly,' she said. 'I just don't want you thinking...'

'Yes?'

'I don't want you thinking I'm a ditz,' she said. 'You know. A waste of space.'

'If I thought that…' He was watching her steadily, holding her gaze. 'I wouldn't have asked you for a coffee. No, wine.' He looked at her empty glass. 'Would you like another?'

She hadn't even realised she'd finished. 'Thanks, I'm good, I'm not really a big drinker.'

And not a waste of space either.

'So tell me more about you,' she said. 'You—well—you don't talk much about yourself, do you?'

'I'm a recovering narcissist,' he said. 'I take it one day at a time.'

'Well, I'm going to make you lapse,' she said. 'Tell me why you belong to the Greens. Why you've worked with them for years.'

'You don't mind a long story?'

'I don't mind if it's an epic poem.'

Because now that she knew he liked her, liked listening to her, even found her funny in a warm kind of way, she could sit there for hours, just looking into his eyes.

'Well, I used to be a Labor voter, just like your parents,' he said. 'But then the party started wheeling to the right, trying to privatise everything under the sun, introducing uni fees. That was under Keating and Hawke. Do you know about—'

'Keating was the prime minister who collected French antique clocks,' she said. 'A working-class boy who ended up being an art connoisseur.'

'Did you read that somewhere?'

'My dad told me. He also called him a wanker, not because of the clocks but because of his massive ego.'

Adam grinned. 'He was never short on that. Just like Bob Hawke.'

'Did he collect clocks as well?'

'I think he preferred women.' She could see his hands

clutching his glass. 'Anyway, I switched to the Greens because of asylum seekers. When I heard about a leaky boat.'

'The *Tampa*?'

'No, but it was around the same time. This one was called the *SIEV X*.'

'I've never heard of it.'

'That's not surprising, Hazel. Both major parties have been keeping it under wraps for years. Anyway, SIEV stands for Suspected Illegal Entry Vessel. That's a cracker of a name, isn't it, for a boat carrying more than four hundred desperate human beings.'

'And the X?'

'It means the government hadn't assigned the boat a tracking number. Because they were hunting down the boats, sending them back to whichever blighted country they came from. And they're still doing it, of course.'

He said *hunted them down* as though he'd just seen something ugly creeping through the door.

'It's just a devastating, heartbreaking story,' he said. 'People throw the word *tragedy* around like confetti at a wedding. You know, some vacuous, pampered celebrity dies of a drug overdose and we're meant to see this as some profound kind of loss. But the *SIEV X* was a genuine tragedy. Over four hundred people in a boat built for forty.'

'That can't be—'

'True? It's absolutely true. And three hundred and fifty-three of them drowned at sea. Some Indonesian fishermen found the survivors a couple of days later. Imagine how terrible they must have felt.'

Hazel studied his earnest face. 'Maybe the government didn't know about the boat,' she said. 'All those deaths.'

'That's what they claimed. But it beggars belief, really, because they'd been doing intensive surveillance operations in the area for some time.' He tapped his glass again. 'There were four government investigations by both major parties.

Four. But it's the old game: set up inquiries with terms of reference that will let you off the hook.'

'And so that the public forgets?'

He nodded. 'And do you know the official name for all those deaths? *A Certain Maritime Incident.*'

'That sounds like the novel *1984*.'

'It was two thousand and one, and entirely real.' He gave a slight shrug. 'So that's my story,' he said. 'My conversion, if you like. And what about you, Hazel? What made you political?'

'Well, I wouldn't call me political, really. Not like you, I mean.' She heard her voice sounding small when she didn't want to be small. But not really big either, not self-inflating. 'I didn't have a moment,' she said. 'It was my mum and dad, really. They've talked politics for as long as I can remember, so I grew up listening about workers' rights and women's rights and Indigenous rights and, well, everyone's rights except big business. Like that billionaire coal baron who tricked the workers into voting him into parliament so he could get even richer at their expense. That's my dad talking, he can be a bit of a ranter and, well, you have to do more than rant, don't you?'

'Well, it's not a bad place to start. And I wish I'd had parents like yours.'

'So they're...'

'Dead. My father ploughed their Volvo into a bus. Which is wonderfully ironic, since they never made way for anyone. Loathsome people. Oh, don't look so shocked, Hazel. I don't believe in speaking well of the dead when they were rotten people in life.'

She was less shocked than saddened by this dismal revelation.

'How were they rotten?' she said. 'I mean, what did they do?'

'Well, my father was a businessman who—I can't say this

politely—fucked people over. And my mother was something called a socialite. Social-lite, who did fuck-all with her life.'

'So—how did you get to be you?'

'Good question. How does anyone escape their family?' He gave her the warmest smile. 'Maybe it's the same as reading,' he said. 'You meet certain people in the same way you meet certain books, the ones who give you the words for what's already inside you.' He leaned back, as though ready for another drink, then suddenly looked at his watch. 'Jessie,' he said, and sprang from his chair. 'I have to get home. His aunt—she picked him up from school because I had a meeting, and I have to get going.' He tugged at his collar. 'She has an important date.'

Yet he wasn't making a move, stood looking down at her, his hands on the table.

'It's early days for her, with a new man,' he said. 'I don't want to cramp her style.' But still he wasn't moving. 'Jessie adores his aunt. I'm very lucky to have her help.'

Hazel saw the crinkles round his eyes; that mop of greying hair she wanted to run her fingers through.

'Maybe it's not luck,' she said. 'Maybe you deserve it.'

She wished he would hold out his hand. Wished she could feel the warmth of his skin.

'Thanks so much for...' He trailed off, not taking his eyes from hers. 'I had a good time.'

He sounded nervous, even anxious, building up to something and then drawing back. Hazel felt her hands tighten under the table. Should she offer him her phone number? Give him her address? Leap up and kiss him on the mouth?

'Maybe we'll meet again,' he said. 'On the campaign trail, I mean.' Then he said a hurried goodbye, turned, walked briskly to the door without looking back.

A kind, sensitive, principled man. A man, not a guy.

She tried to picture him but his face was already blurring

and she didn't know how this was possible: to have seen him so clearly, every curve and line and shadow on his face, and then watch him disappear. She thought about another glass of wine after all and how he'd said they might meet again. Remembering their words and glances and her flutters of emotion and wanting him to like her, like her so much, wanting him to make a move. And now some guy was asking for Adam's chair and this made her feel even emptier, with couples all around and people trying to be coupled and here she was, *alone again, naturally*. Who used to sing that? Might still be singing it in some moody, wine-drenched bar?

She knew what she had to do: message Simon.

You said you'd send me details of the training. The Greens.

Sorry been flat out

So when is it?

A couple of days

Hell. Talk about disorganised. OK. Next step.

Do you know a guy called Adam in the Greens? In his forties I guess

Solid looking guy?

Yes. And striking pale blue eyes

Not very subtle but she wanted to be sure, as she watched the bubbles of an answer form slowly on the screen.

Sure Adams a legend in the party

He's a trainer isn't he? For doorknockers.

Yeah training on Friday with you on his list with me and Felicia

She could have kissed him. And Felicia. Anyone who happened to be passing.

So how come you know Adam

Not that she knew him, as such.

We got talking on a train

I bet he chewed off your ear about the Greens

Something like that yes

Yes and yes and yes.

To speak or not to speak

'She wasn't home, was she?' said Beth, stomping into the living room. 'She sent me a text to say she forgot and didn't even have the decency to say sorry.'

Beth had been to see her mother. One of those *you're getting too* kinds of mothers — *you're getting too fat, thin, lazy, wild, big for your boots.*

'Not a complete waste of time, though,' she said, and plumped herself into the red beanbag. 'I flirted with a very cute guy on the bus. And someone left a magazine on the seat in front and I got to reading about a bunch of celebrities, all the things they're afraid of. Apart from losing their celebrity, that is. There was some B-grade actor who's really afraid of antique furniture, which is seriously weird. I mean, why would anyone be afraid of a seventeenth-century chaise longue? And other weird stuff, like the fear of bellybuttons or holes in cheese. Apparently that's some existential thing, about a hole being a nothing surrounded by a something, so whoever looks at the hole feels like they're facing the void.'

'I don't believe that, Beth. That has to be made up.'

Should she tell Beth about the man?

'It *did* sound pretty whacky to me,' said Beth. 'There was other bizarre stuff as well, about the fear of buttons and the fear of big words — no chance of you catching that one, Haze. But the one that really amazed me was the fear of gravity. They say it's a phobia caused by a trauma, like falling from a very great height.'

'I know you're afraid of rats,' said Hazel. 'Which I totally understand because they're so—'

'Don't go there, Hazel, or I'll scare you with an image of sharks.'

'OK, sorry.'

'I won't go on about those rows of teeth and—'

'Stop. Please. I won't mention rats, ever again.'

'Hey,' said Beth, 'I just thought of something. What if gravity ceased to exist? You'd get to float around in space, feel at one with the universe. You might even see God.'

'I thought you were a rational materialist,' said Hazel.

'WTF?'

'It means you believe that everything comes down to the physical.'

Beth laughed. 'I wish I'd had the chance to get down and physical with the guy on the bus.' She checked her phone. 'Six o'clock. My alcohol gene just kicked in.'

She stumbled out of the beanbag, headed for the kitchen, returned with a bottle and two of their biggest glasses.

'I have to fill out my Newstart form after dinner,' she said.

'Me too.'

Newstart, Hazel thought: it sounded like a cross between a self-help manual and Orwell's *1984*. No wonder she felt depressed.

Should she tell Beth now? Wait until the wine charged her up? What would Beth make of her silly agitation over a brief encounter with an older man? Beth, who she always confessed to, told her everything there was to know.

Beth started waving her glass about because she'd seen something *truly disturbing*, she said, *an ad* in the local paper, *set out in huge pink font: WHAT'S THE DESIGNER VAGINA?* She'd nearly toppled over when she read it, she said, all the stuff about tightening this and rejuvenating that, collagen and creams, making women feel even more ashamed of their bodies than they already did.

'Cosmetic surgery,' she said. 'It's —'

'Ideologically pernicious?'

'I'd call it a pile of crap.'

Almost spilling her wine now, denouncing all the women, thousands there were, having surgery on their bums because they wanted a perky one like Pippa Middleton's. That kind of thing drove her nuts, she said, and who the hell was Pippa Middleton anyway? Hazel tried to explain but Beth said she already knew and that's not why she was angry. She was angry because Pippa Middleton was only famous for having a sister who was only famous because she'd married a prince who seemed like a nice enough guy, cheering up disabled kids and all that, but that wasn't the point, was it, about the monarchy? An accident of birth, unearned wealth and privilege and the next girl who told her they *adored* Kate Middleton because she was so pretty and wore such stylish clothes and had such a cute baby was in serious danger of being punched. Hazel was confused for a moment because she thought Beth wanted to punch the baby, and then she wondered aloud what they could have for dinner.

She took a gulp of wine. Now was the moment. To tell Beth.

I met a man on a train, she might say. We talked. Went for a drink. But, well, he must be at least forty.

But she didn't want Beth to laugh at her. Not about something so serious.

***

The next day Hazel took the train to see her mother, feeling... what was she feeling? That she wanted to see her mother. To ask about an older man. Except that nothing had really happened, had it? And nothing might happen at all. Still, it would be good to catch up with her mother. Have a coffee. Think about asking. About the idea of an older man.

Hazel looked through the window of the train. Wished

Adam were sitting beside her, with his messy hair and solid body and those pale blue eyes.

She really had to get a grip.

Her mother would probably be doing her father's accounts, or pottering in the garden of their weatherboard house, bought in a distant decade when you didn't have to sell your body to afford an ocean view. Well, a glimpse of the Indian Ocean, if you stood up on her parents' roof, preferably on a trampoline, looking through a telescope. And now Hazel was beginning to puff because she wasn't very fit. She was seriously under-fit, which was why she didn't have a perky bum like Pippa Middleton.

She could see the garden up ahead, with the native bushes she'd persuaded her parents to plant. She'd told them that natives looked beautiful, would reduce their water bills and celebrate Australian fauna. The trifecta, her father would have called it. He liked saying things in groups of three. Like: a glass of red with dinner helps your digestion, lowers your cholesterol and supports the local wine industry. Her mother had hit back in one go: Far too many calories, she'd warned him, but he'd waved her away because *it's just what happens when you get older, a couple of kilos here and there*. Unlike her mother, Hazel was lousy at maths, but she reckoned her dad had added fifteen kilos to his middle-aged frame.

Walking up the path, she felt that tug of connection again. It was the only house she'd ever lived in before moving in with Beth. All the emblems of her childhood were there, proudly displayed on shelves or kept safe in boxes. School certificates and badges, a trophy for winning some debating competition, the reports full of comments like *Hazel is a pleasure to teach, always tries her best*. Talk about a loser. Still, it was sweet of her mother to preserve these ancient achievements. Not like Beth's carping mother, and a father who'd taken off because he decided he didn't like kids. *Shame it took five of us to find out*, Beth had told her. The first time Hazel had gone to her friend's house she'd seen and heard the damage. The mother's sour face and sarcastic voice, yelling at them to go outside and play. Later, shoving a plate of biscuits across the table and snapping that she *didn't do* Tim Tams. *Nice* biscuits, they were called. They'd tasted like cardboard but tried to trick you into pleasure with a sprinkling of sugar on top. And the noise: Beth's four bellowing siblings prodding with eight sharp elbows and calling Hazel names, their mother slapping them round those elbows, and the ears as well. When it was time to leave, Beth had walked Hazel to the letterbox and cried, while Hazel clasped her hand and felt her friend's shame and wished she could take her home forever.

Years later, she'd asked Beth what she remembered about her father, and her friend had pulled a face. She remembered how he'd looked at her as if she wasn't there.

Hazel rang the doorbell. A work day, and her father's car wasn't in the driveway, but she wasn't going to take a risk by letting herself in. Last Saturday she'd opened the door to see her parents scrambling out from their bedroom, smoothing down their clothes, rosy with that telltale afterglow. A bit embarrassing, really, but still, it was kind of nice to know your parents desired each other after nearly thirty years of marriage. She rang the doorbell again, and there was her mother, opening the door and — she saw it straight away. The tears. Her mother wiping her face. Hazel was aghast. She hadn't seen her mother cry in years.

'Mum.'

'I wasn't expecting you.'

She ushered Hazel inside, steered her to the sofa. Hazel took her hand, asked her what was wrong. Her mother pointed to a magazine on the coffee table.

'It's this article I was reading,' she said. 'About babies.'

'Babies?'

'They died from SIDS. Do you know about SIDS?'

Hazel nodded, unsure.

'It's heartbreaking,' said her mother. 'To bring a child into the world and then...' There was a tiny throbbing in her throat. 'It wasn't quite like that for me, but I had a baby who died inside me, just before she was due to be born. Three years after you were born. We called her Juliet.' She took a raspy breath. 'And then everything just kept getting worse. I lost three more babies. Three miscarriages, two early on but the last one—I was over four months pregnant.' Her tears welled again. 'I didn't even give them names. I should have given them names but it was too hard, just all too hard.' Picking up the magazine, putting it down again. 'Your dad wanted a tribe of children, but I gave up in the end.'

'You didn't *give up*, Mum. It wasn't your fault.' Hazel watched her mother closely. 'Why didn't you tell me this before?'

'But there was nothing to be done, was there?'

'At least I would have stopped pestering you for a sister.'

'You didn't *pester*, Hazel. And besides, I didn't want to put you off having babies. It's bad enough when mothers carry on about the tortures they go through when they're giving birth. Those women who wear their pain as a badge of honour, when all it does is scare the living daylights out of their daughters.' She patted Hazel's hand. 'I didn't want to burden you, sweetheart, that's all, and I'm sorry for burdening you now. It's just that sometimes it comes back to you. It's like a pocket of sadness in my heart that I'd almost forgotten was there.'

'Do you know my first memory of you, Mum?' Hazel nestled in close. 'I was sitting by a window and it was raining. I can't remember how old I was but I remember the feeling. As if the world had suddenly turned grey, as if it might stay like that forever. Then I heard your voice and there you were, standing by the doorway and smiling at me and everything turned into colour again.'

'And my first memory of you?' said her mother. 'Holding you in my arms just after you were born, your eyes looking into mine, and I felt so peaceful and content.' She laughed, softly. 'You have all this ahead of you, Hazel. It's the most wonderful thing in the world, to raise a lovely child.'

This desire that Hazel had never felt, had only read about, heard women talk about, that drove them to clinics and donors, or to use another woman's body. It smacked of desperation, she thought, or some egotistical need to replicate the self. But remembering her mother's pain—those four, sad babies who never came into the world—how could she possibly protest?

Her mother rose from the sofa. 'Let's have coffee,' she said, and headed for the kitchen. 'How are things with you, anyway? Been on any dates lately?'

Now was the moment. But Hazel couldn't take it.

'I'd tell you, Mum, you know that.'

Her mother tut-tutted. 'I don't understand it,' she said. 'Any male with half a brain would snap you up. What about that young man you mentioned, Simon, wasn't it? The young man from the Greens?'

'He has a girlfriend. Who seems very nice.'

Her mother set out cups, began to slice some fruitcake. 'What about going to their meetings, then? There must be lots of intelligent young men in the Greens. Or have you thought about online dating? June King's daughter, Sasha, she met a very nice boy online. They both like cats and Italian food.'

'And sunsets.' Hazel laughed. 'Plus walking in the rain. And jogging. I bet they both go jogging while they gaze at the sunset and knock back tubs of ravioli.'

Her mother frowned. 'You're not taking this seriously, Hazel.' She stood by the kettle, waiting for it to boil. 'June's other daughter, the younger one, Billie—they were obsessed with having a boy, of course—Billie's just enrolled in a nursing degree. Have you thought about nursing? It's only a three-year course, or maybe it's three-and-a-half. Anyway, they have bridging courses. You know, if you haven't done much science. Biology and things.'

Trying to sound casual.

'It's a possibility,' said Hazel. Thinking: more years of slog, more essays and exams. Not to mention wading deeper into debt. But her mother was pressing her, saying she'd make such a fine nurse because she was *smart and thoughtful, with a great sense of humour*, which was a blessing in a hospital, apparently. And *kind*.

'Kindness goes a long way, she said.

Not very far, thought Hazel, when you were trying to keep people alive.

'You could specialise in looking after babies,' her mother said brightly. 'That would be so rewarding.' She pointed to the magazine. 'Mind you, I'm sick to death of baby George. There's a million photos of him in there, with all the carrying on about the trials and tribulations of being his mother, when she must have a whole fleet of nannies. I bet she has a nanny just to wipe his royal bum.' She sipped her coffee, set down her cup. 'I have to tell you, Hazel, I'm worried about your father,' she said. 'You must have noticed he's been piling on the weight but he won't do a thing about it. Smaller portions, I said, no snacks, and why don't you come for walks with me? But do you know what he said? I could have killed him—he said that sex uses up a lot of calories. As though that would solve the problem.'

'That reminds me of an ancient Greek play,' said Hazel. '*Lysistrata*.'

'Ancient Greeks?' said her mother. 'They didn't have a problem with their weight, did they?'

'It was something much more serious, Mum. The women threatened to withhold sex if their husbands went off to war.'

'That was a great idea.'

'A much better one than getting slaughtered in Peloponessia. The men invented astronomy, philosophy and algebra, but they couldn't negotiate for peace.'

Her mother nodded, took a delicate bite of cake. She was

still what old people called a looker, with golden lights in her hair, slim hips and slender legs. Not like me, thought Hazel, with hips and bum too big for the rest of me, like a woman in a medieval painting.

Did Adam think she looked like a medieval painting? Any kind of painting at all?

'Cake, love?'

'No thanks. Too much sugar makes me come out in spots.'

'Are you sure it's sugar? It could be, you know, stress.'

Hazel made reassuring noises, said she was fit and healthy and would definitely check out that nursing degree as soon as she got home. Because sometimes you had to lie to a mother to stop her from worrying. Did mothers ever stop worrying about their children? And why was there no word in English for a person's adult child?

'June's been talking about online dating herself,' said her mother. 'Some website called Plenty of Fish. I think she's very brave.'

Hazel remembered the names: eHarmony. RSVP. Naughty Date, presumably for adults who said *winky* instead of *penis*, *lady garden* instead of *vagina*. She hadn't bothered to look.

Her mother leaned in closer. 'I wasn't supposed to tell anyone,' she said. 'June doesn't want her girls to know.'

'Why not?'

'She's worried they might laugh at her. Do you know what she said to me? *I don't want to lose my dignity, it's one of the few things I have left.* She never saw it coming, with her husband and that woman from down the road. She said it felt like life had punched her in the face.'

Then her mother screwed up her own face, apologised for gossiping.

'It's not gossiping, Mum. You're being a good friend. And I'm really sorry about what happened. With your four babies.'

She couldn't begin to imagine a life growing inside her, a life dying inside her. And *Juliet*. A sister. She would have been—what—twenty-one or twenty-two by now. This too, was unimaginable.

Her mother sighed. 'They were your father's babies, too,' she said. Then she looked Hazel straight in the eye. 'Are you sure there's nothing wrong, sweetheart? You look a bit worried. I didn't upset you, did I?'

'I'm just a bit preoccupied. Job applications again.'

'Well, give that nursing degree some thought, won't you?'

'Sure, Mum. I'll check it out as soon as I get home.'

At least she hadn't made a promise.

Encounters

Hazel and Beth began their day by eating virtuous, boring Weetbix. Eat your Weetbix, brush your teeth, wash your undies in the bathroom sink because you couldn't be screwed lugging a bag of dirty washing to the laundromat, which was often full of weary mothers and electronic kids and the occasional hopeless male chatting up a hopeful female. But today wasn't really an ordinary day. Beth's dress, for starters: bold red and electric blue, with some snaky green things that looked like tropical plants. Her interview dress, apparently, because she'd actually managed to snag one with the owner of a travel agency. *Consultancy,* Beth had corrected herself, *it sounds much classier that way.* She was bright with possibilities, as well as her dress, because she'd done some preparation by having coffee with a guy who used to be a travel agent—oops, consultant. Patrick. Very helpful and very good-looking but married, alas, with two kids and another one on the way, and he didn't look a day over thirty. Anyway, she'd contacted him through Facebook, via the cousin of a friend of someone she used to work with, and he had nearly two thousand friends.

'Patrick told me that sales skills top the list,' she said. 'As long as you can charm people into forking out thousands to reach their destination, it doesn't really matter if you don't have destination knowledge yourself.'

'What's that?'

'It means you've done some travelling. It has more

authority if you call it the other thing. So it's no big deal that I've only been to Sydney and France and Hong Kong with my cousin Carson. That's always a mouthful, my cousin Carson, so I should just call him Carson and you know who he is anyway, although I don't think you've ever met Carson. My cousin.' Beth shoved in a spoonful of cereal, chewed quickly, swallowed. 'And I've never been to Bali, which might be a point in my favour cos everyone's been to Bali.'

Hazel nodded. Tried to look encouraging. Wondered if people actually booked face-to-face these days instead of buying their tickets online.

'Anyway, I tick the other boxes,' said Beth. 'Solid academic results and a passion for travel. Well, I would have a passion for travel if I could afford it. Plus Patrick gave me a whole lot of other advice about ticketing and computer skills and multi-tasking and de-stressing because it can get really full-on, and other things I can't remember. All that for the price of a decaf soy latte. Except I forgot to ask for decaf when I ordered at the counter. What if he's one of those people who reacts really badly to caffeine? What if he gets a giant headache or stays up all night with the jitters? I'd never forgive myself. Anyway, he was impressed by my out-there personality. Another plus in the travel industry when you're dealing with customers. Oops. Clients. You're meant to call them clients.'

She pushed away her bowl, smoothed down her dress.

'I bought this at David Jones,' she said. 'Two hundred bucks knocked down to eighty. What do you think? I want to look—you know—ready to take on the world.'

Hazel thought the world wasn't ready for a dress like that.

'I think something—more professional—would be good,' she said.

Beth sighed. 'I think you're right.'

She picked up her spoon, began slurping her cereal again. Hazel had grown used to the slurping, after three years of living together. Like an old married couple, Todd had once joked.

'I guess I'll wear my sensible navy blue suit,' said Beth.

Their teaching clothes, which they'd worn in different but equally ratbag schools in order to set high standards for the students. Although they'd both turned a blind eye to the shirts that weren't tucked in, the multiple piercings and clumps of mascara: all the gestures of youthful defiance. Hazel knew she'd been ridiculously naïve. The idealistic, please-feel-free-to-walk-all-over-me teacher who hadn't taught her semi-literate, often rude and probably unhappy students one goddamned useful thing. But now she was finally doing something useful, in a puny kind of way. Three hours of doorknocking for five weeks in a row. That's what Simon had messaged her, along with the details of the meeting. The meeting. The very words warmed her but she had to keep her cool.

Beth dashed off to change, dashed back, gave Hazel a here-goes-nothing grin and headed for the door.

Hazel went in search of distraction. Tried to block out what might lie ahead at a house in Wright Avenue, Swanbourne. When everything might go wrong. She thought about cleaning the living-room window, then decided she didn't really need a clearer view of the congested highway. She cleaned her bedroom window instead, which offered an unimpeded aerial shot of the desolate car park with its massive potholes from last winter's heavy rains. Next she tackled the fridge, one of her more courageous acts in recent times: broccoli gone to seed, tomatoes squashed and dripping, yoghurt that could have strutted off by itself, plus two mouldy bananas. Then she sorted out her wardrobe, throwing out dresses that were too dull or fussy or desperate, packed them in a bag destined for Vinnie's. All that waste: food and dresses and a pair of red boots that pinched her toes horribly. Two years ago, she'd bought them, thinking she'd look cool, and she just couldn't wait for them to order in her size.

How could she not feel ashamed?

She'd seen homeless people huddled in the streets. One of them had played a guitar as a mark of self-respect. Sometimes she dropped a coin into a tattered hat.

Next she tried to pass more time with *Persuasion*, although the tone was beginning to annoy her: a bit woe-is-me with a dash of English-stiff-upper-lip. But still, it was the book that had brought them together. Adam. Hazel. It was the book he'd held in his hands, the story that — her phone buzzed — an SMS: Todd, asking them to dinner, because *would you believe it a job in a bookshop and Dora wants to show off her ring.* Wasn't there some dopey golden oldie about that? That you'd have to be drunk to sing along to? *Third finger, left hand, that's where he placed the wedding band.* Probably sung by one of those all-girl bands with beehive hairdos and bright red lipstick, belting out their manufactured bliss.

She messaged back: *Heaps of congrats on the job will make a huge difference and can't wait to check out the ring*

She deleted the part about the ring because it sounded sarcastic. It was sarcastic.

She heard a quiet knock on her bedroom door, saw Beth's drawn face in the doorway.

'I was shit,' she said.

She sank down on the bed. 'After all the effort it took to write my application. I'm sick to death of writing applications and so fed up with people telling me I was a natural as a teacher. That'll look good on a CV, won't it: a Dip. Ed. in natural talent.'

'But you were a brilliant teacher, Beth. The students all loved you. I saw all the cards, the gifts.'

Beth pulled a face. 'I was *entertaining*,' she said. 'As well as being fucking exhausted. Perform, perform, perform, every single day, to kids who couldn't tell the difference between a plateau and a plate of chips. I was heading that way myself.' She looked on the point of tears.

'And that's why we left, Beth, remember? To save our sanity.'

Beth sniffed. 'I'm just so sick of feeling dumb,' she said.

Hazel put an arm around her friend's shoulder. 'I wish your mother's voice wasn't lodged in your brain,' she said.

'Ha! Do you know what happened the other day, Hazie? Aunty Dot was round for afternoon tea and she was boosting me up about how clever I was, with my two degrees and all, then she turned to my mother and said, *Aren't you proud of her, Lisa?* And do you know what she said, the cow? Not a fucking word. She didn't even have the grace to pretend.' She put her head on Hazel's shoulder. 'Todd told me I should try and laugh it off,' she said. 'I thought that was really funny.'

***

Hazel had tried on four dresses and all of them looked wrong—too boring, too flashy, too short—until she found the one that would do. Cool and floaty, without being shapeless, and if you looked closely, it matched the colour of her dark grey eyes. But as for her hair: flat and mousy brown again, now that she'd washed it a dozen times to get rid of the brazen copper. She used to buy a lot of product for that flat, lank hair, in the days when she was a keenly paid-up member of capitalist consumer society: special shampoos and conditioners that were meant to add volume, make your hair billow and swirl. Or if you wanted to be funky, there was sticky gel or fluffy mousse (sometimes one helped, sometimes the other: there was no logic to it at all), as well as spray, foam, de-curl and do-curl. Hundreds of dollars she'd spent, in her quest to be appealing. No wonder she'd been more or less broke when she quit her job. Ran away.

She could still feel the girl's slimy spit on her cheek. She could still see the girl's vindictive eyes.

But now it was finally time to head for an unknown house, to an unknown man, who all this time had been living just a few kilometres from her doorstep. She decided to walk instead of catching a bus, because she needed the exercise, the late afternoon was balmy, and it would give her more time to settle down, take in the outside world, even if that world was a little bizarre: a For Sale sign on a massive brick-and-tile, with its bold red words across the top: CIRCA 1987. Circa? Was that white Australia's version of ancient history? And which real estate guru had dreamt that up? Next she saw an ancient woman (circa 1929) watering her English country garden. More like flooding. Didn't she know that water was precious, that Australia was the driest continent on the planet? She turned the corner and saw a front verge stacked with a computer and chair, a microwave, a sofa, a mattress, a table, because new ones were always beckoning. And now another house for sale, with a sign boasting five bedrooms, a formal dining room, three bathrooms, etc., etc., and something called a powder room. But women didn't powder their noses anymore, they injected their skin instead, stretched it, tried to turn back time. Like Nicole Kidman, with her rabbit-in-the-headlights look. Our Nic. The woman hadn't lived in Australia for years.

Hazel knew she was filling her head with garbage. She, the great consumer, railing against consumerism to stop herself feeling afraid. Because she was almost there, turning into his street. Cars parked on his verge. A brick-and-tile with an overgrown native garden, bushes leaning into one other. A front porch with a worn, comfy-looking sofa. There was no turning back now, climbing up four steps, standing at the open door, and there he was. Sitting at a table. His back to her. She knocked. He stood up, turned around and walked towards her, opened the door and her heart was *lubdubbing* madly and surely he would see it beating underneath her dress. They said hello. As people do. Was she meant to offer her hand? Wasn't it the woman's place to offer her hand? Even if they'd already met?

'I saw your name on the list,' he said, in his low, quiet voice. 'I thought there couldn't be too many Hazels.'

It was only now she understood how much she loved that voice.

He was stepping aside now and letting her pass and she couldn't even look at him, saw nothing but a blur of sunshine through a window, then faces coming into focus. Simon and Felicia waving. And then the introductions: a woman called Molly, maybe in her fifties but most definitely decked out in turquoise. Her dress, necklace, earrings, bracelets, some streaks in her hair. A man called Neville, maybe older, with a sour kind of face.

All this waving and shaking of hands, and still she hadn't touched him. Adam.

She heard offers of *tea, coffee, milk, sugar*, as she willed her hands to loosen. *Would you like tea or coffee, Hazel?* She looked up into those bright, pale blue eyes that were — she saw it now — the exact colour of his shirt, and it was the melting feeling all over again and she heard herself say that she'd prefer a glass of wine — again — if that was alright — again, and now everyone was starting a chorus: *me too… red if you have it… I can pop down to the bottle shop…* She was beginning to like these wine-drinking people as she glanced around the room, trying not to look like a snoop. A simple room, yes, but charming. Polished floorboards, off-white walls, a plain wooden table and six wooden chairs. A small white bookcase with a few rows of books. But not an ornament in sight, no shiny, pointless things, no fuss or display.

Adam handed her a glass of wine and then called for their attention in a non-commanding kind of way. She heard papers shuffling, saw people nodding, told herself to keep her mind on higher things. Adam thanked them all for their commitment, handed them each a file, guided them through the steps as she dutifully turned the pages. There were summaries of policies — whoever invented bullet points deserved a medal — protocols for introducing yourself, strategies for meeting with resistance, how to answer questions, how to jog people's memories, because sometimes they forgot the issues.

'Or they don't really care,' said Neville.

Adam ignored him, reminded them to put leaflets into letterboxes when no one answered the door. To watch out for snarling dogs lurking in a front garden. And never accept an offer to go inside a house, he said, *especially you women*. Next up he showed them some forms, and how to tick off people's responses: Strong Support, Weak Support, Strong Opposition.

'Most of all,' he said, 'we need to listen to voters' concerns. It's courteous and strategic. It's killing two birds with one stone.'

Molly laughed. 'Did you hear what you just said, Adam? A Green, killing birds?' She looked around the table. 'That's dear Adam for you,' she giggled, and thrust out her chest, showing not so much a hint of cleavage but a highly explicit statement.

Who was this goddamned woman? Hazel decided she had to speak.

'Maybe we shouldn't say *concerns*,' she said. 'That's an invitation to complain. Maybe we should ask people what *matters* to them. You know, encourage them to think constructively. Or to speak from the heart.'

'I like that,' said Felicia. 'I like the heart.'

'*Matters* it is,' said Adam, and looked around the table. 'Good call, Hazel. I should have thought of that years ago.'

Hazel flushed with pleasure.

'So what do people *really* care about?' said Molly.

'Their taxes,' said Neville.

'Asylum seekers are a big issue,' said Simon.

'Keeping them out, you mean,' said Neville.

What a pain, thought Hazel. And wasn't a cynical Green a contradiction in terms? She could see Adam grimace but trying to move on, making some points about climate change.

'And if people don't seem to care'—jumping in before Neville could speak—'appeal to their children's future. Their grand-children's future.'

Silence. A few nods from Simon. Was Neville the serial pest? Why was there always one in the classroom?

'One more thing, Adam,' said Molly. She was doing the fluttering eyelash routine. There was always one of those, as well. 'What would you like us to wear?'

'Thanks for reminding me, Molly. It is important: that moment when a person first sees you and wonders who you are.'

Tell me about it, thought Hazel.

'We should wear green-coloured clothes,' said Neville. 'But only if people already have some. Why should we fork out money when we're already giving up our time?'

He was still sounding grouchy but Hazel took his point. And she didn't own one green item of apparel.

Others were chipping in now: Molly wanting Greens T-shirts, important for verification, while Simon felt strongly that people were put off by the slogans. Felicia agreed with Neville, although Hazel was thinking that Felicia's dress was bound to be irrelevant, since unknown men at unknown doors would be undressing her with their non-political eyes.

She cleared her throat. Ready to say her bit. 'What about everyday clothes?' she said. 'As long as they're neat and clean. You know, look mainstream so people don't feel antagonistic. And then hit them with your radical views.'

'Not exactly hit them,' said Molly.

Adam nodded. 'Every year we have this discussion about clothes,' he said. 'And every year there are different opinions. And, well, I'm with Hazel.'

Who tried not to look triumphant.

Neville was glowering now, said he wasn't very happy with *all this*.

'What's the problem with neat, clean clothes?' said Adam.

'I mean doorknocking.' Neville waved his hands about, suddenly agitated. 'I'm feeling like a Jehovah's Witness. I mean, what right do we have to go knocking on people's doors?

Invading their space, telling them how to live their lives.'

Silence.

Adam folded his hands on the table. 'We're not preaching,' he said. 'We're meant to listen. And use the art of persuasion.'

'Then it's only a difference in method,' snapped Neville.

'Neville. What are the two principles that always guide us? Compassion and reason. How can it be wrong to—'

'Yeah, yeah, I know.' Neville drained his glass of wine, drew himself up. 'You're so bloody high-minded,' he said.

Hazel heard an edge in his voice of—what? Animosity? Malice? She felt tension ripple round the table, saw people looking down at the floor or through the window. And then Felicia laughed.

'It is right to be high in your mind,' she said. 'My father is low in his mind because he is only thinking of his male organ.'

Which made them all laugh, even Neville.

'One more thing,' said Adam. 'This is a five-week campaign, so pace yourselves. Don't let your emotions run too high and try to stay hopeful. The election's a long way off, so people might not be engaged. Oh, and don't forget to bring water. Keep up your fluids.'

'That is five things you are saying,' said Felicia.

Adam gave her the warmest smile.

But not once, thought Hazel, has he smiled at me, or cast me a meaningful glance. Whatever the meaning might be.

'OK, time to organise partners,' he said.

Partners! Hazel's heart thumped. Molly and Neville. Were they a couple? Simon and Felicia, of course, Simon gushing his thanks for her support, as though this was his first time doorknocking, or they'd just had bad sex and she was jollying him along. And how would Felicia manage, with English as her second language? But how good of her to try.

'So that leaves you and me, Hazel.'

Who wanted to place his head on her breasts, stroke his greying hair.

'We'll be doing one of the easier suburbs,' he said. 'Leafy Nedlands. A more educated demographic.'

'That's near my leafy suburb,' she said. 'Except I don't live in a mansion, just a run-down flat. With a woman. Only we're just friends.'

Thank god no one was listening to her adolescent signals. And thank god for mobile phones, since everyone except Adam was glued to their screens as they rose from their chairs. Could she hang around without being too obvious? Did he even want her hanging round? Everyone was beginning to trail out the door and so she had to trail behind and onto the verandah, trying not to feel disappointed. Because what had she expected, after all? That Adam would lift her up and carry her to his bed? Offer ardent protestations of undying love? She must keep things in perspective.

She heard a car pulling up and saw a figure leaping out onto the footpath, heard the blast of a horn, an excited shout at the gate, Adam waving. A blur of legs in red shorts hurtling up the steps.

'Dad!!!' In a tiny, gleeful voice, launching himself at Adam, being hoisted into his arms.

Adam wrapped the child in a bear hug, then turned him round to face her. 'This is my son, Jessie,' he said. 'And Jessie, I want you to meet Hazel.'

A boy with a heart-shaped face and huge brown eyes, who didn't look a bit like Adam.

He eyed her cautiously. 'I don't know you,' he said.

What was she supposed to say? I won't bite you? Is that what you said to very small children?

'Well, I don't really know me either,' she said.

The child screwed up his face.

'You could look in a mirror then,' he said.

'I do when I brush my teeth. And then I poke out my tongue at me.'

'Hey, I do that too.'

He was wriggling in his father's arms and she was waiting, unsure. Then he slid down onto the porch, plonked his hands on his hips and looked up at her. She'd never felt like a giant before, had never seen such a tiny child in close-up.

'Do you wanna see my train set?' he said. 'It's got bridges and signals and heaps of animals and lots of ducks. Little teeny weeny ones.'

'Do they stand and watch the train go past?' she said. 'Wonder where it's going?'

He looked puzzled. 'How come you know that?'

'Because if I was a duck, that's what I'd do.'

He nodded like a sage old man. 'They're going to a magic land,' he said. 'It's a island wiv lots of purple mountains and big trees wiv monkeys in the trees and the monkeys swing around and make growly noises and eat bananas.'

'Sounds good to me,' said Hazel. 'I really like bananas.'

'Why?'

How could you describe taste? 'Because yellow's my favourite colour,' she said.

'Why?'

'Well, I guess it's a happy colour.'

Jessie gasped. 'It's a duck colour.'

'So ducks must be happy then,' she told him.

Was that a syllogism? Possibly. Jessie looked like he was thinking hard as well.

'But you can't tell if ducks are happy,' he said. 'They can't talk.'

Hazel searched for some kind of answer. 'Sometimes you can tell just by looking,' she said. 'Like, right now, you look happy to me because your red shorts make you look cheerful.'

'I got green ones too,' he said. 'But they make my bottom itch.'

She tried not to laugh. She didn't want to condescend.

'Did you know about that?' she said to Adam.

'I certainly do now.'

'Do you get an itchy bottom, Hazel?' said the child.

Adam put his hands on a pair of bony little shoulders. 'That's enough now, buddy,' he said. 'Say goodbye to Hazel and hop inside. I'll run your bath in a minute.'

Jessie ignored him, turned back to her.

'I'm four,' he said. 'I'm gunna be five.'

'In three weeks,' said Adam. 'I'm reminded every day.'

'Well, I hope you have a very happy birthday when it comes,' she said.

What else could she say? Maybe it was better to say nothing. Did children always need to be talked at? Impressed?

'You can come to my party,' he said. 'But I'm not gunna have balloons. My friend Aziz is really scared of balloons cos one bursted in his face and he cried.'

Adam put his hand on Jessie's back and moved him gently towards the door. Jessie began jumping into the house, hollering something that she didn't understand.

'Sorry about the itch,' said Adam. 'And all the questions. And the noise.'

'He's very sweet,' she said. 'You have nothing to be sorry for.'

He shuffled his feet on the floor.

'He doesn't look a bit like you,' she said.

'He looks exactly like his mother.'

'Is that difficult? I mean, it must be painful.'

He gave her that earnest look again. Chastisement. 'Can I tell you something, Hazel? I don't want to be treated as if I have a huge black raincloud hanging over my head. And I don't want to dwell on the past. Or in it.'

'I'm sorry. I just thought—'

'Yes, I know. And I appreciate it. But I'm not the only person who's lost someone they loved. It doesn't make me special.'

All the time his eyes were fixed on hers, as though he were offering her a challenge. Nudging her into a new kind of space, a serious space, even though he was smiling now. She felt herself loosen as well, as though something had been settled between them.

'Jessie certainly warmed to you,' he said.

'Well, there's no pretending, is there?'

He was looking at her intently. Did he even know that he was doing that? Then he suddenly looked away and out into the street.

'I think your lift's waiting,' he said.

She turned around. Simon and Felicia, sitting in a car. She'd completely forgotten their offer. When had they made the offer? She turned back to Adam, thanked him for all his help and advice and said she felt much better about doorknocking now, thanks to his guidance, and she was prattling on again.

She didn't want to leave. It was as simple, as difficult, as that.

'I'll see you on Wednesday, then,' he said.

'Definitely.' Five whole days to go. 'And please say goodbye to Jessie for me.'

He nodded, then took out his phone, gave her his number, asked for hers. She could barely remember it.

'In case you get lost,' he said. 'Or change your mind.'

'Oh no, I would never...get lost...'

And now she was walking down some stairs and opening the door of a car, *sorry to keep you waiting*, doing up her seatbelt, falling back into the seat.

'Are you OK, Hazel?' Simon was peering into the rear-view mirror.

'I just met Jessie.'

He laughed. 'Jessie runs poor Adam ragged.'

Felicia swivelled round. 'He is attracted to you,' she said.

'The child?'

'No. Vladimir Putin. I mean the nice man, of course. The father.'

Hazel swallowed hard, asked Felicia how she knew that.

'I know what I was seeing,' she said. 'All through the meeting he couldn't look at you because he felt no comfort with you. This is often a first sign.'

'And what's the second?'

'I would have to be there to know,' said Felicia. 'But I know he is not a dog with his tongue hanging out because he did not look at my breasts. I know they are big but that is not who I am.' She swivelled round some more. 'Hazel, I think you must be moving first. He is very—how do you say it? He is not making the plunge.'

'Shy?' said Hazel.

Simon laughed, again. 'Look, Adam's a great guy and all,' he said. 'But he's way too old.'

'Too old for what?' said Felicia.

'And that little kid,' he said, ignoring her. 'He's full-on. You wouldn't ever have time for sex. You wouldn't even have time to take your clothes off.'

'You would not have to undress,' said Felicia, and began to stroke the back of Simon's neck. 'Sex with your clothes on is good. Very good.'

Hazel tried to slow her racing heart, tried to piece together the fragments of that last encounter. Because a meeting was always a contest between the spoken and the silent, between the words that came out of your mouth in a stumble or a rush, and the words that you needed to keep hidden inside, anxious and afraid. Where might she begin with Adam? He was uncomfortable in her presence. Did this really mean he was attracted? Did Felicia have some kind of Latin intuition? Had she known hundreds of men? And what could you know about a man who'd lost a wife he loved, who'd been left to raise a son? All Hazel could be sure of were her own, brand new feelings: wanting to embrace him and yet see him from a distance. Try to work him out.

He had a wriggling bundle of questions to care for.

Jessie, I'd like you to meet Hazel. Not: Say hello to Hazel.

Was there a difference? Was there a subtle kind of subtext? Was she going slightly crazy?

Quite possibly.

Knock knock, who's there?

It was time for a different kind of reading: the policies in the file that Adam had given her. The four Green pillars. The first was ecological sustainability, which made perfect sense for the Greens but not for the current government, intent on boosting corporate profits at the expense of the environment. The second pillar was participatory democracy. Which had to be better than representative democracy, given that one of the politicians who currently represented the nation insisted that coal was good for humanity and another who declared that we all had the right to be bigots. Number three was peace and non-violence: was there a substantial difference? She would have to find that out. Number four was social justice: OK, that was self-evident. So. The four pillars. She would keep that in her head in case people asked. She decided to check out the Greens' website, and it took her by surprise as she scrolled down all the pages, tried to take in all the details: Aboriginal and Torres Strait Islanders, Agriculture, Air Pollution, Animals, Arts and Creative Industries, Biodiversity—she skipped a few pages—Disability, Drugs, Education—this was hard-going— Health, Housing and Homelessness—skipping a whole lot more—Media and Communications, Multiculturalism (as opposed to the mono-cultural idiots in the government)—still more, this was endless—Overseas Aid—Sexuality—respected in all its variety, praise the lord—Sustainable Agriculture,

Sustainable Planning and Transport—flipping through to the end now—Water, Women...

Who said the Greens were a one-issue party? And how would she ever take this in?

Then she remembered the importance of listening.

So maybe, with a bit of luck, she wouldn't have to talk at all.

**

She and Beth always looked forward to their monthly Sunday lunch, especially since her mother's sumptuous spread lasted them until Monday. The food was straight out of *Pleasantville*: meat and three veg, plus a homemade apple pie or cherry pie or lemon meringue pie, and once, when her mother decided to experiment in a highly alliterative way, a poached peach and pistachio frangipane. But what wasn't *Pleasantville* at all was the genuine affection between her mum and dad. They didn't play for the cameras, performing some 1950s version of sappy happy families. Not like so many of their friends: separated or divorced and onto their second marriage, sometimes their third. So much for marriage equality destroying the sacred institution of marriage, Hazel thought. The straights were doing a fine job themselves.

And *sacred institution*? Hadn't people read their Friedrich Engels?

Today was the kind of lunch where her parents asked about employment prospects. Encouraged them. And for a change Beth kept it short, made a joke about the interviewer having curly red hair, so maybe she was in with a chance. Hazel's parents wished her luck; Hazel knew she needed truckloads. She saw her mother stroke Beth's arm.

'If you get that job,' she said, 'tell your mother to go and jump in the river.'

And she'd only had one glass of wine.

She turned to Hazel's father. 'Hazel's been talking about doing a nursing degree,' she said.

Which, strictly speaking, wasn't really true. In fact, it wasn't true at all.

'It's going to cost, of course, and she's already finding it tough.'

'But Mum—'

'I know you can put off paying the fees, Hazel, but you'll need some more to live on.'

'We'll look into it, then,' said her father.

The two of them all hearty cheer, like a pair of salt and pepper shakers: Mickey and Minnie Mouse, Master and Lady Chef. They were wonderfully generous, her parents, would do anything to help, but Hazel couldn't help feeling embarrassed, unable to stand on her own two feet, the ones she couldn't squeeze into those stylish red boots. Three hundred dollars, they'd cost her. These days she'd have to cut off a leg to afford a pair like that.

Hazel the Stumbling Uniped, with barely enough money to pay the rent.

'So, nursing, Hazel?' said her father. 'I didn't know that was a passion of yours.'

'It's not. I just—I don't want to keep failing all my life.'

He gave her his stern-Dad look. 'Deciding what you don't want doesn't mean you're a failure. It just means you're still looking, love.'

She saw his hands spread out on the table. A carpenter's hands: strong but supple. Dependable. He'd made all the floorboards in the house, and built the cupboards, their elegant, burnished dining-room table that he'd promised to leave her in his will.

'Do you remember those wooden animals you made me?' she said.

'An owl, a duck, and a pig.'

'Do you remember what I called them?'

'Wise, Quack and Snort.' He laughed. 'You were always an odd little thing.'

'Literal-minded, you mean.'

'Hazie has them perched on her bookshelf,' said Beth. 'We found them in a box —'

'And thought we should release them,' said Hazel. 'They remind me of your workshop, with its sawdusty smell and all your tools organised so neatly. The claw hammer was my favourite because you let me pull out nails.'

'Your thumb seemed to like it as well,' he said, and laughed.

He'd wanted a tribe of children and ended up with one. Hazel hoped she wouldn't disappoint him, or her mother.

He was off on one of his Sunday rants now, all fired up about the government's fact-finding mission to the south of France to research the *bloody warthog industry*.

Hazel's mother laughed. 'It's the truffle industry, Jim,' she said.

'Truffles or warthogs, it's all the same, with their first-class travel and five-star hotels. Now they're spending millions to bring out some royal git and gitess so we can all bow and curtsey like peasants. Having the hide to make us pay more to see a doctor, forcing people to wait six bloody months for the dole.' His face was blazing now, turning to Hazel. 'It's you and your kids and your grandkids,' he said. 'What sort of a world are they leaving you?'

Hazel could have said there might not be any world at all, just or unjust, kind or cruel, if climate change had its unstoppable way. But she didn't want to make his face even redder. And he really *was* stacking on the weight. She tried not to think *heart attack* or *stroke*, wondered if her mother was having any more luck persuading him to look after his health.

'One day,' he said, 'I'm going to fly to Canberra, march into Parliament House and give those wasters a piece of my mind.'

'I'll come too, Jim. I'll make sure you don't make a spectacle of yourself. You have to be civilised.'

'Don't talk to me about civilised! The way they treat those

poor people in those awful camps.'

Hazel stabbed at a piece of pie. What would happen on Wednesday, after all? Knocking on those doors. Walking and talking with Adam. 'Did I tell you'—when of course she hadn't, waving her fork, putting it down—'I'm going doorknocking for the Greens. In a few days time.'

Three other forks were suspended in the air. And then a battery of comments, questions, praise for her courage and commitment, as though she was a soldier marching off to war.

'I'm sure I'll be fine,' she said, airily. 'I'm going to be in very good hands.'

She saw Beth raise an eyebrow. She saw her mother raise an eyebrow. She saw her father tucking into a piece of pie, then lean back in his chair.

'Nan, that was your best ever,' he said. He was beaming now, replete, as he looked around the table. 'Did I ever tell you how we met?' he said. 'It was a Saturday morning, raining cats and dogs, and there she was: Nanette. Taking shelter under an awning.'

'Let me guess,' said Beth, eagerly. 'You offered her your umbrella.'

'I didn't have one. I was dashing across the street, trying to get out of the rain, when I saw her. She had this bright gold hair and the most beautiful legs and I stopped dead in my tracks, getting soaking wet. I just knew I was going to marry her.'

His beautiful Nanette laughed. 'You tell me that story at least once a year.'

'More wine, anyone?' he said, and reached for the bottle.

'One glass, Jim, remember?'

'But it's Sunday. And I have a hard day at work tomorrow. And one more glass won't hurt. See: three good reasons to—'

'Not be convinced for a moment.'

He pouted, like a child.

***

Meandering back to the station, she and Beth were heavy with food and just a bit tipsy with wine. Waiting for the train, Hazel remembered: two people on a train, reading a book. Only not the same one.

Beth sat down heavily. 'Your parents are amazing,' she said. 'Keeping up the romance. Your mum's still so pretty, and your dad – the way he looks at her – I'd be over the moon if a guy looked at me like that.' Beth gasped. 'Not your dad, though, I don't mean your dad. That would be really gross. Hell, not that your dad's gross, I didn't mean that.'

'Well, he is putting on a lot of weight. I know Mum's worried about his health.'

'She should tell him sex uses up a lot of calories.'

'I think he's already worked that out.'

Beth gave her a sly kind of look. 'And what's all this about you being in good hands?' she said.

Hazel shrugged. 'It's nothing, really. It's just that, well, the man I'm doorknocking with is –'

'You're attracted?'

'Well, yes. I mean, definitely. A whole lot.'

'Well, I hope it goes better for you than it did for me,' she said. 'The guy I flirted with at Todd's party.'

'I didn't see you.'

'Cos we went to another room.'

'So what went wrong?'

'His hands.' Beth sighed. 'He was a great kisser, gentle, not the tongue-ramming kind. I was all set to take him home and then he started squeezing my boobs like a couple of stress balls. I'll spare you the rest of my body. Anyway, tell me about this man of yours.'

'Well, here's the thing. He's a lot older than us. Me. In his forties, I guess.'

Beth didn't even blink. 'I always thought an older man would appreciate your depths,' she said. 'No innuendo intended.'

'Look, I'm not even sure if he's interested. And he's a widow. No, I mean, widower.'

'So is he still in a deep state of mourning?'

'I don't think so. I mean, he seems quite happy. Content, really. He leads a very simple life.'

'Boring, you mean?'

'I don't mean.'

'Where did you meet him, then?'

'On a train.'

'That's so romantic, Hazie. It's one of my fantasies, meeting a handsome stranger on a train.'

'But he's not making any moves, Beth.'

'Well, maybe he's not a sleazebag. Maybe he's just—well—lovely.'

Beth had one thing right, at least.

'We'll have to find you something great to wear,' she said. 'Something seductive in a subtle kind of way.'

'Beth. It's not a date. It's politics. Doing my bit to raise awareness. Maybe change a mind or two.'

'If you say so, Hazel.' Beth leaned into her. 'So does he have a name, this lovely man?'

'Adam. And he has a child. A nearly five-year old son.'

Beth whistled. 'Well, that's a whole new ball game,' she said. 'If you're serious.'

Hazel laughed, nervously.

'You are serious, aren't you?' Beth grinned. 'So what's the big attraction? Let me guess. He's sexy and charming and intelligent and—'

'Different. He's just different.'

***

She could watch him from a distance again, standing to the side of the Rose Garden, head down, absorbed in reading, possibly a map. He was wearing light brown trousers and a pale blue shirt, and didn't even notice her arriving.

'You look very dapper,' she said, trying to sound breezy.

He looked up, seemed to force a smile, then tilted his head to the side.

'So you decided to wear green after all,' he said. 'You look very—bright.'

Hazel looked down at her lime-green shirt. 'It belongs to my flatmate,' she said. Which was why it was a bit on the tight side. 'Do you think, I mean, is it too much? Beth, my flatmate, she likes these vivid kind of colours and she's vivid but in a good kind of way.'

What did she want him to say, after all? That you, darling Hazel, look absolutely irresistible?

'Your friend must be fun to live with,' he said.

'Oh, she is, she's always entertaining. Always sees the funny side of things. Only now she's feeling a bit down because she can't find a job.'

Adam nodded. 'That's not good. The problem of your generation.'

Saying they'd better get moving now. Ten am, they'd be finished by one, and did she have a hat? He put on a beaten-up cane one, which made him look even more attractive. Raffish.

'Are you ready?' he said. 'We have a stack of houses to cover.'

Hazel tried to look ready.

'Let me do the talking first up, OK?' he said. 'I want you to listen and observe, then you can write the responses on the form. See. Right here.'

His hand was suddenly so close to hers, and she flinched. Surely he must have seen it? But he was telling her something else now, something she needed to keep in mind: that educated people weren't necessarily informed about politics, let alone engaged.

'But you told me it would be easy,' she said.

'I said easier, Hazel, easier than a lot of other suburbs. And if we get one new commitment to vote for the Greens, even make a few people more receptive, we can call it a promising day.'

'Seriously? Only one?'

'But multiply that by all the volunteers, over many months of grassroots campaigning, and we might get enough votes to make a difference. Hold the balance of power in the Senate and stop bad legislation.'

'Like increasing uni fees? Cutting funds to women's refuges?'

'Exactly.' He pulled down his hat. 'Bad legislation is anything I disagree with,' he said.

'Because you're very high-minded.'

'Correct. Neville's my conscience. Everyone should have one.'

He waved her on and they walked in step, approaching their first challenge. Adam opened a creaky metal gate and... well! It must be a student rental, she thought. A burnt, weedy lawn, torn curtains in dirty windows, two broken cane chairs on the verandah, an ashtray overflowing with butts. Adam went *knock knock knock*. They waited. No answer. *Knock knock knock* again. Still no answer.

'This happens,' he said. 'People at work, or maybe avoiding us.'

She remembered Adam's instructions. 'We have to put a leaflet in the letterbox,' she said.

Which was stuffed with envelopes and flyers, a bunch of local papers. Maybe it wasn't a student rental. Maybe no one lived here anymore. Or maybe whoever lived here was dead. You heard those stories, how the body wasn't found for days, weeks, even more, because no one came to visit.

'Hazel, are you OK?'

'I was thinking about death,' she said. 'And love.'

'You were what?'

'Sorry, I forgot to segue,' she said, and pointed to the letterbox. 'I was thinking about all this junk and how there could be a dead person inside the house, lying there for a very long time and no one came to see them because no one loved them.'

'OK. Then just tick the box that says No Answer,' he said. 'There's no category for Possibly a Corpse.'

Was he laughing at her now? She didn't want him laughing at her.

'Time to move on,' he said. 'And here's our next obstacle.'

A high brick fence, a tall iron gate, which they managed to open after several hefty shoves. Confronted now by a two-storey house with massive turrets, plush burgundy curtains in many large windows.

'It's straight out of *Gone with the Wind*,' said Hazel.

And with a front door so heavy, they'd need a medieval cannonball to knock it down. Which was a different period of history. *Knock knock knock*, with an imposing iron ring. They waited. Heard some yapping inside, and then a haughty voice—*Stop that silly barking*—and there in the doorway, resplendent in a gown that matched the curtains, was Lady Catherine de Bourgh. Another period of history: couldn't these people get it right? But it was over in a flash because the woman looked them up and down, then slammed the door with an angry boom.

'We might get a bit more of that,' said Adam. 'Tick the box that says No Support.' He must have seen the look on her face. 'Most people are courteous,' he said. 'Honestly.'

The next door opened onto a scowling peroxide blonde in one of those upmarket tracksuits with fake diamonds on the sleeves, her face a mask of suspicion. Adam did his expert thing: polite introductions, here to *listen to what matters*. My words, Hazel's thought, five long days ago. And now Fake Diamonds, waving her fake red-painted fingernails, was beginning to wail about culling the sharks: *so cruel, so wrong* (Hazel was trying not to listen, trying hard not to picture that shape in the water, the swift, silent movement, those pointed, deadly teeth). She heard Adam moving on to other issues, heard the woman's snappy replies. Refugees? *Send them back to where they came from.* Climate change? *A load of rubbish, it's just the weather.* Cuts to education? *My kids have left school.* Cuts to health. *We're privately insured. Everyone should be privately insured.* She reluctantly agreed to take a leaflet and shut the door in their faces.

Adam shrugged. 'Maybe we got her with the sharks,' he said. 'Put that one down as Weak Support.' He hitched up his bag, ready for the next encounter. 'Mind you, the culling is a state issue, not a federal one, but we didn't need to remind her of that. I'm happy to string people along to sneak a vote or two.'

'That's very Machiavellian, Adam.'

'Absolutely. Or call it realpolitik. Dirty dealing. Whatever you like. As long as there's a vote in it I don't object at all. Although I must say that it gets to me, this endless sympathy for animals, while asylum seekers are left to rot, to fall into despair.'

He was sounding angry. Not like the Adam she barely knew.

'So you're not a fan of Peter Singer?' she said.

Adam looked surprised. What did he think? That she'd never heard of one of the most famous philosophers in the world?

'Well, I agree with Singer about many things,' he said, 'but not when it comes to species equality. I mean, if you had to choose between saving the life of a person or — I don't know — a gerbil, which one would it be?'

'But that's an extreme case.'

'And extreme cases can be instructive,' he said. 'Ethically speaking.'

'But doesn't it depend on the person? I mean, I'd choose to save the life of a gerbil any day over the life of — let's see — the Minister for Immigration.'

'And don't forget Border Protection,' he said.

'You're right: Immigration and Border Protection. I think that's called conflation.'

'I'd call it scaremongering.'

They laughed, together. She liked it, this to-ing and fro-ing, their lighthearted, serious repartee. They moved on to the next house: no one at home. Ten in a row and it was beginning to feel like a waste of time, even worse when a man adorned with a chunky gold necklace snarled that politicians were all a bunch of crooks determined to shaft hard-working people. Then more No Shows, ten or eleven, she was losing count, until they finally found another real live person: a preppy guy in a striped pink shirt who denounced the Greens as *communists plotting to abolish private property.*

Not one intelligent conversation so far, let alone a conversion. And in between each house, Hazel would tick No Support and they would head off doggedly again.

'This is supposed to be an educated demographic,' she said. 'All we've had so far is ignorance, complacency and selfishness.'

'Don't forget cynicism,' said Adam.

What a huge relief, then, indeed, a lifting of the spirits, when the next two people announced themselves as Greens. Even if one of them—a gangly, bearded guy with a disconcerting squint—went on at length about some infighting in his local branch. And when he'd finally had his say, Adam nodded at Hazel, waved her on.

'Don't let that put you off,' he said. 'The party's not immune from ambition or egotism.' He hitched up his satchel. 'Shall we have a quick break?'

He pulled out a paper bag, opened it.

'This is mostly Jessie's work,' he said.

A congealed mass of something yellow and sticky, studded with plump raisins.

'Campaign biscuits,' said Adam. 'We baked them last night.'

Hazel broke off a piece, bit into it carefully. 'It's an interesting flavour,' she said.

'You're being very polite.' Adam chewed quickly, then swallowed. 'So you and Simon are friends? He's a hard worker for the Greens. A bit scatty in organising things, but very focused in meetings.'

'He told me you're a legend,' said Hazel. 'In the Greens, I mean.'

Adam shrugged. 'He means I've been around for years. You get brownie points for longevity.'

'I'm sure you're being very modest. I bet you have a lot of influence.'

'Not at all. I just take things day by day, and what with Jessie, it's hard to do as much as I'd like.' He took another bite, swallowed. 'These are my guilt biscuits,' he said. 'Whenever I spend a lot of time away from him, I let him run amok in the kitchen.'

Hazel asked what he meant by *a lot of time*.

'Well, it's been flat out preparing for this new campaign. Meetings at night and on weekends. And he's home from school today, pre-primary, a pupil-free day. I've had to leave him with his aunt again.'

'Well, I'm pleased to hear that,' she said. 'I was beginning to think you tied him to the clothesline and left him a bowl of water.'

He grinned, looked at the biscuit in his hand. 'They're not too bad, are they?' he said. 'I should have given some to Neville.'

'So what's story with him? I mean, he seems a bit of a—'

'Moaner?' Adam laughed. 'He hasn't been a Green for long and I'm not sure he'll last much longer. He's a retired GP, would you believe? Can you imagine how he spoke to his patients?'

'I can. What seems to be the trouble, Mr Smith? Well, you think you've got it bad? Let me tell you about my lumbago and my Achilles tendon and my gout and my ulcers.' She remembered his simpering, eyelash-fluttering companion. 'And Molly?'

'Neville's wife.'

'Was she a nurse?'

'She still is, actually. How did you know?'

'Because as a rule, men like to — well, you know.'

He frowned. 'No. I don't.'

'Men like to marry women who aren't as smart as them. Or who have a less prestigious social status. Who are shorter. That kind of thing.'

Adam brushed a hand through his hair. 'If you say so,' he said, and put the biscuits back in his satchel. 'Are you OK to keep going?'

'Never better.'

She didn't want the three hours to end.

They reached another high brick wall. All these walls, she thought, the drawn curtains and closed blinds: so many people looking inwards, unwilling or afraid to look out. But she was determined to give it a shot, to prove something to herself, if not to Adam. So she offered to try the next house, and before he could protest, she rang the doorbell decisively, heard heavy footsteps, saw a bulky man towering at the doorway.

'May I help you?' he said.

Polite, at least. Not a bad start. She introduced herself and Adam in a crisp tone of voice, proceeded to follow the drill.

'So you want to know what matters to me?' The man folded his arms, huffily. Not so promising after all. 'The fact that you lot voted against an emissions trading scheme.' His shook his balding head. 'You lost my vote when you betrayed the country.'

'But—'

'And then we were left with nothing. Nothing.' He unfolded his arms, waved them about. 'We've gone backwards since then. Global warming going through the roof and we're standing by doing jack shit, pardon my language.'

'Sir.' Adam took a step forward. 'The Greens voted against the scheme because they knew it would ultimately fail.'

'So nothing's better than something, is it? That's the problem with you lot, too bloody idealistic for your own good. Do you know where all or nothing gets you in the end? Nowhere.'

Hazel stepped backwards. 'The point about idealism...' She petered out because the man was glaring now and she felt Adam watching her, waiting. She tried again. 'Idealism is about long-term goals, and sometimes you have to hold out for the greater good. Or something.'

The man closed the door.

Hazel turned to Adam. 'I'm sorry,' she said. 'I guess I started something I didn't know how to finish.'

'Well, there's no easy answer. It's a decision that still divides the party. People left because of it, just like the man told you.'

'Let me try the next one, Adam. It's the last house on the street.'

It was falling off a horse, wasn't it? Or was it a bike? And she wouldn't be put off by the rusty gate in front of her, a gate topped with malicious-looking spikes, by the rubble in the driveway and — bloody hell — you couldn't miss the car with a huge bumper sticker slapped on the rear window: *Fat chicks shit me.*

'Seriously?' She pointed at the sticker. 'Words fail me.'

'Do you want me to —'

'No, really. I can do this.'

Knock knock knock. No answer. She tried again. Heard a shuffling and a groaning inside, and then a door opened onto a scruffy, skinny guy wearing a pair of stubbies. He looked about twenty, twenty-one, and he was scratching his balls, for crying out loud, before letting out an ugly yawn.

'I'm so sorry if we woke you,' she said, hearing the strain in her voice.

'Yeah, so whadda youse want?'

She made the introductions, was courteous and concise. Then asked if he was a shiftworker, because — He shook his head. Asked if he was a student, but he shook his head again. Asked if he was currently unemployed, but he was stepping back, about to shut the door. Hazel knew she should let him go, consign him to the realm of lost moronic causes, but something snapped inside her: the long, fruitless morning, the boy's yawning indifference, the crudeness of the fat chicks who gave him the shits.

'Do you mind me asking your age?' she said.

He looked baffled.

'Like, how old are you?' It was like talking to a child.

He mumbled that he was eighteen and she asked if he'd enrolled to vote. Because if not, then—but he was shaking his head, muttering *Nah nah nah, not interested in politics, lady.*

'Sir,' she said, 'you might not be interested in politics, but politics is always interested in you.'

He slammed the door in her face.

She felt embarrassed beyond all measure but Adam was laughing. Actually laughing.

'You were terrific,' he said.

'Terrific?'

'Admirably persistent.'

'But it's stupid trying to argue with stupid people.'

'You were astonishingly restrained. I was ready to shake him by the shoulders. And that line about politics being interested in him. Spot on.'

'It's Pericles,' she said. 'An ancient Greek philosopher. I'm a walking bundle of useless quotations.'

Then her phone rang and Hazel saw the name on her screen: Beth. Excited and gabbling and breathless because *I got the job, I got the job, I start next week!* Hazel stopped herself from saying *You must be joking*, as she watched Adam walk away, give her some space.

'The manager liked me,' said Beth. 'She liked that I seemed prepared to work hard and she liked my confident manner. She didn't see my knees trembling under my skirt.'

'I am SO proud of you, Beth. And SO THRILLED for you.' Was she sounding like Dora?

'We have to celebrate, Hazie. Maybe we could do a really fancy restaurant where all the food's *nestled in* or *draped over* and we can wear our best dresses and it's all on me, three courses and a bucket of wine. Just for once in our lives we can sacrifice our principles or pretend we don't have any at all.' She took a breath, at last. 'So how's it going, all those doors you're knocking on?'

'Pretty awful. Maybe one vote so far, and that was under false pretences.'

'And the man?'

'I seem to make him laugh.'

They said their goodbyes and Hazel made her way back to Adam. Told him that her flatmate was over the moon because she'd finally landed a job.

'A travel agent. No, consultant. Beth, my friend, she thought maybe we could celebrate in style, which means eating three tiny scallops and a lonely bit of seaweed on the side. With snooty waitpersons rushing up to our table with silver dustpans to sweep up our expensive crumbs.'

'Not really your style, then?' He cleared his throat. 'Speaking of food...I mean, would you like to come back for lunch? Jessie would be pleased to see you. He keeps talking about the ducks, and the fact that you poke out your tongue.' He stopped, started again. 'As long as you don't mind the noise. The constant questions. The lack of adult conversation.'

'It sounds wonderful,' she said, without a trace of irony.

He beckoned her to start walking. 'It won't be like your seaweed restaurant,' he said, 'but I guess that's a bonus in your eyes.'

Everything was a bonus. All those ignorant, selfish people of the last few hours had simply melted into air.

'You sound like very good friends,' he said. 'You and Beth.'

'Oh, I couldn't live without her. Or my parents. Or books.' She was brimming with happiness now, glancing at his profile: that slightly hooked nose and the curve of his mouth, his beautiful mouth. 'Do you have something *you* couldn't live without?' she said. 'Apart from your son.'

'Love,' he said, in a flash.

As if she should have known the answer. Or maybe she shouldn't have asked.

Animals

What else did she learn, as they walked down their final street, where there were another ten No Shows in the middle of the day because people in this suburb were likely to be working or working out at the gym or working on their golf game. She learned it was marginally better than doorknocking on weekends, when people were often home but preferred drinking to thinking, recreation to investigation. The timing was always a toss-up, Adam said. She also learned that this was the worst round of doorknocking Adam had ever experienced; that he was relentlessly optimistic; that she was madly attracted and didn't know what to do next. Because he wasn't exactly rushing her, was he, and she was much too uncertain, even afraid, to make her feelings known. She'd made a fool of herself before, declaring her hand with guys she'd liked, and her ego had been wounded. Well, maybe for a week or two. But this feeling—whatever it was—with Adam: it wasn't a matter of ego but of precious self-respect.

As soon as they arrived at his house, she saw another sign of difference: Jessie bounding down the steps and flinging himself at his father, Adam rubbing his stubbly face against his son's willing cheek. Jessie had a mop of dark curls in need of brushing, and he was wearing a very grubby T-shirt. He slid down from his father's arms, told Hazel in a bossy little voice to *come see my animals*.

'Jessie.' Adam placed a hand on his son's head. 'Remember

your manners, please. Hazel has come to have lunch with us, and it's polite to say hello first.'

The little boy shrugged. 'Hello first Hazel,' he said. 'Now *come see my animals.*'

'Of course, Jessie. I've come especially to see them.'

He scowled. 'No, you didn't. Dad said he was gunna ask you to come to lunch.'

Well. She'd learnt two new things today: that lunch was Adam's secret idea, and that you should never lie to a child.

'Where's Aunty Candace, buddy?' said Adam.

'Doing a wee,' said Jessie, loudly. As though this was a matter of great public interest.

Hazel tried to settle her nerves. She would be meeting the aunt, the great helper, who might look askance at a strange young woman walking in off the street. Because—ah, there she was now, drying her hands on her dress. No airs and graces there. A tall, slender woman with an intelligent, open face, and dark curly hair like Jessie's.

'Hazel, this is Candace. My wife's sister.'

My wife. Because there was no other name for the person you'd been married to after that person had died.

'Candace, this is Hazel. Our latest recruit for doorknocking, and a great one to have on board.'

They shook hands.

'You must be terrific, then,' said Candace, warmly. 'Adam has very high standards.'

'So you've been doorknocking with him?'

Candace threw back her head and laughed. 'Not on your sweet life. I had enough after just one meeting with the Greens. Adam persuaded me to go, become a member, but the talk just dragged on and on and on.' She laughed again. 'At one point the people in charge of the meeting said—hang on, no one's in charge with the Greens, they facilitate, or some nonsense like that. Anyway, whoever was meant to be *facilitating* realised they were running late and so everyone spent fifteen minutes debating how to speed up the meeting!'

Adam placed a hand on her shoulder. 'It's called consensus,' he said.

'It still doesn't change the fact that it's so damned inefficient.'

'You take care of Jessie. That's your contribution to the cause.'

'And because I love him,' she said.

Adam began to clear the table, scattered with crayons and paper.

'What's consensus?' said the boy.

His aunt bent down and cupped his face with her hands. 'It's when a whole bunch of people do a whole lot of talking,' she said. 'And then they all agree. It can take a very long time.'

The child nodded. 'Like when Dad makes me go to bed. He feels like a whole bunch of people.'

'And it can take a very long time,' said Adam, and ruffled Jessie's hair.

Candace kissed Jessie on the cheek, said she had to dash.

'I have another date with The Bearded One,' she said.

Jessie screwed up his nose. 'Aunty Candace has a new boyfriend,' he said. 'He's got this ginormous beard what goes way down to here.' He pointed to his stomach and his aunt rolled her eyes.

'Jessie's inclined to be hyperbolic,' she said.

'What's hyper — that thing.'

'It means that Derrick's beard only comes down to his shoulders.'

Candace was jangling her car keys now, gave Jessie a quick hug, a peck on the cheek for Adam, and *nice to meet you, Hazel, hope to see you again.* What did that mean, anyway: nice to meet you? And would she actually see her again?

Adam brushed back his hair. It seemed to be a nervous habit.

Jessie suddenly grabbed her by the hand and dragged her

away, into a little boy's room scattered with blocks and Lego. In the middle of the mess she saw a train set surrounded by a zoo of plastic animals. Jessie told her to sit on the floor while he pointed out the tracks and lights and every single animal, making animal noises and train noises and when lunch was finished, he said, his dad would turn on the train and make everything happen all over again.

He had the darkest brown eyes and a rosebud mouth. He was a very pretty child. His mother must have been a very pretty woman.

'Pick your favourite animal,' he said. 'Go on, go on, pick one.'

Hazel surveyed the zoo. 'OK. The cat.' Because kids always like cats, didn't they?

'My friend Martin has a cat,' said Jessie, 'and all he does is sleep sleep sleep on the couch or his special rug wiv stripes all over and he only ever wakes up to eat. And one time he got really mad at me when I went to pat him.'

He struck out a hand and made a loud hissing noise.

'Pick another animal,' he said.

'OK. A dog.'

'One day this dog ran after me and bounced up at me and made me really scared. Only Dad said it wouldn't hurt me cos you could see the waggy tail.' He gasped. 'If we all had waggy tails, then no one would get scared.'

'That's an excellent idea, Jessie. As long as the tail doesn't give us itchy bottoms.'

He puzzled up his face. 'You'd put your tail on the outside of your shorts and then you wouldn't feel itchy.'

'Well. That's another excellent idea. You're full of them.'

'I'm not full cos I'm hungry and I'm waiting for my lunch.' He pointed to his animals again. 'Go on. Pick another one.'

'OK. Let me see.' She took a closer look. 'I'm keen on the dinosaur.'

Because kids always liked dinosaurs, didn't they? She'd

been fascinated as a child, knowing that those huge, scary creatures had once ruled the world.

'Dinosaurs are dumb,' said Jessie, waving his arms about. 'They've got big fat legs and really tiny flappy arms what couldn't hurt no one and they look really stupid.'

'You're right.'

'So go on, pick another one.'

Hazel sighed. But then she saw the boy's pout.

'The pig,' she said.

Jessie pinched his nose. 'Yukko. Pigs are really dirty. They roll around in the mud and their noses are full of snot.'

'Pigs are actually very clean animals.'

He looked at her, suspiciously. 'Have you ever seen a clean pig?' he said.

'Seven,' she lied.

'But I haven't seen one for me so I don't want you to pick the pig.'

'Alright then. I think—*on reflection*—I like the elephant best of all.'

'What does on reflection mean?'

'It means I've thought about it again, more carefully. Harder.'

Jessie took this in. 'So why did you pick the elephant when you tried more harder?'

'Because'—she thought of the obvious—'I like its long, swaying trunk. It makes the elephant different from all the other animals.'

'But if everyone was different, everyone would be the same.'

Well, what an interesting, curly-haired child. A philosopher in the making.

He suddenly looked up and shouted. Hazel turned to see Adam standing in the doorway.

'Dad! Dad!' Jessie scrambled to his feet. 'Hazel likes the elephant best and I told her all about the dog what nearly bited me.'

'I'm sure you did. Now go and wash your hands, please. And how about changing that shirt while you're at it?'

'But Dad…'

'It's good to be clean when you're eating. You don't want to look like a pig.'

'Hazel says pigs are clean.'

'Then I stand corrected,' said Adam, solemnly. 'Now go and clean up, please.'

'Because you said to?'

'Got it in one, buddy.'

Jessie nodded, then scampered away, and Adam was smiling like, well, a cat.

'Thanks for putting up with him,' he said.

'Not at all. I liked talking with him.'

'You mean you did a lot of listening.'

'Well, you know what they say. We're not learning anything when we're talking.'

'Still. I can't seem to stop him running at the mouth.'

'Have you tried industrial strength gaffer tape, then? It worked a treat with my year eights. Or try putting a bag over his head. It's more humane, although not nearly as effective.'

Adam was smiling as she hauled herself up from the floor, wishing he would offer his hand — it would make life so much easier — but he was keeping his distance, gesturing for her to pass. And then she felt him touch her lightly, ever so lightly, in the small of her back. A courtly gesture to guide her, a new erotic charge.

She tried not to buckle at the knees.

***

Lunch was wholemeal bread, cheese, olives and salad, plus some peanut paste and Vegemite for Jessie. She couldn't have asked for a more lavish spread.

Jessie shoved a piece of bread in his mouth and turned to her, said something incomprehensible.

'Jessie, please.' Adam leaned across the table. 'You know not to talk with your mouth full.'

'Why not?' he said, sloppily.

'Because people can't understand what you're saying.'

Jessie mumbled something else, food spilling onto his chin. Adam picked up a piece of bread, slapped on a hunk of cheese and stuffed it into his mouth. Chewed roughly, then opened his mouth for Jessie.

'Yuk. That's really gross, Dad.'

'That's what other people see when you eat and talk at the same time.' He turned to Hazel. 'Excuse the display,' he said. 'Sometimes showing works better than telling.'

'Exactly like teaching. And you *were* pretty yuk, I have to say.'

Jessie held up a piece of bread for inspection. 'Why are you called Hazel?' he said.

'Because my mother liked the name.'

'But Hazel's a nut, like a peanut. It's my favourite ice-cream what we get from the shop.' He suddenly threw back his head and laughed. 'You could be called Pea. Ha-ha.'

'Jessie. Hazel might not like being called that.'

'Sorry, Hazel.' He shrugged his skinny shoulders. 'Dad's always telling me to say sorry,' he said. 'I like him much better when he tells me stories, really good ones about the sea and the stars and buckets and things.'

'Buckets?'

Jessie sat up. 'He pretended to be a bucket so I could pick him up and take him where he wanted to go.' His big eyes grew bigger. 'Dad could be Superbucket. I could make him fly through the air and he could see all over the world and come down and rescue people what get stuck in trees or if their house was on fire.' He waved his hands about. 'Whoosh! Fire!' he shouted.

'That's a great story,' said Hazel. 'Maybe you could make up another one about your friend Martin's cat.'

'But he doesn't do nothing.'

'Well, you could pretend he does.'

Jessie's eyes widened again. 'I could take him for a walk,' he said, 'and he could scare the dog what nearly bited me.'

'Did you ever think about teaching primary school?' said Adam. 'You're a bit of natural.'

'No way. I had enough trouble with the older kids. Good thing I wasn't a brain surgeon, otherwise there'd be a lot of people walking round with lobotomies.'

'What are lotomies?'

'Oh. Well. It's a special kind of animal, Jessie.' Which was a whole lot better than a special kind of doctor cutting out a piece of someone's brain. 'It's a really big animal, bigger than a dinosaur, and it walks very slowly and never makes a sound and only opens its eyes when you pull its tail. Which has a loud bell on the end of it.'

'Is it as lazy as Martin's cat Frisky?'

She decided not to define *frisky*. Or try to explain irony.

'Frisky is most definitely the laziest cat in the world,' she said.

'But you didn't see him. How do you know?'

'Well'—some quick thinking—'it was the way you described him. You made him sound like you'd need a huge steam shovel to lift him from the sofa to his food bowl.'

Jessie screwed up his face. 'You're funny,' he said. 'Only you didn't ask me about school. I go to school, you know.'

'Oh, I'm sorry I didn't ask.'

'That's OK. Everyone asks me all the time and it's boring.'

'Do you mean school's boring? Or are you bored by everyone asking you?'

He shrugged. 'Both,' he said.

He turned to his father, asked if he could go and play. A skinny, knock-kneed child sliding off his chair, in a hurry to find something new, or return to the old: wherever his imagination might take him.

Hazel toyed with some lettuce on her plate.

'Do you know why he thinks school is boring?' she said.

'Well, they seem to do a lot of cutting out and gluing. But I'm not one of these parents who think their child's a genius. There are some like that at his school, and they're, you know…'

'A pain in the arse?'

'Yes. As soon as I hear that word *gifted* I run a mile.'

'But what if Jessie *is* gifted? There is such a thing, you know. He seems very smart to me. Very curious.'

'I just want him to feel loved,' said Adam. He looked down at the table, then up into her eyes. 'I remember when I first saw him. His tiny fingers and flawless skin, and such a peaceful little body, as though he'd already decided it was good to be here. I had no idea I could feel that way.' He was smiling now, with the memory. 'I was enchanted. And then I became besotted. Utterly transformed.'

She'd never heard a man talk like this before, about a baby, and she was touched by his words, by his wanting to give her this moment. This epiphany, you might call it. But it seemed to come from a distant country of which—she could have said *no conception*, but she didn't want to make light of this baby business, couldn't bat it away with a joke.

'Anyway, enough about me,' he said. 'I really wanted to say, about the doorknocking: try not to feel discouraged. I'm sure it will get better.'

Hazel pulled a face.

'It's early days,' he said. 'And if nothing else, it's something to tell your kids. Your grandkids. That you stood up to be counted.'

She tried not to bristle. 'I numbered exactly one,' she said.

'Meaning?'

'I don't know what to say to people when they trot out their clichés. Like the shark woman, who wants to send refugees back to where they came from. If I hear those words one more time…'

'It might be different if people actually met refugees,' said

Adam. 'Got to know them at work or through their kids at school. Talked to their neighbour when they were taking out the rubbish.'

'Like Jessie's friend? Not putting out the rubbish, I mean.' She rummaged around for a name. 'The little boy who cried when a balloon burst in his face.'

'Aziz. Yes. He's a—'

'Dad. I wetted my pants. I forgot to listen to my penis.'

A worried face peered up at his father. A little boy tugging at his shorts. Adam took Jessie by the hand, quietly led him from the room, without scolding or fussing or even jollying him along. Should I stay, Hazel thought? Of course she should stay. It was only a pair of wet undies. She looked around the room, saw the bookshelves on the opposite wall. Did she have time to take a peek? See what else she could discover? And picturing Adam's beauty, hearing and seeing his kindness, she felt an ache in her breasts, longing for his return so that she could look at him again and think: you're a very good person and I admire you deeply and I'd like to take off your clothes and have sex.

But she had to keep that thought in her head: the sex part.

'Hazel.'

That chirpy little voice again. Jessie, now wearing a pair of yellow shorts.

'My friend Alice knows lots of riddles,' he said. 'She knows lots about elephants, only I can't remember any.'

Hazel had a million of them. 'Does Alice know the one about the elephant and the fridge?'

Jessie shook his head.

'OK, how do you know an elephant's been in your fridge?'

Jessie turned to his father. 'Have we ever had a elephant in our fridge?'

'Never. Even though I've looked very hard.'

Jessie threw up his hands. 'See. If Dad's never seen one, then a elephant never got inside our fridge.' He turned away, started walking to his room, called back over his shoulder. 'If anyone wants me, I'm talking with my animals,' he said. 'They need me to tell them what to do.'

Hazel turned to Adam. 'He's, well, unexpected, isn't he?'

'Indeed.'

'And he clearly worships you. You're the fount of all knowledge.'

'Except I don't know how you can tell there's been an elephant in the fridge.'

'You'll see footprints in the butter.'

'Well. Who would have thought?'

He offered her tea or coffee and of course she said yes. To both, before she realised her mistake. She would happily have swallowed litres of anything so that she didn't have to leave, didn't have to go back to her pokey flat and a view of the dismal car park.

'I do like this room,' she said. 'There's no fuss and bother.'

'Well, I threw a lot of fuss and bother away after my wife—Thea—died.' He rose from his chair, went to turn on a kettle. 'People seem to give you things over the years. Knick-knacks and geegaws. Whatever a geegaw is.'

'A trinket. A knick-knack is more of an ornament.'

'Now, how could I not know that?' he said, and grinned. 'There was one thing I really enjoyed throwing out. You know those china figurines from France or Germany or wherever? Hideously expensive, and, well, just plain hideous.'

'Like a shepherdess without any sheep?'

'Exactly,' he said. 'Not an ovine in sight.'

'But ovine isn't a noun. It's an adjective…pertaining to sheep.'

He leaned back on the bench. 'Is that right?' he said.

He was watching her closely. Was he flirting with her now?

'I used to know a word that meant the fear of big words,' she said, trying not to fluster. 'It's hippopotomon…something or other phobia.'

'You mean you've forgotten? You're not infallible?'

'Infallibility's reserved for the Pope,' she said. 'And for the gullible people who believe him. Religion is the opium of the masses.'

'Opiate, actually,' he said.

She would have said fifteen-all, except that she was losing count and trying to listen to what he was asking, offering her a glass of wine instead of tea. Or was it coffee she'd asked for?

'I have some very good bottles of red,' he said. 'It's one of my indulgences.'

'Just one?'

'Well, there's Jessie, of course. I do like to buy him *stuff* now and then. But just small things, you know, like his plastic animals. And plenty of books, of course.'

'And that elaborate train set?'

'Oh, that's from Candace and her two boys. They spoil him rotten.'

'But it's a coal-fired train, Adam. What happened to your principles?'

He laughed. 'So: tea, coffee or wine?' he said.

'Coffee, thank you.'

He turned on the kettle, apologised for only having instant. And then, turning back to look at her, he asked if she wanted children. Just like that.

'It's not on my agenda,' she said. Keeping it matter-of-fact.

'Ah. Well. You're still very young. You have plenty of time to decide.'

Still very young? 'I've pretty much decided,' she said briskly. 'The world already has too many people and the planet's resources are running out. It would be an ethical decision not to reproduce.'

'You sound very sure of yourself,' he said.

'I'm simply mounting a case. A case based on reason.'

'But what about felt experience? Things will happen to you, and you might feel very differently. And like I said, you're still very young.'

Hazel drew herself up. 'And I'm intelligent enough to know what I want.'

'But the world needs intelligent, decent parents,' he said. 'Think of it this way: it's also an ethical choice for people like you to—as you put it—reproduce.'

'Well, having a child isn't the only way to make a contribution,' she said. Now that they'd started, now that she was saying what she'd never said before.

'I didn't say that. I—'

'In any case'—she could feel her hands clenching—'people don't ask a man that question, do they? But they keep doing it with women, all the time. It's the big question for us, always the big question, and I wish it wasn't. I wish we could get past it.'

'But it's biological, surely.'

She hated people saying *surely*.

'A woman's fertility is limited by time,' he went on, 'and so by definition the question arises. But a man can father a child until well into his nineties. Look at Charlie Chaplin.'

'I'd rather not,' she snapped. 'I hate slapstick.'

How they had come to this, and so quickly? She felt an ominous thud inside her. Because their debate, this batting back and forth, was beginning to feel uncomfortable, oddly personal, as though he was pushing her down a road she had no desire to travel. Fucking roads. The one less travelled. All that folksy Frosty wisdom that had bored her to sobs at school.

'I don't like this,' she said.

'What do you mean?'

'Us. Arguing.'

He reddened. 'We're just having a difference of opinion,' he said.

If only he would take her hand. Everything would feel right if he just took her hand.

Then, to her relief, Jessie scooted back into the room with

questions and commands, wanting his father to make the trains go round and Hazel had to come and watch, right now. Please.

'I'm afraid I have to go home, Jessie.'

'I haven't made your coffee,' said Adam.

'I really should be going.' She rose from the table.

Adam stood too but didn't make another move. 'Maybe Hazel can see your train another time,' he said.

'Or we could go to the zoo,' said Jessie. 'We could see all them real animals and I could show Hazel the bears.'

Hazel was strongly opposed to zoos.

'Why do you like the bears?' she said.

'Cos they're big and scary and you can see them look big and scary but they can't hurt you cos they're in these really big cages.'

'There's an elephant as well,' she said.

'They got three at the zoo,' said Jessie. 'The first elephant got lonely so they found him other elephants to play wiv. Dad said.'

'Well, I'm sure your dad is right.'

Fucking lonely elephants.

'So will you come wiv me? To the zoo?'

She told him she would try.

'Would you like a lift home, Hazel?'

She said no, politely, her mother's model child, then said she'd like to walk because it was such a nice day. And yes, she would wait for the details of time and place. And yes, she was sure it would be better the second time around. And then, out of nowhere, Jessie gently took her hand, as if—and this was very strange—he felt the need to comfort her. She looked down at his bright little face.

'You have quiet eyes,' he said. 'Dad's girlfriend had shouty eyes and I didn't like her one little bit.' Then he released her and ran back to his room.

Adam cleared his throat. 'You don't have to go to the zoo,' he said.

She nodded, unsure.

'So. Next week, then?' he said.

'Why not?'

'And, well…thanks for listening to Jessie.'

They seemed to be locked into something she couldn't understand, that made her feel lost when she wanted to be found. So all she could do was to pick up her bag, say goodbye, make her way to the door.

As she walked along the street, trailing her hands along a white picket fence, she couldn't help wondering—how could she not—if there'd been other girlfriends with different kinds of eyes. Did she think he'd been monastic since his wife died? Even if having a young child meant having little time for sex. That's what Simon had declared: staunchly ethical Simon, whose words struck her now as rather crude. Was it only sex that men wanted, while women were longing for love? Were men from Mars and women from Venus, as some guru had declared, with his half-baked degree or no degree at all but with a nose for making money? Millions of people had bought his message and yet she felt it wasn't true. Didn't men fall madly, profoundly, in love with one particular woman and long to make it last? Mr Rochester for Jane, Heathcliff for Cathy, Abelard for Heloise? Didn't men, too, yearn to be known and loved for who they were, with all their imperfections?

She looked up at the bright blue sky and those fluffy white clouds that, when you were a child, you would turn into pictures. Flying saucers and castles, and so many different animals: birds and dragons, monkeys and tigers, the occasional kangaroo. She and Beth would lie on their backs in Hazel's garden and float along with the clouds, call each other sisters and swear they would always be sisters and believe they would never be happier.

Pricks

By the time she made it home, Hazel was feeling stuck again. She'd had more time to think along the way, about Adam's lecture: more or less saying she was obliged to have kids because she was intelligent. Telling her she was too young to know what she wanted. Putting her in her youthful place, and no doubt out of sight, out of mind. She opened the door of the flat, relieved to see that Beth was home. Sitting on the kitchen floor and polishing her shoes, looking up and smiling.

'Did it get any better?' said Beth. 'Did you make a lot of converts?'

'Well, maybe we got a couple of people to start thinking. Adam did, anyway. Pretty much the only time I spoke, I messed up.'

She sat down next to Beth, tucked up her knees.

'I'm sure you did your best,' said Beth. 'You always do.'

'And I want to give you a gigantic hug. Because you're very clever.'

'Don't forget confident and prepared to work hard.' Beth grinned. 'Wait til I've finished these shoes before you give me that hug.'

When was the last time she'd polished a pair of shoes, she said, or worn a uniform, chirping now about a prim white blouse and a prim black skirt which wasn't very cool but it would save a lot of money.

'And I feel like saving money now I have a job. Which

doesn't really make sense, but there you go.' Her face suddenly fell. 'I'm sorry, Hazel,' she said, quietly. 'I didn't mean to be, you know, about me having a job.'

Hazel placed her hand on Beth's shoulder. 'I'm pleased for you,' she said. 'Really pleased.'

'Thanks. I just wish you could find something too.' Then she gave one shoe a vigorous rub. 'I'm making them really shiny,' she said. 'Someone told me — when I was a kid — that you should shine your shoes so much that you could see your knickers in them. I think it was the local shoe fixer-upper man who told me that.'

'A cobbler,' said Hazel.

Beth laughed. 'Which now that I think about the knickers, is a bit gross. That cobbler must have been dodgy.' She went back to buffing a sensible black shoe. 'Anyway, I think I'm going to like my new boss. Wilhemina. She said to call her Willy but I wouldn't be able to keep a straight face.'

'Does she seem OK?'

'Relaxed. Friendly. Although she did let me know she's sacked three workers in the past two years. So I'm on notice, aren't I?' She held up the shoe to inspect it. 'I remember my father spitting on his shoes to clean them,' she said. 'Which was pretty much how he treated us.'

Hazel moved in a little closer. 'Have you told your mother about the job?'

'Yep. Do you know what she said? *You'd better not quit like last time.*' Beth slammed down a shoe, picked up the other one. 'She told me once she was only happy when she was pregnant. Which is why I guess she kept popping the whole damned lot of us out. I used to think she was longing for a girl after four idiot boys but' — she shrugged — 'it was never me she wanted. She just wanted to fill that hole in her body to match the fucking hole in her heart. Head. Or something.'

She groaned her way off the floor — she wasn't fit either — and then pulled Hazel up with a hand.

'Enough about me,' she said. 'Tell me about your man.'

'He's not mine, Beth. What can I say? One minute he seems to like me and then he backs right off. And, well, we had a bit of a disagreement. He asked me if I wanted children.'

'Holy shit. On a first date?'

'It wasn't a date, Beth. Please.'

'So what did you tell him?'

'It was more like *him* telling me. He thinks I should have kids and I'm not even thinking about it. I don't even *like* babies. The idea of them, anyway.'

'So is he one of those parents who wants everyone to experience his pain?'

'No, no, not at all. He's very happy with Jessie. Who's a very winning child, I have to say.'

'So is he one of these religious types who wants you to see the light?'

'No. No, that's not it, either. It seems important to him. Like it's a matter of ethics to raise a child.'

'Well, la di da,' said Beth. 'In any case, he has no right telling you how to live your life. He sounds like a bit of a tosser.'

'No, definitely not. He's thoughtful. Modest.' Hazel held up her hands, by way of surrender. 'I suspect he's not even interested.'

'Give it time, Hazie.'

'Well, whatever happens, or doesn't, he's a good man. So I hope we can be friends.'

Beth put an arm around her. 'You're full of shit,' she said.

***

Thea. It sounded like a whisper, or a sigh. Hazel said it aloud to make it seem more real. Was it short for Theodora? Had she been a bit loud and zany, like her sister, or more subdued? And how long had she and Adam been married? Why didn't Adam wear a ring anymore? Or maybe he never had. Maybe he'd been one of those married men who liked a bit on the side. Which was a very ugly expression and didn't sound a bit like Adam.

All these pointless questions and puzzled speculations. It was like stumbling in a room, blindfolded.

She turned her attention to checking for jobs to fill up her weekly quota. She had to find something vaguely relevant to her qualifications (since she had no skills or experience to speak of), and adjust her CV accordingly. She finally managed four applications in retail (she could talk literature or philosophy to customers as she wrapped up their sexy lingerie); two jobs in admin (she knew how to spell *prioritise* and *excel*); one as a librarian's assistant (given her voracious reading, she hoped to be of assistance). Next she applied for a tutoring job in a private coaching college (in the unlikely event of succeeding, she'd need to make sure it wasn't one of those companies that ripped off foreign students and didn't pay the staff; thank you, federal government, for deregulating the education system). Finally, exhausted and at the point of self-immolation, she applied for a position as the editor of a literary journal. Why not aim for the stars? Especially since the government insisted that you could be anything you wanted to be if you just pulled your lazy finger out or were prepared to relocate to the ends of the earth to pick strawberries for $8.50 an hour, or had a father who'd left you a hugely profitable iron ore company massively subsidised by the taxpayer and on which you paid a piddling amount of tax. Or you could fork out a few more thousand dollars on top of a hefty HECS debt to get another qualification so you could keep applying for jobs you were never going to win because winning was the name of the game.

In desperation, she checked out the nursing degree online. Three-and-a-half years. She was hoping it had been shortened since her mother had tried to enthuse her. Still, she'd only be twenty-eight when she finished. Or was it twenty-nine? Numbers had never been her strong point. Which could lead to serious consequences if you were sticking a needle full of morphine into a patient's arm.

Then she limped towards the end of *Persuasion*, with its predictable happy ending. But what took her by surprise was the absence of an answer to its central moral dilemma. Had the heroine been right to follow her mentor's advice? Or should she have believed in the Captain from the start? Because seven years after Anne had rejected him, deeply disappointed him, he'd amassed a tidy fortune, while she had lost the bloom of youth, begun to wither into spinsterish gloom. But then again, maybe Austen was rewarding Anne's constancy, her enduring love for the Captain. Or was his return just a stroke of good luck? And wasn't comedy meant to give you the answer to that unruly, vexing thing called life?

Hazel was not impressed. Had Austen dragged her through all these pages just for this? Leaving her to decide for herself?

Still, there was always the Captain's letter, his passionate declaration as the story drew to a close, to lift her flagging spirits. *I am half agony, half hope*, he'd written, hoping to persuade Anne to marry him.

I am half agony, half hope. Now who wouldn't fall for a killer line like that?

***

The next day, at a loose end (some might call it frayed, she thought), Hazel phoned some friends to suggest a movie, but everyone was studying or working overtime. Even Chloe was thinking of going back to her PhD because she'd figured that research in cultural anthropology was far less daunting than serving ice-cream in a shop called Heavenly. (*Would you like a ton of chocolate sprinkles with that...a fistful of jelly beans...a bucket of double whipped cream...a heart attack...honestly, Hazel, people are disgusting.*) In the end Hazel was glad no one could spare the time; movie tickets were expensive, even with a discount, and you'd have to raise the limit on your credit card if you wanted to buy a choc bomb. She'd checked her bank account online and the forecast was grim: storm clouds approaching, possibly a tornado. And it didn't help, either, when the landlord put up their rent by a heartless thirty bucks a week. What had happened to the reasonable old guy who'd once changed their light bulb?

What do you call one hundred landlords lying at the bottom of the ocean?

A good start.

Beth had insisted on paying the extra rent until Hazel found a job. Which made Hazel feel both immensely grateful and even more despondent. A touch humiliated.

The week dragged on until Saturday and the dinner party: Todd and Dora, their first ever dinner party as a different kind of couple, as though the baby and the ring had changed everything. *The Baby and the Ring*: it sounded like the name of a weird English pub. But how great it was to celebrate Todd's brand new job, even if the bookshop was more like a gift shop, he said, selling hand creams and scarves and tea towels, while the books cringed with shame in a corner. But the children's section was terrific, he said, as Dora smoothed her hands over a tiny pregnant belly. There was Beth's brand new job to toast as well, as she filled them in on what she had to learn and how much she was looking forward to helping people have adventures. Because everyone needed an adventure, she said, everyone needed to have fun, as long as it was safe, legal and didn't cause any harm to any living creature. Hazel felt happy for all of them, even as she wished she wasn't so broke. Broken and aimless and watching her two best friends about to begin a new life. Beth had even decided to stop drinking during the week. I'd better slow down myself, Hazel thought, so I don't slip from low-grade self-pity into brutal self-laceration. Three glasses usually did the trick.

'So there was this woman...'

Simon. Entertaining them now with darkly funny stories about his doorknocking day. A tale about a woman who knew, just knew, that the Greens would let all those people out of detention and there'd be terrorism and disease and mosques sprouting all over the place and then where would we all be?

'I told her we would be in Australia,' said Felicia. 'But she kept throwing words and I was throwing back and we were wobbling all over the place.'

Beth laughed, in a warm kind of way.

'Then there was this dumb med student,' said Simon. 'He said he knew the Greens were planning to force every doctor to work for the government for peanuts. I was about to give him some facts but Felicia sorted him out.'

It seemed that once she'd understood working *for peanuts*, Simon told them how Felicia had *flared her nose* and lectured the guy in a very stern voice that medical care was for *all the people*.

Felicia looked around the table. 'My father is a doctor,' she said. 'But he is a doctor of cosmetics. A prick.'

Simon put an arm around her. 'One of Felicia's first Australian words,' he said.

Beth was looking captivated. Little wonder, since Felicia was at her smouldering best: thick black eyeliner and a slash of bright red lipstick. Those cheekbones. That flawless, sunfire skin.

Felicia pursed her lips. 'My father in Roma makes women large or small in different places,' she said. 'And my mother is telling me how the size of his stomach is now inversely proportional to his brain.'

'Your mother's English is very good,' said Beth.

'Her English has always been very good. And she does the maths, like me, so she knows about inverse proportional. But my father, he runs along with young girls with plastic breasts who only want him for his money. He is—how do I say this? He is not real?'

'A cliché?' said Beth. 'Your father is a cliché?'

Felicia nodded vigorously, which made the two sparkling

chandeliers attached to her ears tremble in the candlelight.

'I owe him no respect,' she said. 'But he has given me a beautiful apartment in this place because he wants me to love him. I still have no respect but I use his guilt to have a beautiful apartment. So now he is happy and I am happy but not in the same way.'

She turned to Beth. 'Your hair is like fire,' she said. 'It is dazzling me.'

Beth glowed with the compliment. It was like Jessie and the quiet eyes. Which was a touching thing to say, Hazel thought, as though the child had been observing her, appraising her, liking her. Then, as if on cue, Felicia asked her what had happened with the *shy Green man*. Hazel picked at a bread roll and tried to change the subject but Felicia kept pressing and Hazel kept resisting because she didn't want advice or cheering up, and she didn't want Adam being served on the menu. What she wanted most of all was a new kind of silence in her head. A space in which to think about a mind she couldn't read, a body that she longed for, as she dipped her spoon into the soup, one dip and swallow, another dip and swallow, focused on the creamy texture.

'Still, it wasn't all bad news,' said Simon, jolting her back. 'We even had some good conversations' — turning to Todd and Dora — 'we call the good ones a Meaningful Encounter, people being open to thinking about stuff. Climate change especially. Once you get the chance to explain that the government's Direct Action plan has to be one of the most ironic policy names ever invented. Paying polluters to keep polluting. Opening more coalmines. But hey, plant the odd tree and we'll all be saved.'

'So you just give people the facts?' said Todd, as Dora gave a mighty yawn.

'Doorknocking's crucial,' said Simon, 'because the mainstream media doesn't analyse the issues. Or hold politicians to account.'

'And they think the Greens are loony,' said Hazel.

Wanting to say her feeble bit.

Simon gave her a sheepish look...*Clean forgot to ask...how was your day, Hazel.*

'I'm learning,' she said, quietly. 'Learning to stay positive, for a start.'

'Well, I'm sure Adam's debriefed you.'

When she felt brief enough already: truncated, abridged, a five-hundred-word short story.

'Adam's a very positive kind of person,' she said.

One spoonful, then another.

'This soup is amazing,' she said.

She watched Dora stroke Todd's cheek.

'Toddy made it,' said the girl with the diamond ring. 'He's just as AMAZING as the soup!' She looked around the table. 'I'm SO THRILLED to have you all here!! I HAVE NEVER BEEN SO HAPPY IN MY LIFE!!!!'

At least four exclamation marks, Hazel thought. But how could she possibly diminish sweet, happy Dora? How could she refuse to smile, like everyone else at the table?

***

On Monday, Beth came home from her first day at work with stories about her trying-to-do-fifty-things-at-once kind of day: the computer meltdown, the problems with ticketing, old people wanting luxury accommodation at budget prices, plus all the bits and pieces that cheap airlines added on when you weren't looking, even when you were. She told a story of a cashed-up client who'd already *done* Paris and Rome, Cairo and Istanbul, and then rolled his eyes when Beth suggested India because he'd already *done* India, and the Taj Mahal had been *such a disappointment.*

'How can it be a disappointment?' Beth wailed. 'Just the pictures in the brochures are enough to make me giddy. And then there was this grumpy old couple who wouldn't stop arguing. All that money to go all over the world and all they could do was snipe at each other. As for my boss! Talk about a slavedriver, only she doesn't live in Egypt. How does that happen? All sweetness and light when she interviewed me and then she gives me a twenty-minute break for lunch. It's worse than bloody teaching and probably illegal.'

She was just so tired, she said. So damned tired.

Over dinner on Tuesday she was all fired up about all the pricks she'd met in a matter of a few measly hours. First up there was a military-looking man who refused to make a booking with an airline employing *coloured people*. Beth's jaw had dropped to the floor, she'd said. Hadn't people like him died out with the Tasmanian Devil—no, the Tasmanian Tiger? Then she'd tried to disguise her outrage by telling the douchebag that white was also a colour.

'Although I remember from school that white is the absence of colour, scientifically speaking,' she said. 'Or maybe it's black. But anyway, morally speaking, he was just a racist prick. So then I told him there was no such airline and he told me I was lying, and he got up and left. Except I had to keep it quiet in case the boss was listening. I mean, she might have backed me up, who knows, but I wasn't prepared to risk it.'

Another guy had kept asking her age, like a bouncer at the door of a nightclub, she said. Not to mention the old guy with a warty face and spindly comb-over, wanting to book a flight to Adelaide. She'd wanted to send him to Timbuktu by the time he'd finished staring at her boobs and asking her out on a date.

'I'm constantly amazed,' she declared, 'how even plumb-ugly men can have so much confidence with women. And then, when I dashed out for lunch at the café next door—god, it was awful. I ran into my cousin Carson and I started telling him all that stuff. Except I don't think you've met my cousin Carson.'

'No.'

'In any case, I was telling him, shouting really, cos the place was so noisy, I was shouting how some men must think women are always gagging for it, and right at that very moment the whole place went quiet. The coffee machine and people talking and — thank god — Mariah Carey on the sound system. Everyone must have heard me cos everyone was staring. And then as I'm leaving, some sleek-looking guy hands me a card and he's written on the back: *When you feel the urge to gag.* I swear, Hazel, I'm giving the male of the species one more chance and if it doesn't work out, I'll either, a, take a vow of chastity, or b, throw myself off a cliff, or c, have sex with women so I don't have to deal with predatory men. Which one would be easier?'

'Definitely c,' said Hazel. 'But it's *easiest*. Grammatically speaking.' She poured herself more water. 'I'm sorry about your day, Beth. I guess the travel business isn't that romantic.'

She remembered reading a poem at school about a girl who longed to travel. How something had stirred inside her.

'*She wanted to travel to the edge of the world … saw herself dancing to jazz in a flimsy dress on an ocean liner.* Isn't that entrancing, Beth?'

'Well, I love the image of a flimsy dress, but the ocean liner would be a bit of a drag. Third-rate entertainers, deck quoits and shitty movies. Hundreds of people stuffing their faces with prawn cocktails and triple-decker chocolate cake.' Then she laughed, tossed away her gloom. 'There was this shy kind of guy who came in to book a ticket today. He was really sweet and looked like Joaquin Phoenix when he first started in the movies and his real name was Bottom.'

'The sweet, shy guy?'

'No, the actor. He changed his name from Bottom to Phoenix.'

Hazel had to smile. 'Thereby rising from the ashes of his cinematic arse,' she said.

Knock knock, round two

After a dull Sunday and an even duller Monday, Hazel took a bus to the shops to check out a birthday gift for her father. Wishing she knew how to knit or cook so she could make something on the cheap. Wishing she'd inherited her mother's domestic skills, as well as her long legs and golden hair. She passed the shop that sold lustrous pearls, remembered looking in the window last year and imagining a sign: *Look on my jewels, ye impoverished, and despair.* And then she saw it: the toyshop. She'd never given it a second glance, because no one she knew had a child, of either the small or large variety. Jessie. She would buy a little something for Jessie. Maybe another animal to reflect on or object to, to help him decide for himself. But the instant she stepped inside she was overwhelmed by so many objects, colours and brands: board games like Monopoly Millionaire, Cranium, the old-fashioned Snakes and Ladders. Bouncing putty, Slime Barf and Barrel of Slime, robots, transformers, water shooters, lawnmowers, tea sets, doll sets, Pie Face, Duplo, Lego, light projectors, Chubby Puppies, My Little Pony, Peppa Pig, Hungry Hippos, Play-Doh, magic sets, computer games. A person could go mad in here with so much choice. No doubt parents *did* go mad, with their kids whining and screaming for more.

And then at last, back to the basics: a jumble of plastic animals in a basket on the counter. What did Jessie already have? Cats and dogs, pigs and elephants, a lion. There was a lion, wasn't there, among all the beasts he'd so oddly disapproved of. Ah, there it was! A gnu. With a long head, and a beard and mane made out of wool. She hadn't spied a gnu in Jessie's menagerie. He'd love the beard, wouldn't he, and the horns, the way they curved like upside-down commas? She could already hear his questions when she handed it over. Because she would be seeing him again, wouldn't she? There would have to be another lunch. Maybe even that trip to the zoo, compromising her principles for the sake of an outing with Adam.

She remembered the joke: *Those are my principles, and if you don't like them, I got others. Groucho Marx*. Who was a whole lot funnier than Karl.

***

She was wide awake at six am on Wednesday. Doorknocking day, round two. She knew she had to stop fussing and worrying about what might happen or not happen and what she hoped might happen, tried to settle down with a book borrowed from the library. She'd decided to skip the rest of Austen and move on to the letter B, because art was long and life was short, as well as *nasty and brutish, solitary and poor*. Thomas Hobbes. Another man you wouldn't want to wake up to in the morning. She'd made a start on Balzac's *Le Père Goriot*, in English, and a doorstopper. He'd written a hundred weighty tomes, apparently, about poverty and injustice; people clearly couldn't get enough of the nasty stuff of life.

A buzz on her phone. A message. From Adam.

Would you like me to pick you up? Mosman Park is a long way from your place and you'll be doing enough walking as it is.

Only a man in his forties—well, Adam, anyway—would send a text with grammatically complete sentences, plus one apostrophe to denote a contraction.

Thank you. That would be great.

It's the least I can do.

After what? And then another message coming through:

I'm sorry if I hurt your feelings. I didn't mean to but I'm worried that I did.

She looked at her screen but her fingers were frozen, even as she wanted to write a grammatically complete sentence to tell him that he mustn't worry but how kind of him to apologise and worry about her feelings when what she really wanted to say was that she was standing on the edge of the world, falling from a dizzying height, plunging headlong into desire.

Then another message!

Jessie has a new animal. Guess what it is.

She hoped it wasn't a gnu.

Maybe a hippo but I don't know how to spell it. Did you hear the one about the PhD candidate who could never remember how to spell Nietsche. So after a few months he changed his topic to Kant

Ha-ha. But I think you'll find that Nietzsche has a z.

Smartarse

I'm not being a smartarse. I'm being correct.

Then nothing. That was it. Then another message!

It's a tortoise.

Are you sure it's not a turtle

You like the last word, don't you?

Look who's talking

I'm not talking, I'm texting

You're being very literal

OK Hazel. You win.

She didn't want it to end this way, with winning and losing and jokey banter.

You didn't hurt my feelings, Adam. I know you are the kindest man. That's why I like you so much.

She waited. Waited some more, but it seemed he had no more words to give her.

***

It was awkward now. Unmistakably. Standing on her doorstep, Adam could hardly look at her. Had she pushed him too far? Declared her feelings and made him back off? But it was OK to tell someone you liked them, wasn't it? Or had *so much* been too much? All she could do in the face of her confusion and his evasion was to quip about his hair looking mysteriously tamed. But he just shuffled his feet, darted his eyes about. Should she ask him to come in? For a glass of water? For anything? But he was saying they needed to get going, a fifteen-minute drive, and did she have an umbrella, because it looked like rain. They climbed down the stairs, Hazel in front, weighed down with disappointment. Stepping aside as he opened the door of his car for her, giving each other the widest berth. She slipped into his shiny blue car, spotless inside, but still he wasn't speaking. She knew by his silence that she must have misread the signs: those telegraphic messages she'd begun to turn into a novel, her first fucked-up sentence of *Shredded by Desire*. But she refused to show her deflation. She was, after all, a woman on a mission, trying to do her bit for the greater good.

'I'd like to do the first house,' she said. 'If that's OK.'

He threw her a quick glance, then turned back to look at the road. 'Of course,' he said. 'But only if you feel comfortable.'

She wouldn't have offered, she said, if she didn't feel comfortable. Then she felt churlish and silly and there was silence again. Unease.

'Do you have enough leg room?' he said.

'My legs are very short.'

Churlish again. And he'd probably never even looked at her legs. She listened to the silence, then registered a strange sort of quietness.

'Does this car even have an engine?' she said.

'It's electric.'

'An electric car? Don't they cost a lot of money?'

'My father left me a bit,' he said, matter-of-fact. 'I got rid of my old rust bucket and bought this. It's much safer for Jessie, and much better for the environment.'

Of course. Did Adam ever do anything ignoble?

He cleared his throat. 'You seem a bit down,' he said. 'I mean, is there anything...'

'No, no, I'm fine. Nothing to complain about.'

'You're not a complainer, are you?'

Hazel gave a fake laugh. 'I do it a lot in my head.'

'Like saying *fuck* in your head?'

'Yes. That too.'

Taking her back to the train and the first time they'd talked: when he'd noticed her, and she'd noticed him, and they'd discussed books and love and death, which pretty much covered everything.

'Complaining in your head is a good thing,' she said. 'You don't lose your friends, for a start, by wallowing in self-pity.'

'You don't strike me as self-pitying.'

'Oh, I am. Really. I'm full of it. Just ask my former friends.'

Which made him laugh.

'Why should you feel sorry for yourself, anyway?' he said.

Was he having a go at her now? It brought her up short.

'I know I have distinctly first-world problems,' she said. 'Although I would like a job very soon. I couldn't even score a job in a fish market. Which is just as well, I guess, because the smell wouldn't have helped my prospects in the romance department.'

There. Take that.

'So. You're...not with anyone?'

She heard an edge in his voice, and so she took another plunge. 'I'm a bit fed up with the guys I meet, to be honest,' she said. 'Young men are immature. Clumsy. Superficial.'

She saw his hands tighten, just a little, on the steering wheel.

'That's a huge generalisation,' he said.

'Well, I'm using a statistically valid sample, Adam. I've had seventy-eight young lovers since I turned sixteen.'

He kept a straight face. 'That's not enough evidence. A statistically valid sample is at least a thousand people.'

'Then I have a lot to not look forward to, don't I?'

She waited. He didn't say a word.

'I have an animal for Jessie,' she said. 'A gnu. I found it in a toyshop.'

'Well. A gnu. He'll love that, thank you.'

He looked at her again, a little longer this time. She was measuring out her life with the length of his glances and his different tones of voice and his slightly tight hands on a steering wheel.

'I'm sure you'll find a job one day,' he said. 'Something that satisfies you, I mean. Work that does some good in the world.'

He didn't mention the possibility of lover number seventy-nine.

***

So far no rain. So far so good. But then the first ten doors were No Shows and Adam was hardly saying a word and she was almost beginning to wish it would pour buckets so she could turn back. Go home. But then — finally — an elderly man with an open face who was always happy to talk, he said. But as soon as Adam said *Greens* that open face closed down. It wanted to send the *illegals* back to where they came from. Adam was standing back and so Hazel took a chance, told the bolshie man at the door how the government used that word to make asylum seekers seem like criminals.

'They're people seeking asylum,' she said. 'And under Australian and international law, they're allowed to enter the country without authorisation.'

The man scowled. 'Well, aren't you the clever one?' he said.

She flushed. 'I'm not trying to be clever. I'm giving you the facts.'

'Well, the fact is they have the money to pay people smugglers, so they sure as hell can't be doing too badly.'

Hazel sighed. But wasn't this what she wanted, after all? Some semblance of debate?

'Having money doesn't mean they're not fleeing persecution,' she said. 'Most asylum seekers, the vast majority actually'—she couldn't remember the figure—'almost all of them who reach Australia are fleeing persecution or war. They're not just looking for a more comfortable life.'

'And you know this because?'

'Their claims are assessed. Case by case.'

He was leaning against the doorframe now. Was he being casual before trying to catch her out?

'They could have stopped at other safe countries along the way,' he said. 'They're just country shopping. Picking and choosing.'

She seized another chance. 'The countries along the way won't let them work. So they can't support themselves, let alone their families.'

'Name one.'

'Indonesia.'

'Name another one.'

She couldn't. And Adam didn't rush in to help.

The man stopped leaning on the door, stood up straight. 'Of course people want to come here,' he said. 'But we already take more than our fair share of refugees. How about other countries pulling their weight?'

This time she did remember a number, found in Adam's kit.

'We actually take less than one percent of the world's refugees,' she said. 'And we're a prosperous nation. With lots of space.'

'And a high unemployment rate, my dear.'

He was like one of those big, blow-up plastic toys she'd had as a kid: she kept knocking him down and he kept bouncing back.

'Let's look after our own first,' he said. 'All the poor people living in cardboard boxes who don't know where their next meal's coming from.'

'Well, we could help the homeless a lot more,' she said, 'if we didn't spend all those billions on keeping people in detention. We could save an awful lot of money'—*billions, an awful lot of money*—but then she remembered something else. 'We're the only country in the world that detains asylum seekers while their claims are being heard. It would be so much cheaper, and more humane, to put them into the community.'

The man nodded, as if he agreed, but then narrowed his eyes.

'And so we take them in, treat them well,' he said. 'And then what? They'll keep coming in droves. Look what's starting to happen in Europe, millions of people flooding into countries that can't look after them. That's your solution, is it? Just let them all start pouring in. It's not going to work, sweetheart. It's already breaking down, all across Europe. They'll have blood in the streets before they know it.'

'Look,' she said. Which wasn't a good way to start. 'Sir. I understand it's a complex problem. That war and poverty are the root causes and—'

'Complex! So what makes you an expert?'

'I know we're not helping by bombing other countries,' she said. 'We're only creating more refugees.'

'So you're one of those people who think the West is to blame. You think that—'

'It would have been better if the West had...' She stopped, started again. 'If we'd dropped plane-loads of flowers and chocolate instead of bombs.'

The man shook his head. 'You Greens have really lost the plot.'

'I was using a metaphor, Sir. I meant we should have made friends with the people in Afghanistan, Iraq, the other troubled places. We should have—'

'Thrown money at regimes and watch them waste it.'

'We should have built schools and hospitals,' she said. 'That would have been a good start. To include people, give them a sense of hope.'

'Shoulda, coulda, woulda, it's all too late. We have to deal with the problem we have now. Because—'

'But the bottom line right now ...' She'd interrupted again. She pressed on. 'We have a moral obligation to treat asylum seekers decently. Wherever they've come from, whoever is to blame. Not lock them up and make them sick, not degrade them and destroy their sense of hope.'

'They're adults. They made an adult choice.'

'What about the children? That's no way to treat children.'

'Well, why did their parents put them in harm's way?' He drew himself up, triumphant. 'We've stopped the boats, haven't we? We've stopped all the deaths at sea. That's all that matters.'

He waited for a moment, then turned around and swiftly closed the door. Hazel kicked the ground with a frustrated toe.

'You gave him some valuable facts,' said Adam. He was trying to reassure her, she knew, yet she couldn't look him in the eye. 'And it is a complex problem, Hazel, you're absolutely right. And you're right to say we should treat people decently. That's non-negotiable.'

She finally met his gaze. 'But this all feels...' She didn't want to say pointless, didn't want to give up. 'Maybe I should be helping to raise money, or teach English to a refugee. Storm a detention centre.' She shrugged. 'Maybe I should have suggested building thousands of McDonald's in the Middle East so the terrorists would get so fat and slothful they wouldn't be able to move.' She pulled a face. 'I'm sorry, I shouldn't make a joke of it,' she said. 'I'm beginning to feel like Neville.'

He took a step towards her. 'You're doing your bit, Hazel. And you're not going to change the world. Except, well, you could try to tone down your voice, just a little. Be a little less—'

'Abrasive?'

He nodded. She swallowed.

'You did well,' he said. 'Honestly. Maybe he'll think about what you told him. You might have nudged him just a little. It's like teaching, I guess. On a good day.'

She shrugged.

'What about your parents?' he said. 'How did you persuade them to start voting for the Greens?'

'I guess they were decent people to start with. I didn't have to work all that hard.'

'And that's what you have to keep believing in. That basic sense of decency.'

They drank some water. They moved on. More No Shows, then Adam doing the talking, she doing the listening again: to the cynicism on the threshold of too many polished doors with stained-glass windows, with so many people chorusing that *politicians are a bunch of crooks…snouts in the trough…just in it for the money and the ego.* She straightened her back, which was meant to be good for your spine as well as your morale. *Knock knock knock.* A middle-aged woman in tiny pink shorts, looking Adam up and down, clearly liking what she saw.

'So what matters to me, you say?' She was positively purring at him. 'Childcare. Do you know how hard it is to find a decent place? And the cost! It's astronomical and going up all the time and …'

On and on she went, a self-interested, burbling pink machine, Adam nodding sympathetically, chipping in with details of Greens policy…*over two billion dollars in a boost to funding…more money for parents using long-term daycare…money for assistants…*and Hazel was growing impatient, wanting to butt in with the BIG issues: asylum seekers, climate change. And when Tiny Shorts was finally done and closed her parochial door, Hazel turned to Adam, indignant.

'Why are people so selfish?' she said. 'Where's their sense of proportion?'

'But childcare's a crucial issue,' said Adam. 'I'm lucky I

have Candace to help me out. A lot.' He stopped, started again. 'People's daily lives matter. They worry about having someone to look after their kids or whether they can afford their medication. New brakes for the car.'

'But none of that will matter if the planet is dying. Can't people see that?'

'Most people see and yet they don't. It seems too remote from their more immediate needs. I guess that's how it often goes.'

'So you'd call it human nature?'

'Maybe,' he said. 'But it's too easy to call it selfish.'

He was putting her in her place again, and so she simply kept walking, keeping in step. Growing accustomed to more No Shows—six in a row now—and one thin-lipped rebuff. And then: a chink of light. A Greens voter, even if the woman didn't have time to talk because she had a cake about to burn in the oven. Then more light, a burst of illumination, in fact: a retired farmer who'd voted conservative all his life but was now feeling conned by the government...*no long-term plans for the land...salinity...and now this fracking business...*He fixed Hazel with a look.

'What are your policies?' he said.

She recalled words like *biodiversity* and *bio fuels* and other things with *bio* in them. Under A for Agriculture: too far back to remember any details.

'To be honest, I don't really know about that policy.'

'So, why do you support the party, then?'

At least he wasn't glaring, or sounding rude.

'There's a lot I don't know,' she said, battling on. 'Things I should know. I know I should know them.' This wasn't going well. 'But I care about two things most of all. Asylum seekers and climate change, the two most important things for the Greens. And I know we'll have even more refugees if we don't stop global warming. We'll have millions of people without water or fruitful land...' *Fruitful land*? 'All I know is...'

She unclenched her hands. 'Ninety-five percent of the world's scientists believe in climate change and the urgent need to address it. That soon it will be too late to reverse the damage.'

The man nodded. 'My son thinks you lot are mad,' he said. 'That you care more about the loss of the hairy-nosed caterpillar than jobs and the economy.' He laughed. 'He actually said that. The hairy-nosed caterpillar.'

'Of course we're committed to ecological diversity,' said Hazel. 'But what people don't understand—not you, I don't mean you—we can have a vibrant economy and a healthy environment at the same time. Renewable energy, for starters.'

'So that's why you're knocking on doors?' he said. He was gnarled and lantern-jawed in that rural Aussie kind of way. 'Something to tell your kids, then?'

'Something to tell myself.'

'Well, good on you. It's young things like you who give me some hope as well. Not like my son, I'm afraid to say.'

Hazel felt herself beaming. And she didn't even mind being called a young thing.

'You can always look up our policy details on the website,' she said. 'Agriculture tops the list.'

He laughed. 'I'm guessing it's alphabetical,' he said, then shook Hazel's hand, firmly. 'Well done, love,' he said, released his own hand and quietly closed the door.

She felt a watermelon grin on her face.

'Yes, well done, love,' Adam said, teasingly.

It was beginning to feel easier. She knew this wasn't logical and yet the shift in her mood made her think that maybe people could, after all, have a change of mind and heart. Maybe reason and compassion could prevail. And so she was overjoyed when a woman at the door, dressed for the gym, ready to spring into her silver Mercedes, denounced the treatment of asylum seekers as *shameful, disgraceful*. Her husband was a doctor, she said—*a neurologist, actually*—and many doctors were speaking out about the mistreatment of people in detention centres.

Their ethical duty, she called it. Hazel ignored the neurological boast, could in fact have hugged the woman, right there, on the doorstep of her two-storey, environmental monstrosity. But no, the woman went on, she wouldn't be voting for the Greens because they *discourage individual initiative.*

'We'll keep fighting for the closure of detention centres,' she said, 'but we'll do it from within our existing structures.'

Fair enough, Hazel thought. That had to be better than lounging on a couch and flicking the remote to *Better Homes and Gardens*. But still she had to push a little more.

'So you and your husband are in accord,' she said. 'But is there something you can do on your own? I mean, in your own capacity?'

Now she was sounding insulting. But the woman's face was friendly, sympathetic.

'I talk to people,' she said. 'Just like you.'

Hazel nodded, relieved. 'I'm sure you know more important people than I do,' she said. 'More influential, I mean.'

'I'm on a few boards, yes.'

'So what do you say to people?'

'I give them facts. Information. And I appeal to their sense of compassion. For those who have it.'

Hazel put on her best school-prefect smile. 'Do you know,' she said, 'you sound exactly like a Greens voter to me. Reason and compassion are our two guiding principles.'

'I wouldn't press your luck, my dear.' She smoothed down her shorts. 'Now, if you'll excuse me, I'm about to do my bit at the gym.'

Hazel stepped aside and then walked towards the gate, Adam following behind, catching up.

'I hate it when wealthy people are decent people,' she said. 'And I'm glad she didn't bite my head off when I more or less said she didn't have a mind of her own.'

'Do you want to try the next house?' he said. 'You're on a bit of a roll.'

He'd been right about things getting better.

Next up was a tall, willowy blonde, maybe in her early twenties, very pretty in a generic, cheerleader kind of way. *No thanks, I vote Liberal.* But she didn't shut the door, and it was only then that Hazel noticed the book in her hands. One of those rubbish *Twilight* novels that kept topping the bestseller lists.

'Have you read it?' said the blonde.

Who must have caught her peeking.

Hazel scrambled for an answer that wouldn't be insulting. She'd read the first one in the series just to see what all the fuss was about. Two pages in, and she'd already counted three clichés, one mixed metaphor and a laughable feminine stereotype.

'I haven't read it, no.'

'It's on one of my uni courses,' said the blonde. 'Gothic fiction. But it's so badly written, I have to keep forcing myself to read it.'

Well. That was unexpected. And still she wasn't closing the door.

'So tell me,' said Hazel. 'Why do you vote Liberal? If you don't mind me asking.'

'Because they encourage people to work hard and make money.' Her look suddenly turned icy. 'And you Greenies, you're putting heaps of people out of work. Shutting down coalmines, for starters.'

'Well, we haven't actually shut them down.' Not for want of trying, Hazel thought.

'Coal has lifted millions of people out of poverty,' the blonde continued. 'It's reliable, affordable and abundant, and so much safer than nuclear.'

She'd managed to finish *that* book, at least: the coal industry manifesto.

'And before coal, people burned wood, and indoors the smoke killed millions of people.'

True enough, Hazel thought. Where to now?

'You're absolutely right about coal,' she said. 'I'm sorry, I didn't catch your name.'

'Polly.'

'Well, you're absolutely right, Polly. But you need to know...' Hazel paused. Knew she had to rephrase. 'The thing is that coal isn't actually cheap. It's heavily subsidised by taxpayers but the media doesn't tell you that. And the truth is—' Better to rephrase again. 'It's also the case that the disadvantages now far outweigh the advantages, especially the rise in carbon emissions. And we all know how terrible the consequences of that will be. Rising sea levels, massive floods, widespread drought, ravaging bushfires, airborne diseases.'

'I've heard all that stuff before,' said Polly.

Maybe I should have started local, Hazel thought. 'Did you know that climate change will hit Perth really hard?' she said. 'Harder than any other city in Australia? Because—'

'I'll move to Melbourne, then. All my friends are going there, they say it's really cool.'

It was time to put an end to another dead-end encounter.

'And another thing,' said Polly. 'Everyone thinks the Greens are all peace and love and stuff but my last boyfriend was a Green, from New South Wales he was, and he said they were fighting all the time. The loony left and the loonier right, that's what he called them. He was just so glad to leave.'

'Well, your party has factions too,' said Hazel. She could hear herself sounding indignant. 'You argue over economic policy and marriage equality and—'

'We call it a broad church.'

Broad church, my ass, thought Hazel. What did the mainstream media call it? Robust but respectful debate in the Liberal Party, internal chaos for the Greens. She was ready to turn around, walk away, but then, on impulse, she pulled out a booklet from her satchel, offered it to the former girlfriend of a disillusioned Green. 'Would you like a copy of this? Our vision for Perth? There's a lot of interesting stuff—information, I mean—about job creation in renewable energies.'

Polly shrugged, took the booklet just the same. 'Maybe I'll give to my mum,' she said. 'She's a bit infatuated with your senator. She thinks he's cute but she wouldn't vote for him in a million years. Maybe if he switched to the Libs, learned how to grow the economy.'

She finally closed the door.

Hazel turned to Adam. 'People,' she said. 'Honestly. And I think I just wasted a booklet. I just wish I'd remembered some statistics about climate change.'

Adam waved her on, down the path and onto the verge. 'I'm not sure the stats would have made any difference,' he said. 'Less than one percent rise in emissions, a twenty-centimetre rise in sea levels. It sounds so insignificant, so paltry.'

'So how do you make people listen, let alone change their minds?'

'Talk to them about extremes in the weather,' he said. 'Around the world, and at home. That's a start. You have to grab every opportunity to make it seem real.'

He looked down at his map. His face, his voice, seemed tired now, as though he'd had enough. Of her, maybe, as well as the whole damned trudge of knocking on useless doors.

'That was the last house,' he said. 'Shall we get back to the car?'

Would he ask her back for lunch again? Should she drop a hint? They began to walk in silence, Adam seemingly lost in thought, until he turned to her.

'So that book she was reading. Polly. The gothic fiction.'

'Oh, it's garbage for the female masses. I only read one, to see what the big attraction is.'

'And?'

'Well, the romantic hero is a strong, handsome vampire, so for female readers, I guess it's the fantasy of taming a powerful man.'

'I see.'

'Which is such an insulting stereotype,' she said. 'A lot of women like gentle men who aren't into the trappings of power.'

He didn't say a word.

'*Twilight*'s been called an example of abstinence porn,' she said.

He kept looking straight ahead.

'It means the writer gets her female readers feeling all hot and heavy but the characters don't actually have sex.'

And still he didn't speak.

'The author's a Christian fundamentalist,' she said. 'Which doesn't surprise me a bit. Her book's pornographic because it's dishonest. It's dishonest to titillate young women and then—'

'I think I understand, Hazel.'

Had she offended him now? Implied he was obtuse? Or maybe he was a prude. He couldn't be a prude, surely? Sexually repressed?

'I much prefer Jane Austen's version of romance,' she said, keeping her voice steady. 'It's about the importance of integrity, honesty, kindness, when you choose a partner. It's a moral concept of love.'

She was sounding like an exam question: *Discuss the representation of the moral concept of love in Jane Austen's novels in relation to their social and historical context. Refer to at least one novel in detail in your answer.*

Adam suddenly stopped, making her stop in her tracks as well.

'At the risk of being patronising,' he said, 'you did really well today. I'm proud of you.'

She laughed. Overcome. 'I feel like you've just given me a platypus stamp,' she said. 'My year eight English teacher used to give them to us, for effort and improvement. He'd stamp them on the inside of our wrists.'

Adam placed one finger on the inside of her wrist. 'Consider yourself stamped,' he said.

He had touched her only twice in two weeks: a hand lightly resting in the small of her back, a finger on her pulse. As they settled into his car, she couldn't stop herself from leaning over and kissing him on the cheek.

'Thanks for helping me learn,' she said.

She saw him redden as he did up his seatbelt, felt the heavy silence that followed. She remembered Felicia's words: that Adam wouldn't make the plunge.

Felicia had absolutely no idea.

As Adam started up the engine, not taking his eyes off the road, he told her he had a meeting in the city but of course he would drive her home.

Of course.

So she blabbered on about her reading project...moving to the letter B...Honoré de Balzac...needing something now, anything, to lift her sinking heart.

'Balzac was a very lonely boy at school,' she said. 'He used to read a dictionary for company.'

Adam laughed.

'I don't think that's funny,' she said. 'I think it's very touching.'

Prattle prattle blather blather, filling in a space. Yes, she'd finished *Persuasion* and no, she hadn't really enjoyed it, and had he finished *The Man who Loved Children* and no, he hadn't had time. Then she rabbited on some more about her favourite TV crime shows, *Sherlock* and *Fargo*, and did he know why crime shows were so appealing? Because they used reason to make sense of a potentially irrational world...blabbering now but she couldn't stop...giving him a lecture about the powers of deduction, restoring the moral order, Adam saying he didn't watch much TV and so she made a point of saying she'd rather read crime fiction and how most TV shows were rubbish anyway. More silence, so she geared up again. Had he read a novel called *Truth*, it was crime fiction, and when it won the Miles Franklin a few years back—did he know about the Miles Franklin, a big award for literature?—and how some people had objected to *Truth* winning the prize because they thought crime fiction wasn't serious.

'Not serious?' said Adam. 'What does that mean?'

'That if it's enjoyable to read, it can't be any good.'

She was sounding more inane by the minute.

'You're not a reader of fiction, anyway,' she said.

Did that sound sniffy and superior?

'I prefer history,' he said, in a clipped kind of voice.

Was he shutting down the conversation? More accurately, her whacked-out monologue?

He was peering through the window now, muttering something about a change in the weather. Bloody weather. Was that all he could think of to say? She was done with small talk now, possibly forever, looking at all the traffic whizzing past, oblivious to her mood. She was almost relieved when Adam turned into her car park and came to a halt. She reached into her satchel and brought out the toy for Jessie, in a brown paper bag, and handed it to Adam.

'Sorry about the presentation,' she said. She saw the question in his eyes. 'It's the gnu. For Jessie.'

'Ah. Yes. That's very kind of you.'

'It's nothing,' she said, and opened the door.

'See you next week, then?'

'OK.'

'I'll text you the details.'

'OK.'

She slipped out of the car, kept her head held high and didn't once look back.

As she walked towards her flat, flattened by the unromantic state of the ungenerous world, she tried to remember all the good things in her life: her parents and her friends, meals on the table, a roof over her head, books to read and reflect on, physical safety, more-or-less good health. Plus she was smart, if not always up to speed on details.

Trudging up the stairs, Hazel felt some drops of water on her arms. Fat, heavy drops. She looked up to see dismal rain falling from a leaden sky, the world turned grey in an instant. As if her mind had the power to rob the day of colour. As if the day would even care.

Walking backwards

Hazel was having a long, self-pitying kind of bath when she heard the front door open, heard Beth's voice calling out her name.

'In the bathroom,' she called back.

Just me and the water, she thought, with some froth to lift her mood. *Mr Bubble* for kids, because it was on special at Woolies. She saw Beth's face at the door.

'You're home early, Beth,' she said. 'Is everything OK?'

'I'm feeling a bit queasy. I think it's the prawns I had for lunch. But — oh, Hazel. You look really glum.'

Because a best friend, even a queasy one, could tell just by looking. A best friend always had great timing.

Beth sat down on the edge of the bath and Hazel told her about her doorknocking day: the ignorance, prejudice, self-interest, stupidity, venality and indifference and … well … OK, there'd been a few highs among all those lows but not much to speak of in the cosmic scheme of things. A few Weak Supports.

Beth asked Hazel to explain.

'It means people are open to changing their vote. So you pay them another visit, try to talk them round.'

'Well, that's a good thing, then. Try to take some heart.'

Beth was sounding like Adam.

Hazel slipped under the water, rose to the surface again.

'It's Adam,' she said. 'I just can't work him out. He likes me,

I'm sure, and sometimes I think I make him nervous, which is a good sign, isn't it? And he smiles at me and talks to me like I'm an intelligent human being and...well, that's it.'

'Weak support?' said Beth, and scooped up some bubbles, blew them away. 'Hazel, look. He's a lot older than you, right, and he has a young kid. He's probably thinking you're too young. Fancy-free and all that.'

'But I'm not just after sex.'

'Maybe he isn't either. Maybe he wants a woman who's more his age, ready to settle down. With his kid. A family, you know.'

'But I like Jessie. Adam's son.'

Beth looked at her closely. 'You've met him—how many times?'

'Twice.'

'And you'd be prepared to take care of him? Be his step-mother, or something?'

Hazel flushed. 'I haven't thought that far ahead.'

'So it's sex you're after?'

'Of course. But, well, not just with anyone. I like Adam so much. He's the loveliest man I've ever met.'

'Who comes complete with a young child.' Beth scooped up more bubbles. 'Try to see it from his point of view, Hazie. If he's a serious person, like you say he is, he's not looking for a fling, is he? It wouldn't make sense.'

Hazel hauled herself out of the bath. 'Or maybe he doesn't fancy me,' she said.

Beth laughed. 'But just look at your beautiful breasts.'

'These tiny things. You know I've always wanted to be voluptuous.'

'Like Felicia?' Beth suddenly looked serious. 'She told me her breasts give her backache sometimes and how men are always ogling her and it makes her so fed up. Only she called it *oogling*.'

Hazel reached for a towel. 'So you've been seeing Felicia?'

'I ran into her in the café—the one where the prick made me

an offer I could refuse, remember? She was getting a takeaway soy latte cos she's lactose intolerant and when she saw me she said she wouldn't take away her coffee but would *drink it in*— I love the way she says things kind of wrong and kind of right as well—so we sat down and had a long talk.'

'About her breasts?'

'Mostly about our fathers. We bonded over two pricks, ha-ha.' She stood back to let Hazel past. 'Oh, and I nearly forgot—a school phoned me to ask about relief teaching. They need someone right away, until the end of the month. Are you interested?'

Hazel was about to say *don't be nuts, over my dead body*, until she remembered the increase in their rent. Her father's birthday in a month: maybe a pair of runners to help him shed some weight. She really needed to have her eyes checked, too, because she was starting to squint at the pages.

Maybe she'd look cool in glasses. Sort of sexy. If a myopic man should chance to look her way.

She asked for the name of the school.

'Cranfield High. It's a bit on the rough side, but it's only two classes. Years eleven and twelve.'

Until the end of the month. Just over two weeks. Which would mean missing two weeks of doorknocking. Which would be a good thing, wouldn't it, all things considered? Which wasn't very noble of her, but would it really matter if she gave it away? She wasn't indispensable. And she'd have some *distraction by distraction from distraction*. T.S. Eliot again, in his pre-conversion state of secular despair. Maybe she could just get religion and turn a pile of easy answers into fridge magnets. Or maybe she could stop joking around, stop using humour to ward off the blues. The *mopes*, you might call it, a made-up word: a neologism. She'd tried to explain that to her students once—from the Latin, *neo* meaning new, she'd said, and *logos* meaning word—but it was hard for them to see the point of any words when the youth unemployment rate was nudging twenty percent.

She dried her hair, slipped on a dress and decided to phone the school. Heard a feverish female voice tell her they'd been looking everywhere for a teacher. Only part-time but she had to come in every day. The school was *really desperate*.

Good to know that even Hazel West would do in a desperate situation.

No Adam for the next two weeks. She could go cold turkey, release herself from a man who must be wanting something substantial. Enduring. Who wasn't the kind of man to take advantage of a needy young woman.

She wished he'd take advantage of a needy young woman.

Then her phone buzzed. Another message from Adam.

Jessie is rapt with his new animal. He says it's awesome. He says to give you a massive thank you.

Well, at least she'd made a little boy enraptured.

He's very welcome. I was just about to text because I can't do doorknocking for the next couple of weeks. I have a job.

A space. A long one.

Congratulations. What is it?

What could she say? I'm working at going backwards. 'I'm Walking Backwards for Christmas': a Goons song.

Relief teaching. Don't laugh

I would never laugh at you, Hazel.

He sounded so tender. Could a text possibly sound tender? And then:

So will you doorknock after you've finished teaching?

Wasn't it time to bite that damned bullet?

I'm not sure

About so many things, she didn't know where to begin. Then another long gap; more of those slow, pulsating bubbles on the screen.

You don't have to do this if you don't want to.

She took this in. *I will try to make it. OK?*

Another long pause. *OK.*

That seemed to be it. And tomorrow she'd be going back-wards. As if she hadn't already started.

***

That night Hazel dreamed that the carcass of a gnu was being picked clean, with frightening, malicious efficiency, by hordes of ravenous vultures. And while she feared that the dream might be prophetic, she was glad she wouldn't have to tell Jessie about *nature red in tooth and claw*. Because you couldn't sit him down, a nearly-five-year-old child, a cup of Milo in his little hands, and tell him the cruel facts of life. It wouldn't have been her place, anyway. It wasn't written in the stars, if you happened to believe in a light you could see even though the stars were dead.

Yet she wanted to see Adam's face, take his hand, take him to her bed, make love, talk. They would give each other their stories, they would pleat their moments together, and it would be more beautiful than she'd ever imagined.

She'd watched too many crappy rom-coms.

***

She struggled out of bed at seven am—had she really done this for two long years?—showered quickly, put on a respectable dress, ran a brush through her hair. Packed a sandwich, a muesli bar and one juicy red apple for the teacher, grabbed a book to read on the bus: a short story anthology she'd stolen from her former school because theft was meant to be empowering. Or maybe it was a reward for those two long years of *the horror, the horror*. So what was she doing now, returning to the heart of darkness? She told herself it was only for a couple of weeks, and what was the worst that could happen? Backchat, resentment, gum chewing, swearing, being bowled over in the corridor, being mocked, truancy, the odd punch-up or two.

She ran for the bus and just managed to catch it because the driver had seen her coming. Must be my lucky day, she thought.

Slumped in her seat, she could see what lay ahead of her: boring worksheets on plot, theme, character and setting, boring documentaries about drugs and the media, tolerance and intolerance. Showing movies the kids must have seen a hundred times just to fill in the time. What had she shown her students on her more desperate days? *Clueless, 10 Things I Hate About You, Shrek*. The best part of *Shrek* was when the bluebird of happiness puffed up and exploded. Or maybe she'd have to do some real teaching. Proper lessons. She started flipping through her stolen book. Everyone liked stories, didn't they? Roald Dahl: he'd been a hit with the year eights, especially his grisly tale of the landlady who'd killed a young male tenant and kept his body in her bed. Hazel remembered how one of the kids—an observant girl, precocious—had noticed the woman's strange kind of interest in the corpse, and she'd quickly changed the subject. Necrophilia. That was one word she hadn't wanted her students to know. Well, not when they were twelve years old.

She ran her finger down the table of contents. What would fifteen, sixteen-year-olds like? Joyce: too depressing. Hemingway: too flat. Chekov: also too depressing, and probably much too subtle for kids who didn't read between the lines. And then she saw it: a story she'd studied way back in year twelve. Joyce Carol Oates. A woman. Even better. Such a creepy tale, it had knocked her out, knocked everyone out, even the science brainiacs. Everyone loved *creepy*, didn't they? She could talk with the kids about what made their hair stand on end, what made them afraid, and why. Because we were all afraid of something, even if we didn't know it, even when knowing it didn't make it disappear. Like her fear of sharks. Of being useless. Of being alone.

She returned to the title of the story: 'Where Are You Going, Where Have You Been?'

She'd been knocking on doors and hadn't made one definite conversion. She'd been to a toyshop and made a little boy rapt. She'd met a man, and then...nothing.

And where was she going? Back to where she'd started: with a book, a lunchbox, an ache in her heart, and already counting down the hours.

***

Cranfield High had the look of a government school strapped for government cash: too many demountable buildings, straggly gardens, a grey carpet in reception that was thinning in patches. The red-faced receptionist handed Hazel some notes, asked for her Working with Children card to ensure that she was safe. When some of the children Hazel would be teaching might already be driving cars, binge-drinking, having sex, possibly all three at the same time. Still, you could hardly blame them, when they didn't have much else to give them pleasure. She sometimes used to wonder, as she stood in the front of a class, how the hell they managed it: seven hours a day of boredom and frustration, hating every single minute of compulsory education, with teachers who tried to help them see the point of compulsory education and others who *couldn't give a flying fuck*. That's what a teacher at her old school had said: Tony Tucker. Phony Fucker, she'd heard some kids call him, and you couldn't blame them for that either. And now here she was again, about to front up to a bunch of strangers, most of them taller than her and some of them slightly threatening and all of them checking her out. The relief teacher. Who, according to the scrappy notes in her hand, must have some kind of knowledge to impart.

She made her way to the classroom and stood outside for a moment, breathed in, breathed out, made her hands go loose. Year twelve English...she headed inside...maybe twenty, twenty-five, of them...and sure enough, murmurs of derision and rocking back in chairs, making their obvious point: slacking off time, try and make us work, Miss. But she wanted to be strong, hold her nerve. She'd been doorknocking, after all, and survived. So she looked at particular faces instead of an anonymous crowd: the scowling boy with the row of heavy piercings in one ear, the thoughtful-looking redhead, the hulking boy who could knock you for six. She pulled back her shoulders and waited for silence (that much she remembered from her more-or-less useless Dip. Ed.), as they looked her up and down, or looked at their friends, delighted. A woman. Yay. Even slacker.

'Hey, Miss, what's your name?'

It was a member of the acned brigade, the kind of boy who deflected his embarrassment through insult or bravado.

'I'm Ms West. And what's your name?'

'Superman,' he said, and looked around, grinning, for approval.

She refused to be smart-arse, like him.

'Well, I'm pleased to meet you,' she said. 'Now, your teacher wants you to write a feature article. The pros and cons of using social media.'

There was an immediate chorus of *borrrring...we do that every year...* and Hazel held up her hand. She had to agree in her head—*borrrring*—but she couldn't undermine their teacher.

'Let's do a deal,' she said.

Many eyes narrowed, because a deal usually meant them losing.

'If you spend ten minutes making dot points about the pros and cons of social media, I'll read you a story.'

Loud moans and groans all around.

'But it's a really creepy one,' she said, trying not to sound like she was talking to infants. 'It's written by a woman called Joyce Carol Oates.'

More laughter, and wisecracks about breakfast cereal and feeding pigs, but she needed to make a start before she lost her nerve. So she ignored the sniggers, cleared her throat, waited for silence, and began. With the story of working-class Connie:

fifteen years old and restless, fond of looking at her reflection. Whose only source of pleasure was flirting with boys, whose only form of power was attracting them. Someone in the class whispered *cockteaser* but Hazel let it go, kept on reading, sensing that the story was drawing them in to their familiar, garish world: generic shopping malls, fast-food outlets, drive-in this and that, the tacky merchandise, the aimless hanging around. She paused for a moment, looked up to see them attentive and perfectly still, as the girl in the story—pretty, vain, sexually naïve—walked headlong into danger, lured by a charming, flattering man with big dark glasses and a flashy gold car. Who seemed much older than Connie was aware. And suddenly someone called out, *He's soooo creepy, watch out for the creepy man*—as though the characters were real. A plea, a warning, straight from the heart. And then a girl, Asian, wearing horn-rimmed glasses, suddenly put up her hand and flapped it around, announced that she'd discovered a code.

'The creepy man's name,' she said. 'I wrote it down. Arnold Friend. If you take out the letter r, his name spells An Old Fiend.'

Which got the whole class buzzing. *How'ja work that out?*

'It's in the Bible, a fiend is the same as the devil.'

A drumming of applause on desks and *way to go Mavis*, the girl's face glowing with pride.

Hazel didn't tell them the code had already been cracked. She didn't mention the many critics who'd dissected and debated this terrifying story. Because Mavis was entitled to the pleasure of discovery, and the pleasure of being admired. And there were other things as well, to consider. Like what it might mean to be a teenage girl with nothing in her head but vanity and flirting and sex. Where this might lead you, and how there might be a better place to go.

Hazel finished the story, put down the book, and someone shouted out, *Hey, Miss, what happened to the girl?*

'We don't know,' she said. 'That's the end.'

There were grumbles, a few shouts... *but we wanna know ...*
that's so not fair... and then someone waved a hand.

'That's what makes the story creepy.' Mavis again, shouting
now, finding an even bigger voice. 'It's like the girl, Connie,
she's become a missing person.'

'That's exactly right, Mavis,' said Hazel, and took in a sea of
puzzled faces. 'Imagine if one of your friends went missing.
How would you feel, not knowing what had happened to
them? That might be worse than knowing they were dead.'

A girl raised her hand and Hazel asked her name.

'Shareen. You'd feel like there was hope,' she said. 'But
every day they'd still be missing and you'd die a little bit more.'

Hazel was about to praise her—a sensitive, intelligent
response—but another girl with fierce dark eyes waved her
hand about.

'And who are you?'

'Jaycie. I'd feel gutted if my mum was missing, but not my
dad.'

A loud voice from the back row called out: 'So will you read
us something else tomorrow?'

'We'll have a discussion first,' said Hazel. 'About what you
think of this story, and why.'

More moans and groans.

'But we've already done that,' said a dark-skinned boy.

'And your name is?'

'Jamal. Can we hear another creepy story?'

Joyce Carol Oates had set their pulses racing, without the
need for a nurse.

'Do you have a suggestion, Jamal?'

She could have kicked herself. Asking a student if they had
a suggestion could lead to something crude.

'No, you choose,' he said. 'You're the teacher.'

And then the siren blasted. She'd always hated that sound:
piercing and officious. But right here, right now, she saw
open, interested expressions, heard the energy of their talk,

and she found herself wondering if they'd ever been read to as children. If they'd ever sat on a parent's lap, encircled by love and the wonder of words, pleading for just one more story.

'See ya tomorrow, Miss.'

She couldn't tell who'd said it, but a cheery voice had said it and, for the moment, that was enough.

She watched them leaving the classroom, jostling and laughing and—fuck! She'd forgotten to call the roll. Who knew how many kids were missing? And she'd forgotten the dot points about social media as well, the deal she was meant to have done. She looked around at an unknown, familiar space: marked walls, smeary windows, a badly scuffed floor, but there were many bright movie posters of vampires, gangsters, outer space, boy meets girl. A chart about Genre, Audience, Purpose. GAP: there was always a handy acronym to fill the gaps in a student's head. There were the usual laminex pages about text types, grammar, classroom rules, and a map of the world, with some sappy words of inspiration: *A good book can take you anywhere.* Well, maybe she'd taken them somewhere today, those unknown kids with their unknown lives. Maybe she'd raised a few questions. It wasn't a bad start to the day.

Which became steadily worse. She should have known that the next lesson would give her nothing but aggression and indifference: the usual bookends of a teacher's life in a school like Cranfield High. Year eleven. Their teacher had left another lesson plan on social media (he or she must have run out of ideas early in the year), and the kids were beginning to shout, call each other names, stroll casually round the room. After ten pointless minutes, in which she failed to quieten them, indeed barely stopped a riot, Hazel slotted 'The Dark Knight Rises' into the giant TV. They'd seen it twice already, the kids told her, but no one objected to a third.

Thirty minutes of a movie that seemed hammy. Portentous. The siren had never sounded so sweet.

She should also have known, when she went for morning

tea, that three teachers talking in the queue were just twiddling their pedagogic thumbs until they retired in five or ten years' time. She should also have bet heavily on the odds of a male teacher sloping up to her, looking her up and down and resting his lecherous paw on her hip.

'Don't touch me,' she snapped.

'Jeez Louise,' he said, backing off. 'What's your problem?'

And how could she not have foreseen that one of her colleagues deserved to be shot to improve the national IQ: a middle-aged woman with beady eyes and a slit for a mouth who warned Hazel not to do anything *political* in her classes because they weren't her classes, were they? *Teaching ideology*, she said, pursing her lips, as though she'd just tasted something foul in her coffee mug. Literature had nothing to do with gender or race or class, she vehemently declared. *All that reductive business about power and victims, people choose to be victims, everyone can make it if they try.*

Her name was Penelope. *Call me Penny.* And I need to hold my tongue, Hazel thought, or I'll end up calling her a fucking idiot.

What she hadn't expected was the warm welcome from another English teacher, who smiled toothily, took her by the elbow and guided her to another table. Asked how she was settling in. Marcie, or Martha, Hazel didn't quite catch her name, who told her that Penny yearned every day to teach in a private school but none of them seemed to want her, despite the head of department's brilliant reference designed to *give her a hefty shove*. An earthy woman, this Marcie or Martha, smiling now at an approaching figure. The school principal, it seemed. Hazel straightened her back, shook hands with Ms Hipkins, a striking apparition with shrieking blonde hair, a leopard-skin blouse and bright red skirt. She welcomed Hazel, thanked her for helping out in a very tight spot, her voice like a flutter of welcoming birds. Not like Hazel's former principal; the only time he'd made contact was knocking her tea cup to the floor when he'd rushed to get at the Shortbread Creams.

The principal waved to someone in the distance, excused herself, and Hazel turned to Marcie? Martha? Asked if the principal always dressed like that.

'Inappropriately, you mean? She sometimes shows more cleavage but hey, she's a damn fine principal. Knows the names of all the kids. Really cares about her staff. So.' That toothy smile again. 'You must have enjoyed teaching the year twelves,' she said.

'We had a good time with a story, Martha.'

She seemed to have got that right.

'They looked really alive,' said Martha. 'I thought you must have given them a special drug.' She put a hand on Hazel's arm. 'Make sure you come to the office tomorrow, meet the rest of the crew. Just watch out for Darren, though, he likes to thrust his groin at women. He's a good teacher, but I do wish he'd give over with the cock.'

Hazel laughed. How did Martha know she wouldn't be offended? Or wouldn't she even care?

***

She and Beth had cheesy toast for dinner and exchanged their news of the day. Definitely the old married couple. The constancy. The certainty. It was like the end of the TV weather forecast: sunrise will be at 5:32 am and sunset will be at 6:49 pm. Maybe, Hazel thought, remembering those year elevens, she could try for a job as a weather person. Not a forecaster, though, because you'd need to have specialised knowledge, but one of those women with a sing-song voice and a long stick, pointing to gale warnings and sheep weather alerts and alarmingly hotter temperatures all over the madly spinning globe. Hazel knew she should go to bed early: another seven am start to catch the bus. She slathered on some cheap generic sorbolene cream, having read in *The Guardian* that a two-hundred dollar jar of night cream did absolutely nothing to hydrate, invigorate or rejuvenate your skin. Skin: the body's largest organ. She shrugged off those treacherous feelings, put on her non-flimsy nightie and slipped into bed, gave a fleeting thought to some lessons for tomorrow. What the hell would she do with those year elevens: a double period first up, ninety long minutes, and she couldn't bear to finish that movie. She'd need to make them do some work, some thinking at least, and they'd need a break as well. Tim Tams. Except that you weren't allowed to hand out chocolate biscuits or giant snakes because it was meant to be pedagogically unsound and encouraged unhealthy eating. She'd hope for inspiration in the morning.

Why was she taking this so seriously? It was only relief teaching.

She picked up her phone: one last check for messages. Her mother:

I took your advice and now he's more bolshie than ever.

WTF? she messaged back straight away. *What advice?*

About not giving your father any sex.

I was only joking, Mum. I'm sorry.

Don't be. I think it might actually work.

Then she heard another message coming through. Adam. Adam!

How was your first day of teaching?

Which was kind of him to ask. She could almost have cried with his kindness.

It was OK. One lesson went really well, in fact, thanks so much for asking

One really good lesson. That's a good start.

But the second one was a dud

Remember the good one, Hazel.

Was he admonishing her? Or trying to reassure?

I wasn't chastising you, honestly. And I'm sorry if I sounded patronising.

Before she could respond, he sent another message:

Tell me to mind my own business, if you like.

She didn't like.

You're just trying to keep me hopeful. Which is really good of you, thank you

Another gap. Then another message coming through:

Jessie said to say hello.

And say hello from me

Will do.

And he was gone. Courteous, brief, non-committal.

But still she remembered kissing his cheek. The touch of his finger on her pulse.

'What's a word gunna do?'

She was up at five am, doing some research. Not that Wikipedia was proper research, but she wanted to check out the creepy story. She read that it was based on the nefarious activities of a real live serial killer. Four victims. That the story was dedicated to Bob Dylan, because of his song 'It's All Over Now, Baby Blue'. Just the title gave Hazel the shivers. She listened to it on YouTube, keeping it low so she didn't wake Beth, and wondered if the kids would like it. Would they understand the lyrics? Did anyone understand the lyrics? Maybe even Dylan didn't know what he meant. *The painter drawing crazy patterns on your bed sheets?* And what was that allusion to *reindeer armies?* He must have been on some pretty strange stuff.

Beth wandered into the kitchen, rubbing her eyes.

'What are you doing up so early?' she said.

'Preparing lessons.'

'But it's only relief, Hazel.'

'The kids loved the creepy story I read them.'

Beth laughed. 'You actually read them a story?'

'Sure. Why not? You just have to find the right one.'

'I need some inspiration, too,' said Beth, turning on the kettle. 'The boss wants me to come up with some snappy words for the brochures and posters. She's heard me talking to the clients and reckons I'm articulate. And now I'm stuck. You know I'm not creative. Do you know any really good lines?'

'Have you tried the net? All those sites on quotable quotes?'

'They'll all be horribly clichéd. Thousands of quotes about the journey being more important than the destination. Which isn't really helpful when you're planning a client's itinerary.'

They googled some quotes. And yes, there were pages of clichés.

'Here's another useless one,' said Beth. '*A good traveller has no fixed plans*. That's no good for an anally retentive client.' She peered more closely. 'OOOH. I like this one! *We lean forward to the next crazy venture beneath the skies*. Jack Kerouac. *On the Road*.'

Another famous book that Hazel hadn't read.

'It has possibilities,' said Beth.

They busied themselves for work: back to the bad old days, negotiating the tiny space of the bathroom, talking while they brushed their teeth.

Hazel looked in the mirror and poked out her tongue.

'Why are you doing that?' said Beth.

She shrugged. 'Do I have to have a reason?' she said.

***

Sitting on the bus, rushing past the fast-food joints and used-car yards, Hazel was beginning to feel panicked about those year elevens. She felt the bus slam to a halt at a red light, looked down to see an old man sitting in a car, his head bobbing in time to what must have been some boppy music. *Boppy. Bobbing.* They were jazzy kinds of words; jaunty. *Bobbing* was a ducking-your-head-in-a-bucket-of-water-to-find-an-apple kind of word, which all her friends had done at Ed's twenty-first and thought it was more fun than smoking pot. Except for Ed. And then she had a light-bulb moment: she would ask the year elevens to think of a single word, any word, as the beginning to their story. To show them that a single word, like travel, could take you anywhere. To a place you didn't know, or was completely unexpected. That writing was a product of the unconscious as well as the conscious mind. Only she wouldn't use those words, not to begin with, anyway. Except she was only staying for a very short time, so she wouldn't use those words at all. Then she saw a woman in a different car, peering into the rear-view mirror to apply her lipstick. *Lipstick*. A child on the footpath, being led by the hand, his baggy shorts flapping round his knees. *Knees*. The world was full of possibilities, and there were more words in English than in any other language. Her year ten English teacher had told them that, and how Shakespeare had used some thirty thousand of them, which was a whole lot more than most people. And how he'd invented the word *bubble*.

Mr Papadopolis. She hoped he was still teaching.

But it wasn't quite so easy when she fronted up to the class. When her creative idea met the unimaginative reality, kids looking restless in their dull grey shirts, or yabbering loudly, calling out to watch the movie.

'We're going to write a story instead,' she told them.

'We're always writing stories,' said a boy with a very large head.

'And they're always the same,' said a girl with a mass of steel in her ears.

'What does that mean?' said Hazel. 'Always the same?'

A hand shot up.

'Your name is?'

'Amina.'

'Amina's from India,' said a voice from the back. 'She's a wog.'

Hazel was just about to speak when Amina spoke calmly for herself.

'Your parents come from Scotland,' she said.

'So what?'

'We all come from somewhere.'

Again Hazel went to speak but Amina was unruffled.

'Men from Scotland wear skirts,' she said, 'and they don't wear underpants.'

The class erupted into laughter.

And so they returned to the writing of a story. Amina knew the formula: a story, she said, with admirable clarity and confidence, had an exposition, development, *climax* — sniggers then — and a resolution. Hazel thanked her, explained that this was one way to write a story, but you could do it differently, you could... she saw many eyes glazing over.

'Everyone choose a word,' she said. 'Don't even think about it.'

That's stupid... what's a word gunna do... why? A chorus of juvenile dissent.

'You might find out when you do it,' she said.

More dulled eyes, a few blatant yawns. Maybe some of them were tired, not bored. Maybe some of them hadn't had breakfast. She'd forgotten this as well.

'After you've chosen a word,' she said, 'I'm going to ask each of you to give me your name and then —'

'Why d'ya wanna know our names?' said a hunched-up boy. 'You're the relief.'

'Please don't interrupt when I'm... when someone's talking.' Hazel breathed in, breathed out. 'I want to know your names because you know mine. That's only fair, isn't it?'

She'd stunned them into silence, without meaning to.

'So give me your name,' she said again, 'and then tell the class your word.'

She could see the kids screwing up their faces, shaking their heads, but she made herself push on. Beginning with the back row: getting the worst over with first.

'Jaxon. *Boofhead.*'

Laughter. And then a volley of names and words. Magenta, *Tree.* Tahla, *House.* Tahlia, *Chocolate.* Teniele, *Netball.* Beckham, *Revhead.* Next to him, a female Beckham, *Fashion.* All the bogan names, the working-class, aspirational names, and non-Anglo names like Wahleed, whose word was *Cool*, and Kassim, whose word was *Home*. The Anglo names for Indigenous kids: Percy, who gave them *Wheels*, and Maurice, who gave them *Tree*. Someone called out that *Tree* had already been taken but Hazel pointed out that it would be a different tree and please don't shout, she said, no one here is deaf. Next up was the smart-arse, because there always had to be one. Nick, *Sex*. Followed by Rita, *Tonight*.

More fits of laughter.

'Well, I like my word,' said Rita. 'And not because I'm having sex tonight. It's just a cool way to start a story cos anything can happen.'

'Fair enough,' said Nick. 'But you can come round to my place anyway.'

They'd made a start. They'd all made a start. Hazel asked them to write another sentence. Then another. And they did. Until they began to sigh and fidget and mumble *this is dumb*.

'Here's a very different way to start a story,' she said. She couldn't let them get restless. 'Begin with a memory. Something that stays with you. Ask yourself why it's stayed with you and then write a few sentences about what you remember.'

'What for?' said the male Beckham.

'You'll see.'

Lots of puzzled looks, but again they did as she'd asked.

Why did this seem a bit easier the second time around? Because she was only here for ten more working days. She wasn't responsible for them, in the longer term at least. And maybe she'd grown up, just a little, although the thought seemed so unlikely that she nearly laughed out loud.

She collected their writing, keen to read their efforts, then dashed to her next lesson. Year twelves. She was ready to tell them about the real live serial killer, get them thinking about the difference between fact and fiction, the different kinds of truths they embodied. But as soon as she walked into the classroom, the kids were already talking up the story. A couple of the boys, to her delight, had googled it yesterday, but far less delightful was their ghoulish satisfaction in the details of those four grisly murders.

She cut the boys off. 'Why would you do that?' she asked the class. 'Not kill someone. I mean why would you write a story about something as gruesome as that?'

A bunch of hands shot up...*to give us nightmares...writing sicko stuff must be fun...but no one dies in the story...that's cos it's not about killing...you don't get to know what the sicko's thinking.* Which got them talking about hearing the voice of the victim, and why Connie had agreed to get into that gold flashy car. Which made them argue, often boys against girls, sometimes loudly, all over the top of each other, about how much, if at all, the girl was to blame, and whether *blame* was even the right word.

They ended up learning from each other.

A platypus stamp for Hazel.

Even her colleagues looked bright when she walked into the English office. Martha did the introductions: Len, the head of department (flamboyant orange tie), Liz (vivid blue dress), Darren (pink shirt). There was a lavish bunch of yellow roses on the table, in honour of Martha's birthday. And then, as Hazel stepped outside with Martha, she collided with a tall, lean guy with dark green eyes, who asked if she was OK. Looked abashed, asked her again if she was OK. Martha introduced him: Lucas. Who taught chemistry.

'How's the teaching going, Hazel?' he said.

'I'm only the relief.'

'I know. So how's the teaching going?'

She smiled, suddenly shy. Then listened as Martha asked Lucas about a student, a boy who'd told her he hated the noise of the siren because it made him think of the end of the world. Did Lucas think that was a problem?

'I don't think so,' Lucas said. 'Hadley's a genius in chem.

He often stays back after class to talk about matters like the end of the world as a matter of abstraction. He's the most intelligent student I've taught in my seven years at Cranfield.'

Seven years. Hazel took this in. Had Lucas been boasting about his loyal service? Or was he implying he was in a vocational rut? And how old would that make him? Twenty-seven if he'd gone straight from school to uni, twenty-eight if he'd done honours. Older if he'd changed careers or been travelling or spent time in jail, the latter being most unlikely because he didn't look like the criminal type. If you believed in phrenology, that is, which at some irrational level, she must have. And weren't we all guilty of seeing virtue in a beautiful face, vice in an ugly one, to guide us through the tricky maze of working people out?

Whatever the case, she figured that Lucas wasn't too much older than she was. However much was not *too much*.

He had a gap between his two front teeth. It made him look interesting. Appealing.

As she stood watching his tall, loping figure receding, she asked Martha what she thought of him.

'Lucas? He's one of the good guys. I'd go for him in a flash if I were straight.'

***

Friday afternoon faded into evening. Beth had gone for drinks at the Captain Stirling but *sorry, too tired*, Hazel told her on the phone. She was, in truth, knackered. Only two classes for two days in a row and she was ready to drop. One glass of wine would do her in, and quite possibly make her maudlin. She had a weekend ahead of her with nothing to do except look at those year eleven memories, and memories, after all, could be dangerous. They could make you think about a kiss on the cheek and wanting more kisses and knowing it was useless. She thought about making a Milo, decided it was time to kick the habit. Nuns wore habits, didn't they, and managed to live without sex. They were required to keep their mind on higher things. The life of the soul, if you happened to believe in souls.

But why try to satisfy the soul when it was hard enough to please the mind and the body? Especially the body.

And yet she couldn't stop herself from picturing Adam's pale blue eyes, black-rimmed. The freckles across the bridge of his nose. His sensual mouth with the upturned corners. His unbrushed, greying hair, strong thighs and round bum. She could take him apart and put him back together and still he wouldn't be here, sitting beside her, taking her hand.

Who could account for the stirrings of desire?

He'd phoned her to ask about her teaching. She should return the courtesy, shouldn't she? Have a civilised exchange. Ask him what he'd done with his day, or what he might be planning for the weekend. Whether he had replaced her.

She just needed to hear his voice.

But what if he thought she was desperate? She didn't want him thinking she was desperate. Even though she was. Desperate.

She poured herself a drink, guzzled it in one go, poured herself another.

***

Hazel woke up groggily—was it really ten am?—and staggered to the kitchen, turned on the kettle. Saw a note from Beth, something about shopping for clothes. Clothes? That little black dress flashed into Hazel's head but she settled for a strong coffee and a large bowl of Connoisseur ice-cream: Chocolate Brownie and Chocolate Custard. Then she ate an apple so she'd feel less guilty. Decided to read those year eleven memories so she would feel even less guilty. But as she scanned their words, she was utterly cast down by the poor spelling, rotten grammar and mangled syntax. Maybe she could do a PowerPoint: *Meet Ms Verb. Say hi to Mr Apostrophe.* But the kids would think that was lame. And was it really crucial to distinguish between *their* and *there*, or to write *laughter* instead of *larfta*? Because the main problem was the unwieldy length of their sentences.

Maybe she should do a different PowerPoint. She wrote down a beginning: *Short sentences are important because if you write really long sentences you'll forget what you started out trying to say and the longer your sentences become the more you'll forget anything and everything you were trying to say and your head will be a mess and the person reading what you've written will start getting really annoyed.* Because she couldn't say *pissed off* in a PowerPoint, at any point at all. So, yes, she'd try getting them to write much shorter sentences. She wouldn't expect polish but a jab at coherence would be welcome. Coherence might help them unscramble their thoughts and feelings, maybe front up to that interview and do a reasonable job.

Hazel checked what she'd written: *you'll forget what you started out trying to say.* Changed the word *trying* to *wanting* because it sounded less condescending. And it told them that wanting was permissible, that wanting was important, because if you gave up wanting you might as well sink into the muck of life and die. *We are all in the gutter but some of us are looking at the stars.* Oscar Wilde. One of Chloe's fridge magnets. *Our truest life is when we are in dreams awake.* Henry David Thoreau. *For most of history, Anonymous was a woman.* Virginia Woolf. Chloe had dozens of fridge magnets, so many that you couldn't see her fridge, in a flat so messy with research papers that you couldn't see her floors. I should get in touch, thought Hazel, see if she's gone back to her thesis. Maybe see a movie, eat a giant box of popcorn. Have a couple of drinks and try not to blubber as we have a heart-to-heart.

But for now she must focus on her classes. Which weren't, strictly speaking, her classes, but she could try to nudge, even sow the odd seed. Because she couldn't change the world, just as Adam had said. Which was, of course, a cliché, but she wouldn't hold it against him.

Longing. She could begin a story with *Longing.*

Hope

She barely saw Beth on the weekend. She was out with Felicia, showing her the sights that Simon had been too busy to offer. At least that's what Beth's exhaustive note had implied. They'd been to the Freo markets, where Felicia bought a boomerang, then on to the wildlife sanctuary, because Felicia had never seen an Australian animal except back in Rome, where she'd loved to watch 'Skippy', dubbed in Italian, and wonder how a country could be *having such crazy creatures.*

Hazel tried not to feel resentful. Left out.

But she did feel pleased about the prospect of school on Monday. It was a structure, at least, for ten more working days, and she'd had another idea to keep the year elevens writing: a bag full of objects to spark their imagination. One of her primary school teachers had used it, and she'd loved the experience, the whole class had loved it, because it was like a lucky dip. After half an hour of rummaging round the flat, she'd found seventeen items, one for each student, including her father's three wooden animals, a blank notebook, a shell, a lipstick, a lollipop still in its wrapper (how long had that been sitting on her desk?). She'd given the students' memories another look as well, and been surprised by what she'd read beneath the surface mistakes. For while most of the memories were ordinary—the first day at school, a beloved grandparent, a favourite pet—some of them reminded her that nothing was ordinary: that everything was extraordinary if we could only find the words. Like Magenta, who described her first cat, now long gone, as *crouched black on the fence, ready to leap across the night*. Jaxon, whose triumph at learning to tie a shoelace was a case of *me fingers trickin me brain*. Percy, a Noongar boy from the country, remembering his first view of the city: *Them towers were stuck in the ground not reaching the sky cos they aint got the spirit inside em*. And Jamal from Afghanistan: *I am missing the mountains*.

***

She told the class that their memories had been interesting. It was a teacher's cop-out word, a book-reviewer's cop-out word, but as Hazel's mother would say, there was never an excuse for being cruel. Her mother. Hazel wondered if she should call, tell her about her job. Her dad, too. But it might make them anxious, remembering what a mess their daughter had become the last time she—but now a couple of boys were scuffling in the front row and Hazel had to have a word. Then she took out her bag of objects, walked among the rows of seats, told the class what she had in mind. But it seemed there was nothing on their minds right then but mockery and mayhem: she saw a dolt of a boy grab the lipstick and smear it on the boy next to him, saw a girl doing something obscene with the lollipop in her mouth, and before Hazel could stop them, objects were being thrown about, a notebook flung in the air, her father's animals skidding along the desks, kids making animal noises, laughing out loud. Hazel was stunned. Enraged. Told the offenders *to grow up, you're behaving like idiots*. Which did nothing but make them sneery and snarly and everything was collapsing now, everyone staring at her, glowering, as she marched around the room, collecting the objects, ordering them to work on their memories and she didn't want to hear another squeak out of them or they'd all be staying back after school. She sat down heavily with her useless bag of tricks, wished that her cheeks would stop burning.

But at least they stayed more-or-less shut up until the siren blasted and she snapped at them to leave.

As they trailed out, muttering, she caught Percy's eye and told him that his memory writing was beautiful. Told Jacinta that hers, too, was beautiful. Told Jamal she was sorry he was missing those mountains. But the boy was in a hurry to *eat my lunch, Miss, then go play soccer*. He started walking away, then turned back.

'You can come and watch,' he said.

Percy looked back too, gave her an enormous grin. 'Come watch me play Aussie Rules,' he said. 'Soccer's stupid.'

Hazel smiled in return, and was grateful.

***

She took her sandwich to the oval and watched both the boys at lunchtime. Percy was a flash of long skinny legs and a fiendish tackler; Jamal was a weaver through countless legs, hugged by his teammates when he scored a classy goal. Sport: the Great Australian Leveller, she thought, pleased to see Martha approaching her now, giving her a wave. Martha wasn't keen on either form of football, she told her. Cricket was her game, although she loathed the current Australian team, *a bunch of self-important bullies*, she called them. She was also a huge fan of crime fiction, featuring *kick-arse smart women detectives*, and had an undying reverence for country and western music. Did Hazel know the longest ever title of a C&W song? 'It's Hard to Kiss the Lips at Night That Chew Your Ass Out All Day Long'.

'Shame about the misogyny, though,' said Martha, even as they laughed together.

And then Len appeared, rubbing his hands, telling Hazel he'd had two year twelve parents call him that morning to offer their praise. Their kids actually wanted to come to school, he said, thanks to the relief teacher. Hazel was pretty chuffed. Very chuffed. Inwardly made a promise to try harder with the elevens. As the principal strode away, Darren sauntered up, then quickly thrust out his groin as if to say *I have the perfect cock for you.* Hazel stifled a laugh. Did men do this consciously? Well, some men, anyway. Or was it a reflex action, some kind of evolutionary thing to ensure the survival of the species? But men who thrust their groin at women didn't deserve to reproduce. There ought to be a scientific law against it.

So the day hadn't turned out so badly after all. There were things to laugh about and some much-needed boosting of the fragile ego. Because everyone was saying it, weren't they, even if they didn't use the words? Tell me, please tell me, that I matter. That what I do, who I am, has worth.

***

The next two days went quickly. Only one lesson on Tuesday, with the twelves. She'd checked out Poe's 'The Premature Burial' online and cribbed some notes, discovered that people had devices fitted into their coffins in case they needed to let someone know that they weren't actually dead. So why had this fear held such sway? Was it the decline in religious faith? That you couldn't trust god to resurrect you? She hadn't had time to research it: i.e. look up another website. When she read it aloud the kids were enthralled, wanted another one, and so the next day she tried out 'The Telltale Heart' on the unsuspecting year elevens. At first they seemed stunned by the novelty—a teacher reading them a story! but then they listened attentively enough (a bit of chatter and one hefty shove notwithstanding). When the siren sounded and because they'd been well behaved, she promised to show them a video of *Frankenstein*. She told them it was *inadvertently funny*.

'It means the movie didn't *mean* to be funny,' she said, not wanting to miss a chance. 'It means doing something you didn't intend to do. That it was accidental.'

Was that Richie with his hand up?

'Miss, is that like when I'm taking a piss at the urinal and some fuckwit next to me inad…that word…pisses on my leg?'

Everyone laughed, of course, and how could Hazel scold him? He'd certainly understood the meaning of the word, and was probably making a valid point about the male of the species. But she *did* make it clear that swearing wasn't on. Someone shouted out *too fucking right*, and before she could object, someone else asked about saying *the c word*.

At least he'd had the decency to ask.

She told them that neither word was acceptable and why would you want to use them anyway when the English language was so rich and vast and their eyes glazed over and she made herself stop.

And then it was Wednesday. Doorknocking day. She'd tried to file it away and slam the cabinet door, but Beth asked her over breakfast why she looked like the sky was falling down. Was teaching really that bad? Hazel had reassured her it was fine, going well in fact, because she didn't want to talk about Adam, even to herself. But all day at school she was distracted, as though a mark on a calendar, Wednesday 21st May, made the day any different from all the other days she hadn't seen him. Those days when he'd advised her, encouraged her, aroused her, without knowing his effect on her. The day he'd argued with her about having children and then apologised for upsetting her. Those days they had made together, when she'd wanted to be closer but felt him drifting away: to a meeting in the city, to caring for his child.

When her bus pulled up at last and she hurried onto her street, she already knew she would call him, because throughout her busy days he had always been there, like a plaintive melody humming in her heart. She opened the door to the flat, glad to be alone, and took out her impatient mobile. Willed him to answer.

'Adam?'

'Hazel? Is that you?'

'Yes. It's me. How are you?'

'I'm... fine. And you?'

'Fine.'

'That's... well, good. And how's the teaching going?'

'OK. Good, actually.'

'That's good to hear.'

Would they ever get past these banalities?

'I was just wondering about the doorknocking,' she said, her own heart knocking in her chest. 'How it went today.'

A pause. Then a truck roared past and thundered across his words and she had to ask him to say that again. *Good,* he said. *Encouraging.* Four people of varying ages had warmed to the Greens' policy on climate change, *no pun intended.*

'And there was one man,' he continued, 'a Labor voter all his life, who said that a lot of people in the party want to close the offshore detention centres but they're too afraid it's a vote-loser. He's hoping they'll change their policy if they win government.'

'So what did you say, Adam?'

'I suggested he didn't take that risk. And then...' A long pause. 'I don't want to bore you,' he said.

'But I want to know. That's why I phoned.'

Silence. A long one. And then his voice again, faltering.

'I wasn't implying that the day went better without you,' he said.

'But I didn't think that for a moment. You're... you have to stop doing this.'

'This?'

'Worrying about offending me. And in any case, with the doorknocking, the whole thing, it's not about me, is it? I'm just pleased it went well today.'

Another long silence.

When all she wanted was to see him, touch him, tell him he could never offend her, tell him how much she longed for him.

'So school's going well, then?' he said. 'Tell me all about it.'

She stumbled out her minor triumphs and told some jokes and made him laugh.

'And you're on your own now?' she said. 'Doorknocking, I mean.'

'I'm with a young man called Tom,' he said. 'He's very keen. But he's not nearly as much fun. I mean—I don't mean…We had a great two weeks, didn't we?'

She could hardly breathe.

'I'm really hoping I can make week five,' she said.

'And I'm hoping you can make Jessie's party,' he said quickly. As though he'd been holding this back for hours. 'He said he'd really like you to be there and… well… I promised I would ask you… if you have nothing better to do, I mean… On Saturday. This coming Saturday, I mean… if you don't mind a bunch of small children…'

'Oh. Of course. Yes. Of course.'

She gathered herself up, took in the details of time and place, before collapsing onto a beanbag, exhausted with emotion. But what could she buy for Jessie, who really wanted to see her? And what would she wear, so that Adam would see her as he'd never seen her before? And how could she possibly wait until the party?

Three days to go. She checked her watch. Three days, less two hours. Which was marginally better than three whole days.

What had she heard in his halting rhythm and clumsy repetitions? In the spaces between his words? And had she sounded offhand? Should she have sounded more excited? Ecstatic?

She checked her watch again but the numbers hadn't changed. How was that remotely possible?

***

It was the longest two days of her youthful, hopeful life. She felt impatient, increasingly annoyed, openly frustrated. Angry.

Ready to throttle those bullies, girls as well as boys, in her year eleven class, with their cheap shots and sneers, their blatant, nasty put-downs. Retard. Waste of space. Dumb-arse. Moll. She knew they were itching for the weekend, restless, as hard-edged as flint, but she didn't care about their itching or wanting or longing; she just wanted the unkindness to stop. She didn't care that they sulked and shot her dirty looks when she kept them in after school, when they moaned how they'd be late for whatever it was she chose not to care about, because they needed a lesson in respect. But as she surveyed the rows in front of her, saw the sullen or hostile faces trying to stare her down, she panicked. What should she do now, having seized the power to detain them? She breathed in deeply, breathed out, breathed in deeply again.

'Do any of you like feeling hurt?' she said.

No one said a word, or raised their hands.

'I don't like feeling hurt,' she said. Waited. 'So. Do any of you like feeling hurt?'

A few mumbled words.

'So you shouldn't hurt other people,' she said.

Could she possibly get any lamer?

She sensed a thrumming in the room, of simmering rebellion.

'Kindness is important,' she said, trying to sound decisive. 'It means understanding that other people might be struggling, that they need people to be sensitive to their problems, give them a helping hand.' She looked at the crowd of mostly blank faces. 'There's a famous saying about that, you know: *Be kind, for everyone you meet is fighting a hard battle.*'

Like me, right now, she thought. This was going nowhere fast, while the kids were going nowhere at all and probably wishing her dead.

'OK. Let's try a simple rule,' she said. 'From now on, count to ten and see if you still want to call someone stupid or a loser or a shithead.'

Some of them laughed. Because a teacher saying *shithead* was funny.

Someone raised a hand.

'Can we go now, Miss?'

'No.'

More mumbles and grumbles.

'I want you all to promise me,' she said. 'Count to ten.'

'Then can we go?'

She nodded.

And of course her strategy was universally accepted. Lauded. Because she'd finally released them into their weekend: the booze, cigarettes, sex, maybe the harder drugs.

She didn't know a thing about them.

She'd tethered them in a room and given them a patronising lecture about kindness. Which didn't prevent poverty, she knew, didn't stop war or child prostitution, the trade in illegal arms, all the structural, systemic problems she'd learned about at uni. But kindness was important; derived from kindred, of the family. What kind of families did those young people dwell in? And why were some people luckier than others?

What had Adam said about his parents? And how did you get to be you, she'd said.

The you she would be seeing tomorrow.

She picked up her bag and checked her watch. She would have missed the bus, and who knew how long until the next one? It was much too far to walk from this land of the rude, the crass and the socially disaffected to the privileged refinements of the western suburbs. She'd have to sit at the bus stop and wait. Read a book. Except she'd forgotten to pack one, in the rush of Friday morning and not one clean pair of knickers to her name. Friday night would be handwashing night, because she couldn't wear unclean knickers to the birthday party. Not that she planned on removing them, or any item of clothing at all. Unless she got very lucky.

'Hazel.'

She stopped, startled. Lucas. Sitting in an office, swivelling on a chair.

'You're working very late,' she said.

He waved at her to come in, offered her a seat.

'I'm applying to do a masters,' he said.

'More qualifications?' Her mind flipped back to her year elevens. 'Are you trying to get out of this place?'

'Not really.' He grinned. 'I just need a challenge because I'm naturally lazy.'

'I don't believe that.'

'It's true. It's easy teaching science. Well, in this place, anyway, because you mostly have to keep it pretty basic. But I like the kids, even if they don't always like science.' His eyes suddenly brightened. 'Say, can I impress you?'

'Sure.' He didn't sound boastful, or threatening.

He scribbled quickly on some paper and handed it to her with a wink.

'My honours dissertation,' he said.

She saw a whirl of words in dark blue ink: *Characterisation of Novel Macrocyclic Polyether Pseudostationary Phases for use in Micellar Electrokinetic Chromatography and Development of a Chemiluminescence Presumptive Assay for Peroxide-based Explosives.*

'Is that for real?' she said, looking up at his boyish face. 'Or did you just make that up?'

'It's one kind of real. It's scientifically demonstrable.'

'Well, I'm definitely impressed.'

And not just by the title. She could warm to a guy who said demonstrable, and who knew about different concepts of the real.

'Let me see,' she said, and peered more closely. 'The only words I understand are in very different contexts. I mean, I like reading novels, especially ones with memorable characters. I loathe pseuds and I try hard not to be presumptive. No, *presumptuous*.' She ran a finger underneath the words. 'I should try to be less stationary, and I once used peroxide to lighten my hair. And I know that explosives are used in mining, action movies and terrorist attacks.'

He scratched his head. 'You're very funny,' he said.

'Oh, I know.' She laughed. 'People keep telling me that.'

'We should go out sometime,' he said. 'Do you fancy a movie? A meal?'

She liked Lucas, and didn't want to brush him off, but she needed to get home and wash some knickers.

'OK. Sure.'

'Great. Catch you later, then.'

Because that was the way young men talked. *We should go out sometime. Catch you later, then.* Which was fine, if you liked young men.

***

She thought she might mention it to Beth—no big deal, she'd say—a child's birthday party, really no big deal at all. But Beth hadn't been around much in the last few days, had left an unusually perfunctory note: *Gone to Felicia's. See ya soon.* When she usually left a three-volume novel about when, where, with whom and why, and sometimes expressing a hope for a desirable outcome. Still, at least Beth's writing was always legible; impressively neat, in fact. It deserved a golden sticker with the words *Beautiful work!* encircling a smiley face.

Hazel sent her friend a text: *Everything OK?* There was an instant reply: *I'm at Felicia's. Don't fuss, Hazel.* Was she fussing? She thought she was just taking care. And Beth didn't come home that night either, sent another message to say that she was fine. And still wasn't there in the morning. She was, it seemed, always with Felicia.

She could have used her right now, to comb some dye through her hair, make sure it spread evenly. *Tropical Dream*, it was called, offering a promise of pristine beaches and drinks with delicate paper umbrellas and yourself in the foreground, alluring in a see-through white dress. She tried on some of Beth's eyeliner but decided it looked too dramatic. Red lipstick? Same thing. And she didn't want to be dramatic, overwrought. She wanted to be herself, which meant quaveringly anxious and excited. And then her phone rang and she jumped and immediately thought of a cancelled party but it was only Todd. *Only Todd*? Since when had she started reducing him in this way? And since when had he sounded so dismal? Could she meet him for a coffee...*need to talk...no, no, I'm fine...well, no, not really...*and of course she'd meet him, of course, all the time thinking of a present for Jessie and getting to the party on time and wondering how long Todd would need because — She was brought up short again. Todd was one of her dearest friends and yet she couldn't put Adam on hold.

Ten thirty, in the mall. She knew there was a bookshop round the corner, so maybe Todd could give her some suggestions for a gift. She had nothing more than a dim childhood memory of *Spot* and *Postman Pat*. And what could she recall about kids' birthday parties? Cake melting in the heat, some whooping and screaming, a few tears. But she'd read about the recent trend in extravagance: the hiring of clowns, magicians and bouncy castles. Roving superheroes and fairy floss machines.

She was sure that Jessie's father would keep it very simple.

Then her thoughts returned to Todd. He'd said he was fine and then he wasn't. Was he ill? Had he broken up with Dora? Or was it the baby? Hazel tried not to think of her mother.

***

Careworn. That was the word, the moment she saw Todd in the distance. He hurried towards her and wrapped her up, held her so tightly that she gasped. He released her, they sat down, placed their orders.

Hazel searched his face.

'There's something wrong with me, Haze,' he said.

She took his hand, held it gently.

'I just can't feel,' he said. 'I can't feel for Dora or the baby. There must be something wrong with me.' He lowered his head.

'I don't understand, Toddie.'

'It's just that, well, Dora's so blissed out. Her family, all our friends, they're all so rapt. But me? I feel nothing.'

'So you're not overjoyed?' She looked at him closely. 'It's OK not to feel overjoyed.'

'But I don't even feel happy.' He lowered his voice. 'I used to feel so close to her but everything's changed. I can't share what's happening to her. Like, physically, I mean.'

'Hey, that's a perfectly normal reaction for a guy, isn't it? To feel excluded. It's bodily, isn't it?'

She hoped she was sounding convincing.

'Last week, at the ultrasound...' Todd's voice went even quieter and she had to lean in closer. 'I thought the picture would make it all feel real. I thought I'd be all excited, like Dora was. But it just looked like a wriggling mass of shadows and I felt nothing. Nothing. Hazel, I'm a freak, I'm an emotional bloody robot.'

She curled her fingers around his. 'Tell me what you're afraid of,' she said.

'What if I turn out to be a rotten father? One of those fathers who resents his kids or is cold and harsh towards them?' She felt his fingers tighten. 'What if I'm a father who raises his fists?'

'I can't imagine that for a moment, Todd, any of it. And look, you made a commitment. To Dora and the baby. You could have walked away. So, you know, give yourself some credit.'

He shrugged.

'Anyway,' she said, 'you don't know how you'll feel when the baby is born.' She was thinking of Adam, of course, but she kept her eyes on Todd. 'If it's any consolation, if it helps at all, I don't feel like having a baby. I never have. I don't know why, especially as I have great parents like you do. But I just don't feel it and I'm not going to force it or feel guilty because society tells me there's something wrong with me.'

Their drinks arrived and they sat back to make room for the waiter. Hazel took a sip of coffee. Ah, good coffee. Strong.

'Have you talked with Dora?' she said. 'Told her how you're feeling?'

He didn't want to worry her, he said, or frighten her. Hazel watched him closely: his dark brown eyes, his full mouth. She used to fancy him, like she used to fancy Simon.

'Maybe you could give her more credit,' she said. 'Trust her to understand.'

Then somehow, out of nowhere, she began to see Dora: her baby bump, they called it, and her little-girl face, like a doll.

'Do you touch her?' she said.

'What do you mean?'

'Do you lie next to her and stroke her belly and talk? About the baby. Maybe even talk to the baby.'

He stared at her, confounded.

'Maybe you could try it. See how you feel. How Dora feels.'

'But you said you don't feel maternal.'

'Well, if I ever did get pregnant, I figure that's what I'd want. That the man I loved, the father of my child, would touch what we'd made together.' She laughed. 'I must have read one of those women's magazines at the dentist's,' she said. 'You know, the stories you can read in five minutes that transform your life.'

'You're sounding very wise, Hazie.'

Which made her laugh again.

'And you look happy. What's going on for you?'

She tried not to blush. 'I'm going to a child's birthday party,' she said. 'Which reminds me, can you recommend a book? For a boy who's turning five.'

'Sure.' He was calmer now, more settled. 'What sort of kid is he? Does he have any interests?'

'Well, he's smart and curious. And he likes animals. Sort of.' She remembered Jessie's rapid-fire questions, his constant wanting to know. What does consensus mean? What's a lotomy? 'Maybe more for a six-year old,' she said.

'Well, you could try *Alexander and the Terrible, Horrible, No Good, Very Bad Day*. It's really popular, and pretty cool.' Todd looked her straight in the eye. 'So how do you know this kid?'

'I know his father, actually.'

'So what does that mean, Hazie?'

'It's the child who wants to see me.'

'But I thought you didn't like kids.'

'Babies, Todd, not kids. And it's not that I don't like babies as such. It's just—oh, never mind. I'm just hanging out for some cake.'

She squeezed his hand, asked if he felt any better.

'I always do with you,' he said.

Spinning in circles

Just as the bus was pulling up at Matilda Bay, Hazel sent Beth another text. *Are you sure you're OK? Haven't seen you for ages.* Another quick reply: *I'm having fun with Felicia.* What was that supposed to mean? Fun: it came in many guises. But there was no time to untangle the message because she was here now, with a gift-wrapped book in her hand. But not the Alexander one, which she'd skim-read in the bookshop; the story of a mother who fixed her child's problems, so it wouldn't have been right for Jessie. And he was surely way too old for glossy picture books and pop out this and that and all kinds of surfaces for touching. The book as sensorial experience, at $49.95 RRP! Couldn't a kid touch the bark of a tree instead? Stroke the soft fur of a kitten? They could even plunge their hands into a bowl of ice-cream. She'd also seen a book called *My Hiroshima*: for a child! She believed in the value of innocence, for some time, at least. In the end, confused and running late and already picturing Adam, she'd settled for the indisputably safe if quite possibly dull *Stories for Six-year Olds.* Lodged safely in her handbag now, along with a card with a picture of an elephant: *For Jessie with love from Hazel.*

She hoped he wouldn't mind the *love*.

She waited for the lights to change, felt gentle sun on her bare arms and shoulders, her unmade-up face. She was even more nervous. Even more excited. To be so close. Before she'd even glimpsed him. She walked across the road, trying to keep steady, with no idea of how many people she would meet, how many kids — and should she have brought some food? Adam hadn't said. And there it was, it had to be, a bunch of grown-ups milling about and scampering kids, blankets and eskies, and there was Jessie, dashing towards her, heading straight for her knees. She bent down quickly, felt a pair of skinny arms draped around her neck.

'You're here!' he said, and placed his face against hers.

She was overcome, feeling his affection, the softness of his skin. To feel so wanted, when she didn't even know him. What had she done to deserve this, except chat about some animals, tell a few jokes? Then he moved away and his eyes were all agog.

'Dad said you might be busy,' he said.

'I'm really happy you asked me. Thank you, Jessie. And a very happy birthday.'

She handed him the gift.

'You need to give it to Dad,' he said. 'I'm not gunna be five til the night-time. Dad said we could sing happy birthday and eat cake and play games and stuff but my real birthday is night-time when I got born and Dad was holding my mum's hand.'

He pointed to Hazel's stomach.

'Dad says that's where I grew,' he said.

More or less, she thought. Well, less, really.

Jessie took her hand and led her to the group of unknown people. Oh, but there was Candace, bending down to speak to another tiny person, and Adam behind her, in jeans and a loose pale blue shirt and was his hair a little longer? Could hair grow longer in a matter of ten days? She willed her heart to go slowly, smiled nervously at no one in particular and everyone in general, as Jessie ran off and now Adam had seen her and he was smiling too, walking towards her and leaning into her, kissing her on the cheek.

She felt giddy and faint but managed to hand him the

present…*not necessary*…*but thank you*…*a book, of course*…
good choice…and was he nervous, like she was? He seemed
a little on edge. Did she remember Candace…shaking hands
again, saying hello…and in an instant, Hazel saw it. That
Candace knew. She had seen it on her face. But now it was
introductions time, to the parents of the frolicking children.
Max and Elsa and Abdul and Nahal. Nahee? She'd never
remember their names. Now Adam was lifting the lid of a box
and walking over to offer her a cupcake, with bright green
frosting and a fat pink marshmallow on top. Then he was
gone again, offering cake and conversation, as Hazel chatted
to Elsa, an athletic-looking blonde with a strong, deep voice.
And where was Adam? Elsa was a speech therapist and Max
was a plumber and yes, she'd met Adam through the Greens
and yes, he was — and he was back again, carrying a plate of
sausage rolls.

'Would you like some help?' she said.

'Thanks, I'm good. And would you like a glass of wine? I
have some very good red that goes well with kiddy food.'

Jessie was right beside her now, and tugging at her dress.
She looked down into his dark brown eyes.

'How do you make a sausage roll?' she said.

'You push it down a hill,' he said, solemnly. 'My friend Alice
told me.'

'Is Alice here?' Hazel looked around, having no idea what a
riddling Alice might look like.

'She's with her dad,' said Jessie. 'Her mum and dad take her
in turns and her dad lives a long way away.'

Then he ran off again, having forgotten why he'd tugged at
her dress, turning in circles now, and Adam was pouring ruby
red wine into her glass, introducing his nephews, handsome
faces, handshakes, Adam being the good host, organising
something else, as one of the nephews — Mitch, was it? — asked
what she did for a living. So what else could she say?

'I'm a teacher.'

The boy nodded. Because he was a boy, fifteen at most.

'I wouldn't mind teaching,' he said. 'Adam says it's one of the most important jobs a person can do.'

'Which is true.' She took a sip of wine. 'But exhausting, too, if you want to do it properly. Not that I want to discourage you,' she rushed on.

Mitch laughed. 'Adam used to say that too.'

Jessie was bowling up again, dragging Mitch away. Cousins. They were cousins. She was trying to fit names to faces, make connections, build a family, and it was all a little bewildering, with Jessie and his friends shouting now, and jostling, some of them rolling along the ground. What was the collective noun for a group of small people like this? A frenzy? And why did small people look different from adults? It was their heads, she realised: they were much too big for their tiny bodies because their brains were still growing, they still had a lot of thinking to do. Something like that. She didn't know the first thing about anatomy or human biology; she would have made a terrible nurse. And she knew it had never been an option. She saw Jessie whirling round in circles again, a dizzying blur of bright red shorts and a dark blue shirt. Heard Adam call out that it was birthday-cake time, everyone gathering round now and singing very loudly. She saw Jessie's puffed-out cheeks and three mighty attempts to blow out the candles, chocolate cake on paper plates and still she hadn't spoken to Adam, not really, and not a word to Candace. The woman who'd caught her eye and told her, without telling her: I can tell that you fancy him. There's no use trying to pretend.

Jessie was tugging at her dress again and she looked down to see a worried little face.

'Will you make a castle wiv me?' he said.

She bent down to listen. Find out.

'What sort of castle, Jessie?'

'Sand.' His voice was very small.

She looked across to the river, saw the sails of the leisurely yachts, the ripples of slate-grey water. 'You'd need to go to the beach,' she said. 'It's not the right kind of sand here.'

'But can't we try?'

His face looked so worried, intent, as though — Hazel saw it now, in an instant — he was on the verge of tears. So she put down her glass of wine and took Jessie by the hand, walked with him in silence down to the grassy slope. Away from the bustle and the shouting, the two of them jumping down onto the sand, Jessie's clammy hand still holding hers tightly.

'You don't look very well,' she said. 'Did you eat too much cake?'

He shook his head. 'I don't like all the noise. All the singing and everyone yelling at me.'

She saw his lower lip quivering.

'It happens real quick,' he said.

'What does?'

'The noise. I want the noise to go away.'

She looked at his pale face and felt a kind of panic herself. Was this normal for a child? To be so spooked by party noise? She found herself sitting on the sand and patting a space beside her but instead Jessie backed up into her and wriggled into her lap: just like that. She felt his warm, bony little body against hers as they looked out onto the water, and she wrapped him carefully in her arms. She didn't want to overwhelm him.

'Does it frighten you?' she said. 'The noise.'

He nodded, slowly. 'Sometimes. When it whooshes up to me.'

She took in what he'd said. Because you always remembered the fear, didn't you? The darkness; the monsters under the bed. That first day at school. Wasn't every child afraid of a world they couldn't control? And was that what it meant to be an adult? That you simply got better at pretending?

'I used to get frightened, too, Jessie,' she said. 'Shall I tell you the story of my fifth birthday? My Most Horribly

Frightening Day? It was the scariest day of my entire life.'

She was embellishing, she knew, but what did it matter? When all that mattered was Jessie.

'On my Most Horribly Frightening Day, I decided I wanted to spin round and round, faster and faster, my arms outstretched. I just knew I had to do it. And it was wonderful. It made me feel so dizzy in a good kind of way.'

He turned around to face her. 'All speeded up? I did that just now.'

'And didn't you feel like the strongest and cleverest person in the world?'

He nodded.

'But when I stopped, everything was still spinning all around me,' she said. 'That's when I got really scared.'

'Cos you thought it would never stop?'

'That's right. I couldn't understand what was happening.'

He looked at her, his face calmer now. 'I wasn't scared,' he said. 'When I was spinning round and round.'

'Well, then you're stronger and cleverer than me.'

'So how did you stop feeling scared?'

He was thinking of her. She was thinking of him. It was quite possibly one of the most adult conversations of her life.

'I called out to my dad,' she said. 'He came running straight away and I told him what was wrong and he calmed me down, made the spinning stop.'

It was her mother she had called for.

'Did he give you a hug?' said Jessie.

'Sure. That's what fathers do.'

'Dad's busy now,' he said, solemnly. 'So I asked you.'

She didn't need to know why. It was enough that he had asked her.

'Your dad's busy because he wants to make you happy. You know that, don't you?'

He nodded. He was so much looser in her lap now, relaxed and revived, and it made her feel: what did she feel? It made her feel safe. It was the strangest feeling in the world.

'Do you make sandcastles?' he said.

'I did when I was little, like you. My dad was the best sandcastle maker in the world.'

'Why?'

'Because he made really big moats that let in lots of water. That was my favourite part.' She hugged him a little tighter. 'Do you know what a moat is?'

'Yes, yes,' he said, eagerly. 'But I like the towers best. And the shells what you stick on. And the seaweed too.'

'All of that. Every bit of it.'

And still they sat, close and warm, with the breeze lightly ruffling their hair.

'Jessie!'

They turned as one, to see a flustered Adam standing at the top of the bank, towering above them.

'I didn't know where you'd gone.'

He jumped down and his face was white. He held out his hand and pulled Jessie up from the ground.

'I was worried,' he said.

'I'm OK,' said Jessie, quietly. 'I'm good.'

Adam knelt down, spoke to Jessie eye-to-eye. Told him that his friends were waiting to play some very fun games.

'Is that OK with you?' he said. 'Because...' His voice trailed away and Jessie looked up towards the party.

'What sort of games?' he said.

'Aunty Candace will tell you. She has some great ones lined up for you.'

'Do I have to line up, then?'

'You don't have to do anything you don't want to.'

'Except go to bed when you tell me.'

His father patted him on the backside. 'You get a pretty good deal, buddy,' he said. 'Now off you go, see how fast you can run.'

They watched him run up the hill, a lively monkey, ready

for his friends. Because this too, Hazel thought, was what it meant to be a child: to be frightened, and then to quickly forget.

Adam turned to her. 'He just disappeared,' he said. 'He was here one minute and—'

'I should have told you. I'm sorry.'

'So what was the matter?'

'He got a bit over-excited. But, well, he's settled now. He's fine.'

Adam ran a hand through his hair. 'Thanks for looking after him,' he said. 'It was very good of you. And I'm sorry, I didn't ask you here to—'

'Adam.' She took a very deep breath. 'Please don't keep saying sorry to me.'

'But you just said sorry to me.'

And before she could say another word, he sat down beside her and clasped his hands together.

'I couldn't see him anywhere and I panicked,' he said.

She took his hands in her own, uncurled their tightness, held them gently. She didn't say a word, simply let him rest in the warmth of her regard.

'He was so young when Thea died,' he said. 'And she'll never be real to him.'

'Do you show him photos? You must have a lot of photos.'

He nodded.

'Do you tell him stories about her? Thea.' She felt his hands tighten again. 'Is it…too difficult for you?'

'No. No. Not really.'

He was holding her gaze now, wanting or needing to say more.

'I fell out of love with her,' he said, flatly.

'Was there…someone else?'

'For Thea there was. But I'd already fallen out of love with her. Some years before.'

Hazel waited.

'You don't wake up and look at a face and feel differently. It's…' He smiled at her, wanly. 'You know how it goes,' he said.

'No, I don't, actually. But I'll take your word for it.'

They sat in silence, holding hands. A man who didn't want to dwell on the past, and a woman who had taken him back there. For this is how she understood it now, knowing almost nothing about love and grief and betrayal, and most of it gleaned from books. She only knew that she didn't want to move, sitting beside him, touching him, being touched.

He looked down at the ground, then up at her.

'I've never told anyone that before,' he said.

'About the other man?'

'About falling out of love.'

She saw tears in his eyes.

'Thank you for listening,' he said.

***

She watched him walk over to Jessie, bend down and talk with him. She watched him walk over to Candace, lower his head and talk with her. And she didn't mind at all that he'd walked away because she knew there was no distance between them anymore. But she loved that he returned to her, his face lit up with seeing her. She was a twenty-five-year-old woman and a five-year-old spinning child. Elated. Unafraid.

'I want to thank you properly,' he said. 'I'd like to cook you a meal. I'm not a bad cook. Promise.'

She would dine on air if he asked her.

'What about tonight?'

'Tonight?'

'Are you doing anything tonight?'

'No. No, nothing.'

'Shall I pick you up at seven, then?'

'Seven. Yes. Do you know where I live?'

'I picked you up last week.'

'Ah. Yes.' Wanting to say so much more. 'And then you

dropped me back again.'

'So I did. I did.'

She looked across to see Jessie, who seemed happy to be noisy with his friends, while Candace was busy clearing up. Hazel would soon make her way over and offer to help and hope that her hands would stop shaking. She'd give Jessie one last hug before seeing him tonight, and then hurry home to get ready for what must surely happen next.

***

She was in truth relieved that Beth wasn't home because she didn't want to talk. Not to her best friend, not to anyone. It was hard enough saying goodbye to Adam. She, the great talker, tripping up on a single word, *goodbye*. But he wasn't shying away now. He had shown her who he was and he wasn't ashamed and it filled her with such warmth to know him. And she had helped him care for Jessie, shown Adam who she could be, when she hadn't even known it herself.

She knew this was serious. That it might be monumental. But as she looked into the mirror, brushed her hair, she found herself laughing with sweet anticipation. She looked good, even if she did say so herself, in her knee-length grey dress — a different grey dress — that showed off the curve of her arms. But she couldn't be too provocative, could she? Jessie would be there. Even if he went to bed later. She would have to bide her time, because it was only a matter of time before Adam took her to his bed and let her into his life because it wasn't just about sex, it had never been just sex: right from the beginning, when they'd talked. So, yes, serious. Monumental. But they would have to take it slowly, because of Jessie. They would have to consider his feelings, even though he seemed to like her. Maybe even *really* like her.

Knock, knock, knock.

She tried not to race to the door.

He was looking very smart, very handsome, in a dark blue

shirt and dark trousers, even if his hair was messy. Oh, how she loved that messy hair.

'Hello,' he said.

Hello?

'Hello to you,' she fluttered.

'You look very nice.'

Nice?

He cleared his throat. 'I hope you don't mind, but I thought we could go to a restaurant instead. Without Jessie.'

Mind? She had to stop herself from leaning in and kissing him.

'I'm happy wherever we go,' she said.

Still he didn't touch her, hadn't even pecked her on the cheek. She closed the door behind her and they made their way to the car. Silence as she did up her seatbelt, turned to look at his profile, then asked if Jessie was with Candace. He nodded, keeping his eyes on the road.

'Thank you for the book,' he said. 'For Jessie.'

'It's not very—'

'It's great. It will keep us going for a very long time.' He glanced at her quickly. 'Did Jessie tell you about the noise?' he said. 'How it scared him?'

'He did, yes.'

'And what did you say to him?'

'I told him a story.' She kept her eyes fixed on Adam. 'About how I'd once been frightened when I was a child. I told him that my dad made me feel better.'

'Really?'

'Well, it was my mother, actually, but it's different for Jessie, isn't it? And I told him that my father gave me a great big hug because, well, that's what fathers do.'

She saw him shift in his seat. 'Sometimes...' He sighed. 'Sometimes I'm not a very good father.'

What was she supposed to say to that?

'I don't spend as much time with him as I should.'

Did he want her to tell him he was wrong? Boost him up?

'I don't want to bore you with all this,' he said, quietly. 'But Jessie was abandoned. I don't want that to happen again.'

Abandoned? His mother had died, for goodness' sake.

'Adam. You're a—'

'A child needs a mother as well,' he said.

She heard something in his voice, something sharp, and she felt her skin tighten.

'But you've been a wonderful parent, Adam. You said yourself that women bring up children by themselves and—'

'I know what I know,' he said.

She put a hand on his arm and saw him flinch. She had made him flinch and this wasn't going well and everything seemed to be changing again and she didn't want to be confused like this, confused and more anxious by the second. And then without a word of warning he slowed down the car, looked in the rear-view mirror, pulled over to the side of the road and cut off the engine and her heart was knocking as he turned to look at her at last.

'I can't do this,' he said.

'What?'

He didn't reply.

'Tell me,' she said.

'I can't.'

She felt heat rising inside her, told him that he must, but still he didn't say a word.

'I want to understand what you mean,' she said.

And still he didn't speak.

'If you have any respect for me, Adam.'

'Of course I respect you,' he rushed in. 'How could you possibly think I didn't?'

She waited some more. She would wait all night if she had to. She saw him tug at the collar of his shirt.

'This isn't going to work,' he said. 'Us.'

Now where had she heard that line before? Or had she

embarrassed him, after all, made him feel ashamed, because she'd witnessed those extraordinary tears? But he couldn't be like that, surely? And he wouldn't have asked her to —

'Hazel.' His mouth was a grim straight line. 'Look at us. You're so young, and I'm... I mean, it's ridiculous.'

'Ridiculous?' She laughed. Because this was easy, it was going to be easy, after all. 'It happens all the time,' she said. 'Older man, younger woman.'

He flushed. 'I'm not just after sex.'

'Well, I'm not either, Adam. You must —'

'I know that, I know. And that's why we have to finish this.'

'Finish what?' What on earth was she hearing? 'We haven't even started.'

'And I don't want to.'

She had to stay calm, think. Be rational.

'Hazel.' Why did he have to keep saying her name? 'It just wouldn't be fair on you. You're very young, you have your whole life ahead of you. And I have a young child to care for.'

She looked at him carefully. 'So you're telling me... you're telling me... you won't start anything because Jessie might make it more difficult?'

He nodded. It was just as Beth had asked her to imagine. And yet now that he was sitting next to her, in his neat shirt and trousers and looking so dark, something told her she didn't believe him.

'You know I like Jessie very much,' she said. 'And I think he likes me. We're getting on really well.'

Nothing.

He was retreating again, behind his wall of silence, and she needed to make him speak.

'I'm better than the woman with loud eyes,' she said. She heard herself sounding fierce.

'That has nothing to do with it. It's just... look... you need to find someone who... who you can make a life with.'

'And you don't want to make a life with me?'

He nodded. He couldn't even bring himself to look at her.

'You don't even want to have sex with me?'

And then she felt a thought snap inside her head.

'You don't really want me at all, do you?' she said. 'You're just making up a bunch of excuses.'

He didn't say a word.

'Tell me, then. Go on. Tell me.'

She would do this. She would get through.

He tugged at that fucking collar again.

'I'm sorry,' he said. 'You must have read it all wrong. I'm sorry, so sorry, if I gave you the wrong impression. I didn't mean to lead you on, honestly. I just enjoyed talking with you and, you know, just talking and laughing and finding things out. But I didn't…I don't…want to hurt you.'

It was more than he'd said all night, and every word was hateful.

'Don't flatter yourself,' she said, and opened the door, stepped onto the road.

'Hazel. Please. At least let me drive you home.'

'I don't want *at least* anything,' she said, and quietly closed the door.

Because her dignity was important. Dignity, and self-respect. There was always that to hold onto, to keep you afloat, whatever you were doing when you were walking down a street that would kindly take you home, because home was always comforting, even if it was a cramped, mean flat on a noisy highway and your friend of a lifetime wasn't there. Because home was what you knew, and knowledge was welcome. It was important. It might be most the important thing in the world. To know where you stood and where you were walking and she couldn't even picture his sharp ugly face anymore.

***

After half an hour of walking, and three bouts of honking horns and one guy giving her the finger, she decided she was hungry. Starving. She needed a large mug of Milo and a humungous piece of cake, preferably with cheerful pink icing. She finally spotted the new café on the corner—Melanie's, whoever Melanie was, or wasn't—and she walked briskly, shoved open the door. Would they be serving cake in the evening? Yes. Jackpot! Cake with layers of jam and cream and mounds of chocolate shavings. Luridly yellow custard slices, so yellow they looked radioactive. But then looking again, scanning the dressed-up sugar and fat, she suddenly lost her appetite for cake. She'd lost her appetite, full stop. She ordered a cup of peppermint tea instead, relieved that the place was empty, slumped into a chair and told herself she would not, must not, cry.

She saw the café door swing open and a tall, skinny boy come fumbling in. She'd seen that kind of puzzled face before on some of her old students, as if life kept lobbing them hand grenades and they didn't know what to do with them. But now the boy's face was lighting up—he seemed to recognise her—walking right up to her table, goddamn it.

'Hey, Miss,' he said, from on high. 'It's Brett. Brett Marino-vich. Remember me?'

And now she did remember: he'd been a boy with a badly acned face and her heart had gone out to him in a superficial way. Now here he was, two years on, his skin so much clearer.

'How are you, Brett?'

'Yeah, yeah, I'm good, real good.' And still he was smiling, slightly goofy. 'Hey, can I sit down? I start work here in like, ten minutes.'

'You work here?' Because now he was coming back to her more clearly. A very lazy boy as well. It was always an effort to get him to lift a goddamn pen.

'I clean up after the evening shift,' he said, 'and get ready for the morning. I do the lunch shift too.' He folded his body into a chair. 'So it's good. Real good.'

'Well, that's excellent, Brett. Terrific.'

'I'm like, saving up,' he said. 'I'm getting married.' Looking very pleased with himself.

He would have been, what? Eighteen? Nineteen?

'Well, congratulations, Brett.'

What else was she supposed to say? Who's the lucky girl? May you both have a long and happy life?

'My girlfriend and me, we're having a baby,' he said. 'In a month. And after that we'll get married cos she doesn't want to look fat in her wedding dress.'

'Of course not.'

Hazel tried not to look at the clock on the wall. Another five minutes, maybe, and Brett would be getting down to work. But he didn't seem to be in a hurry, spreading his hands on the table, his face suddenly screwed up tight.

'My girlfriend's Kayla,' he said. 'Kayla Watts.'

The spitting girl.

'You remember, don't you?' he said, and reddened.

Hazel tried not to toss her head. 'You're not likely to forget something like that, are you?'

The boy clasped his hands and stared at her.

'Kayla knows she shouldn't of done it,' he said. 'And I should of done something too, you know, said something and that. But we all just like, sat there, the whole class, and we didn't do or say nothing.'

This, too, she remembered. And she'd resigned the very next day.

'Afterwards, but'—the boy swallowed—'afterwards, I said something to Kayla, how what she did was really gross and she like, burst into tears and started telling me stuff, all this really awful stuff about her dad. But that's when we started being friends. Me and Kayla.'

Hazel forced a smile. 'And now you're going to be parents,' she said.

'Yeah. It's cool.'

'So the two of you can make a new start.' No one could say

she wasn't trying.

'That's what I told Kayla. We can make it all better.'

'What a wonderful thing to be doing.'

The boy looked down at his hands, up again at her. 'I told her to say sorry,' he said. 'I said, you have to go up to Miss and say sorry for the gross thing you done. But she couldn't, she said she just couldn't and she was crying so hard and that, so I didn't want to push it. But, well, just so you know. We both felt really bad about it.'

She thanked him for telling her. Was she meant to add something else? Gee, Brett, now I feel a whole lot better? To know that you both felt ashamed?

'Is that why you left, Miss?' he said, quietly.

So he wanted relief, this tall, skinny, father-to-be. He needed absolution, he and his girlfriend with the made-up, sulky face. And so she sighed, dug deep. Gave it a shot.

'I left for a whole lot of reasons,' she said. 'Because it's never just one thing.'

'We were a bunch of shitheads,' he said. 'I sure would of left if I was you. But we liked you,' he said, smiling again. Absolved. 'Even if we didn't learn nothing, nothing I remember, anyway. But' — he looked down at the table, then up again at her — 'there was this kid in our class, Pete, he always looked real stupid and stuff, like a dog you'd wanna kick if you were into kicking dogs. Do you remember Pete?'

She pretended that she did.

'Anyway, he told me once, it was kind of weird him telling me, how your hands looked soft, like they'd be nice to touch. He didn't mean anything wrong or nothing. It was just your kind hands, he said.'

He stopped. Looked shocked. Because former teachers, especially those with soft, kind hands, weren't supposed to cry.

'It's OK, Brett,' she said. 'Honestly. It's not about what you said. Any of it.'

He stood up awkwardly. Unsure. 'I gotta start work,' he said. 'But it was real good to see you, Miss.'

But still she couldn't stop crying, and if she didn't stop, couldn't stop, the whole damned floor would be awash with tears streaming down her fake-jolly clown of a face.

'Please tell Kayla that I wish both of you and your baby every happiness,' she said.

She sounded like Mother bloody Teresa, offering him her worthless blessing. But she saw his face light up with pleasure, because he was, after all, just a boy, soon to be a father, and was happy.

'There's like, one other thing,' he said. 'The whole class, how we all just sat there and didn't say nothing. It was really weird cos everyone must have been thinking how bad it was but no one did nothing. And then you walked out of the room. How come that happened? Like, we just sat there.'

She took his question, walked around it. Searched for some fatuous wisdom.

'Maybe it's about timing,' she said, through her tears. 'Knowing you should do something, but you don't. And then it's all too late.'

He nodded, muttered something, then turned and loped to the kitchen. He'd been saving his money because he'd made a girl pregnant, or she'd made herself pregnant. Who knew how these things worked? Who knew how anything worked? Not I, said the sparrow, with my little arrow, that a man had shot into her heart.

Someone brought her a cup of tea. 'Are you sure you don't want something to eat, Madam?' she said.

First she was Miss, now she was Madam, with no Adam, and she knew that she'd been slightly mad.

'The muffins are really good,' said the girl. 'We've got five different kinds.'

Hair

Hazel woke up feeling refreshed. Not broken. Not bereft. Not jolted into worthlessness by another miserable rejection. Pulling back the sheets, stretching her arms, she felt a welcome looseness in her limbs, a release from whatever had been gripping her, fogging up her brain. She must have been genuinely mad, if madness meant not seeing the way of the romantic world with a necessary clarity. She must have been under some kind of spell, both magical and deranged. She couldn't even name the desire that had driven her. And had it only been three weeks of feeling this way? She could hardly believe this either.

She rubbed her eyes. What day was it? Sunday. Question and answer and purpose, because she had lessons to prepare for tomorrow. She must have slept very deeply, undisturbed by dreams, by wrenching sobs of self-pity. She made her way to the kitchen, in need of a cup of tea. No sugar. Wondered how her father was getting on. Or not. And then she saw a note on the kitchen bench, in Beth's copperplate writing. The woman with the speedy mouth, but with an elegant script straight out of finishing school. Another one of life's mysteries.

Hazie, I hope you don't mind me spending so much time with Felicia because you'll always be my dearest friend even though I find her so interesting and funny and so clever with her maths you should see the stuff she has to know for uni, it's like a foreign language with a whole heap of brackets. And even though she's so beautiful she's not in the slightest bit vain and being so rich too you should see her apartment. It is unbelievably sumptuous. Turkish rugs and so much space and even chanderliers. I mean, can you believe that? But Felicia doesn't flaunt her wealth which is great cos you know I've never liked flaunty people and nor do you which is one of the reasons we've always been friends and always will be friends true blue like your dad likes to say. Did I ever tell you about your dad at our Dip Ed graduation? How we were waiting for the photos and my mother was carrying on about not liking the way her hair had been done and how she'd look awful in the photos and your dad took me aside and put his arm around me and told me he was so proud of me and how my father didn't know what he was missing. I can't remember if I ever told you that cos we've told each other so many things over all our years but it doesn't matter if I've already told you because you need to say it loud and clear don't you when people are doing good. And I'm glad you're enjoying your teaching Hazie which I think is nothing short of amazing although now I think about it you've always had a lot more patience than me. So I'm on my way out again and we'll be back around Sunday lunchtime and I hope you don't take this the wrong way but Felicia wants to cut your hair. She said she wants to transform you and I think that's really cool. But like I said before I hope you don't mind me spending so much time with her lately because there's no one like you Hazel there's no one like you in the world and of course there never will be.

Heaps of love from Beth

Her sentences rambled and circled and jumbled, and then circled back again. Hazel loved every one of them. And then she read them all again. Circled the mis-spelling of chandeliers.

***

Felicia swept into the flat, cast her eyes around the living room and didn't look disapproving. Because even though she lived in a sumptuous apartment, apparently, and this place was only a squeezed-in flat, she didn't seem like a superficial snob. Even if her intuition about men had been right off the mark. Not that one case was statistically valid.

'Your place is so charming,' she said, and took a pair of scissors from her massive leather handbag. They were pointed, shining scissors that looked more alarming than charming. Then she flourished a jumbo bottle of champagne.

'For the fridge,' she said. 'You call it a fridge here. You people are always chopping up words. Vegie and bikkie and barbie and lolly, it is like living in a country full of children. How do you say it?'

'Infantile,' said Hazel.

'There are men who are wearing short pants all the time.' Felicia turned up her nose. 'The knees are ugly, very ugly. And there are people who call me Flick. This is ugly too. That is what I tell people, which makes them laugh when I am not trying to be funny.'

She handed Beth the champagne.

'For later,' she said. 'When we will celebrate the new Hazel.' She turned to look at her model—her victim. 'I am a professional,' she said. 'In Italy, I cut the hair of my two brothers and they are in magazines. The fashion magazines.'

'Felicia's brothers are models,' said Beth, knowingly.

Felicia nodded. 'Now. I want Hazel to look like more of her,' she said. 'More sexy.'

Hazel's panic was rising but she made herself calm down. It was only hair, wasn't it, and hair grew very quickly. It even grew after you were dead. Or was it only your nails?

Felicia looked at her sternly. 'There is still nothing with your shy man?' she said.

'Not a thing. And I won't be seeing him again.' She saw Beth's face, waved away her concern. 'Anyway. I've just met a really nice guy who, well, he seems interested.'

'Then my task is urgent,' said Felicia, and raised those lethal scissors. 'You will show me a mirror and bring a chair to the

bathroom. A towel. A dryer. And Beth, you will assist me, no?'
It was the closest she'd come to softening a command.

There was a flurry of movement: Beth pushing Hazel into the chair, covering her shoulders with a towel, dampening her hair, and then—those deadly scissors, poised. Hazel closed her eyes. Heard a decisive snip. Another snip. An eerie calm descending. More snipping, slowly, carefully. Murmurs from the stylist and her willing assistant and it seemed to take forever and then finally she could hear the whirring of the dryer and all she could feel was mounting trepidation.

'I am done,' said Felicia. 'Look.'

Fuck. She'd been clipped. Shorn. She barely had a wisp of hair on her head. It wasn't so much a radical change as a disappearing act.

Felicia put an arm on her shoulder. 'Very sexy,' she said. 'I knew you would be like this.'

Hazel turned this way and that, anxiously peering. What did she look like, really, her eyes adjusting to her reflection. It had to be her, underneath the cropped little spikes, and—yes, it was OK. It was good. In fact, it was very good. It made her eyes look bigger. It showed off the curve of her neck. Beth put her arms around Hazel's shoulders, told her she looked amazing, and who was the new guy, by the way? Groaned when Hazel told her that Lucas was a teacher. Hazel laughed and told her not to denigrate such a venerable profession and she laughed again because she liked what she'd seen of her haircut, which admittedly was only from the front. Other people saw you from the sides and the back. Took one look and desired you, or didn't.

Felicia returned to her oversized bag, pulled out a hand mirror and showed her what others would see.

Hazel nodded. 'Thank you, Felicia,' she said. 'You've done an amazing job. I love it.'

Felicia ran her fingers through her latest triumph. 'And you will be delighting your teacher,' she said.

Hazel stood and gave Felicia a hug. It was like being enveloped by a pillow.

'Your English is really coming along,' she said. 'I mean, improving. Getting better.'

'It's because we talk a lot together,' said Beth.

'Now there's a surprise,' said Hazel.

Felicia placed a hand on her chest. 'My heart is exploding with my excellent work,' she said, then held out her arms to both of them. 'Now my dears, we drink the champagne. It is only second best champagne but it is still very good.'

***

Hazel was greeted by a gush at reception: *your hair… fabulous…ooh la la…where did you get it cut?*…and then by all her colleagues: *wow* and *chic* and *glamorous*. The Head of Department told Hazel that she looked like a boy in a way that made looking like a boy sound irresistible. Darren did the groin-thrusting caper again and told her she looked *adorable*. By now she was tiring of all this silly praise as she dashed to her first class, running late, hearing the kids chattering and laughing, a few shouts, hurrying in and then: silence. Every mouth fell open. Then someone began to clap. A slow handclap. More clapping, everyone grinning, and then the whole class rising like a wave, giving her—WTF?—a standing ovation. For a moment she'd wanted to shout at them: *It's only a haircut, guys. I'm not the mousy heroine, miraculously transformed.* But then the impulse passed and she felt what they were telling her, so she made a sweeping bow and thanked them.

'Why did you do it, Miss?'

'A friend persuaded me, Ahmed. And I wish you'd call me Ms, all of you. I keep telling you—'

'Are you one of them feminists?' That was Bobby.

Hazel nodded. 'Let me tell you about the word Ms,' she said. 'Let me give you the history.'

Because they needed to know it, whether they liked it or

not. And so she gave them a short lecture about the politics of naming and the necessity for choice, at the end of which Allie raised her hand and said: *Does your boyfriend like your new hair, Miss? Did he get mad at you?*

The year elevens gave her haircut a more raucous treatment. Catcalls and *who was the drunk who did that* and girls wanting to touch. But you weren't allowed to touch, not even tiny wisps on your head, and so Hazel told them instead about changing social attitudes to hair, ideas about being female or male, and eyes began to dim and the first yawn of the morning told her to give it a rest. Because they were tired of being talked to. Lectured, instructed, advised. They just wanted someone to listen.

What had she once told Adam? That we're not learning anything when we're talking. It was in the context of Jessie's chatter, and what would happen to a little boy who liked to prattle as he advanced through the school. He'd be one of those children with their hands always waving in the air, begging or demanding to be heard, told to wait his turn and let other people speak. All of which was right and proper but which might be hard for a child who liked to prattle.

'Go on, Miss, just quickly.' Rita, wanting to touch.

Hazel relented. Which meant nine other girls wanting to do the same.

'Right, now that you've all had your sensorial experience ...'

'What's that?' said Ahmed.

'An experience that uses one of your senses. And since you have five senses—'

'Jaxon's got no sense,' said the female Beckham.

'Right.' Hazel put on her stern voice. 'Which two rules did Beckham just break?'

'She wasn't kind to me,' said Jaxon.

'And I interrupted you,' said Beckham.

'Correct. Now. You have five senses: sight, hearing, touch, taste and smell. Which one would you least like to lose, and why? You have ten minutes to write and then we're all going to listen.'

'I don't wanna lose my dad,' said Teneelle. 'He's going down for six months this time.'

A hand waved from the back of the classroom. Tex. A name from a movie with wide-legged cowboys and guns in manly holsters. And why were they called cowboys instead of cowmen?

'Miss, what do you think about the Muzzies?'

A few sniggers, a female voice sneering: *They're Muslims, you moron. Don't you know anything?*

Was that Clara? Cara? And so much for being kind.

'Do they bite?' said a different male voice.

'Muzzies, not mozzies, Tex.' Clara or Cara was indignant. 'And anyway, they're people. They just believe in a different god from us.'

'I don't believe in no god,' said Tex. 'But my old man, he says the Muzzies here are gunna start throwing bombs and mowing people down with semis.'

A barrage of voices about Muslims and terrorism and cutting off heads. And what was it with all those women covering up their faces, those guys wearing white dresses...*robes, you moron*...how they called Aussie women sluts and—Hazel held up a hand.

'Enough,' she said. 'Just stop, all of you. We're going to have a rational discussion. No insults, no opinions.'

'What da ya mean, Miss, no opinions?' Shayna, who had one lazy eye. It was easy, alas, to put a name to her. 'My mum says we're all entitled to our opinion, and she reckons that Muzzies cut women up inside.' She giggled.

Hazel kept her cool. 'Everyone has the right to an opinion,' she said. 'But everyone has a responsibility to make sure their opinions are based on fact. Wild emotions don't get us anywhere.'

She knew she was sounding preachy. And she didn't know

if there were any Muslims in her class.

Where, then, to begin? By planting a seed, or turning on a switch. Even if she wouldn't be around to see the bloom or the spark.

'Why do you think Muslims are terrorists?' she said. 'Let's start with that one, shall we?'

But then the siren blared and the kids stood up on cue, began jostling to leave, for maths or Home Ec. or science: another forty-five minutes of jam-packed instruction. Dead time for many. Filling in time. Killing time. Just like a prison, really.

***

On Wednesday, someone else touched her hair in the staff-room. But he asked her first, politely.

'It feels even softer than I thought,' said Lucas. He grinned. 'And you now look very cool. For an English teacher.'

Hazel gave him a flirty kind of smile. 'So science teachers are very cool?'

'I was just being defensive. I almost failed English at school.'

'Well, I *did* fail chem, so you're one up on me.' Hazel laughed. 'I was in love with the chem teacher, like every other girl in the school. A few boys as well.'

'Well, we do have a certain animal magnetism,' said Lucas. 'It's one of the job requirements.'

So he could laugh at himself as well.

'Actually,' he said, 'you might be pleasantly surprised to know I'm a bit of a reader. I'm a huge fan of sci-fi but only the challenging stuff. Azimov and Philip K. Dick, dudes like that.'

More writers Hazel hadn't read. And when was the last time she'd picked up a novel?

But Lucas was giving her an education now. Did she know that Asimov had written over five hundred books? And over ninety thousand letters and postcards? Hazel shook her head.

And did she know that Asimov was a claustrophile?

'It's a love of small, closed-in spaces,' said Lucas. 'When Azimov was a child he really wanted to own a magazine stand in the subway. In New York City. He wanted to shut himself in and listen to the rumble of the passing trains.'

'Well, that's unusual.'

And she *did* like that gap in Lucas's front teeth.

'I reckon a subway station would be comforting,' he said. 'You know, you'd feel sheltered, kind of cosy, but you could always come up for air and walk around the city and then go back again.'

'A claustrophile,' she said. 'I like that idea.'

And she liked Lucas for telling her.

He moved a little closer. 'You look amazing with that hair,' he said. 'I mean, you looked great before, but now you look ravishing.'

She blushed. Of course. When was the last time a guy had called her ravishing? Called her anything vaguely erotic?

'Can I message you then?' he said. 'We could do dinner.'

'Sure. Why not?'

Because this sounded perfunctory, even a touch ungracious, she added that she'd really like that. Would look forward to it.

Martha flopped down between them and sighed.

'A mother wants me to give her kid some homework,' she said. 'She clearly doesn't know it has zero educational value, it's just designed to placate anxious parents like her.'

'Be grateful you have one who takes an interest,' said Lucas.

'I'm grateful if they have one,' said Martha. 'Parent, that is.'

Hazel felt a stab of envy. They seemed so easy together, and in two days time she'd be gone.

'The kids spend six hours a day in the classroom,' said Lucas. 'They deserve a break.'

They actually liked their students. Maybe teaching could be different, not feeling strapped on a rack until you wanted to scream. Like the man in the famous painting by Edvard

Munch. She used to think that scream wasn't existential at all but the anguish of a teacher heading off to work. Maybe she could work part-time, or even keep doing relief. She liked the spontaneity of her classes, which she knew was unorthodox, as well as educationally unsound, for children craving order, even if they didn't know that's what they were craving. But for the next couple of days they were having some fun and discussing the meaning of life. Maybe she could bring in a copy of *The Scream*, and say, there: what do you make of that? Let's discuss it. It might be the first time they'd seen a famous painting, even as a print. She could ask them why they thought it was so famous. Tell them it was stolen from a museum. Would they do that? Or if they had money, how much would they pay for it, and why? How would they rather spend the money? She could ask them to give all this some thought and then write it down. The meaning of life, in a very short essay. Then she'd take the essays home and read their reflections and give them back on Friday, after which she'd never see them again.

She'd miss some of them, Rita most of all. The girl who thought *Tonight* could take you anywhere. She'd stayed back after class to talk about going to uni but no one in her family had ever been to uni and they thought she was *up herself*. Hazel had asked her what she wanted to study and the girl, all thick black eyeliner and pouty mouth, had looked at her, stunned, and said that *everything's interesting*. Hazel could have made a joke about an arts degree but she'd taken Rita seriously. Rita had the right to be taken seriously. They'd ended up talking for an hour—more meaning of life stuff—about intellectual pleasure, the value of the humanities, the purpose of critical thinking: all the things she'd cared about when she was Rita's age, until she'd ended up doing a job she hated. That she didn't hate now. Which, if anyone had asked her, she would say had gone pretty smoothly, except for a few speed humps along the way. Rita was thinking of teaching, she'd said, but not with a pack of morons like Jaxon and Bobby and why were boys such morons and did Hazel think that boys were really immature? And Hazel had nodded and said that sometimes boys just grew taller and wore long pants. Which Rita had thought was hilarious.

Hazel would miss Jamal as well. The boy who didn't want to tell his story when she'd asked because he was worried for his grandma, still living in a village in Afghanistan. Unsafe. He was a soft, gentle boy with light, floating hands. But she wouldn't miss Bobby, who liked to goad her and accuse her because she must have stood for everything he despised. Like the spitting girl, Kayla Watts, because she too had a name. She would miss Magenta, who'd turned her image of a black cat into a spiky kind of poem and asked Hazel for her opinion, stood taller with the praise.

Magenta told Hazel that her haircut looked sensual. Which wasn't the same as sensuous, she'd said. She'd checked it out in the dictionary.

Revelations

'What a bunch of wankers.'

Martha's voice.

'Listen,' she said. 'Those cretins at the next table.'

Hazel turned to look. It was the guy who'd felt her up on the day she'd arrived, flicking over a newspaper now, talking to a colleague. Frothing at the mouth, really, about *that woman from the Greens...always poking her nose in those detention centres...making trouble...coaching kids to self-harm.*

'And she's built like a brick shithouse,' said his colleague. He looked like a guy in an ad for luxury cars: suave, darkly handsome.

Lecherous Paws grinned. 'She should spend less time in those places and get on a treadmill instead,' he said. 'Get rid of that big fat arse.'

Hazel wanted to scream. It was *fat chicks shit me* all over again, but these men were teachers. They had tertiary qualifications and children in their care. Lucas nudged her: he must have seen the look on her face.

'Just because people have a degree hanging on their wall,' he said.

'Well, thank goodness the kids are different,' said Hazel. 'They're prepared to think about things. And they'll accept anyone, as long as they're nice kids, or play sport well. I've seen Percy and Jamal on the oval and the kids think they're great.'

'You're idealising,' said Lucas. 'And you've only been here for eleven days.'

So he'd been counting. Keeping her in his thoughts. But Hazel was still put out.

'I can tell you some pretty bad stories,' said Martha. 'Some of the kids in my classes, the way they talk about Indigenous kids. They love the players when they're kicking goals and taking speccy marks but not when they stand up for their culture.'

'It's not their fault,' said Hazel. 'It's the media. And their parents.'

'Or their stepmother,' said Lucas. 'Or stepfather. Or their mother's third boyfriend in six months who uses all her money to buy drugs. So many dysfunctional families, I can't tell you.'

Hazel leaned towards him. 'That's such a class stereotype,' she said. 'I have a friend from a middle-class family whose father walked out on them when she was six years old. Five kids in the family. And my parents' friends, so many with broken marriages. Who says the nuclear family is the best way to bring up kids, anyway? What matters is having a parent who loves them, cares for them.'

Because there was always that, wasn't there? You could never take that away from him.

She could see them looking at her strangely: earthy Martha and thoughtful Lucas. Had she raised her voice? She looked around the staffroom: teachers eating, laughing, whining, making coffee.

'I have an idea,' she said. 'Education sessions for the staff. And then maybe the parents.'

'Education sessions?' Martha and Lucas spoke as one, raised their skeptical eyebrows.

'You know. Information. Challenging racial stereotypes and myths about asylum seekers. Facts on climate change. We could discuss domestic violence, too. Oh, I know that could be tricky, but—'

'It's not that the teachers don't care,' said Martha. 'Some of us sure do. It's just that we're too fucking exhausted.'

'We know you mean well, Hazel,' said Lucas.

They fell into silence and she fidgeted about, opened her lunchbox, closed it again.

'What about lunchtime talks?' she said. 'You know, a captive audience.'

Lucas reminded her that she was leaving tomorrow. Martha nodded to confirm the bleeding obvious. And so when lunch was over, there was nothing to do but stand up, leave, sit in her empty classroom, wait for half an hour until the elevens came sprawling in.

She could see her future dangling before her again. That damned noose was feeling tighter.

At least she had her new haircut to console her. She'd sent Todd a photo and he'd shot back an effusive text. Dora had joined in as well: *!!!!!!!!!!!!* Hazel had asked if he was happier, waited some time for an answer, then he'd sent her a smiley face.

Getting easier and thanks for listening. You're the best. How was that party and did the kid like his book?

Hazel had paused, wanting to pretend. But this was Todd, who was doing his best.

I had a fight with the boy's father

Crap so what about?

It's not important and I can't really remember anyhow

So she'd ended up pretending to help her forget. Blue eyes and the touch of his hands and telling her what he'd never told anyone before. Those unexpected tears.

***

Teaching had been up and down. The good, the bad and the ugly, the light-bulb moments and the predictable blackouts. She'd learned not take things too hard, to be a little kinder to herself. In a matter of twelve days, she had understood what she hadn't grasped in two long years: to take the longer view. To be patient. Except now she was leaving. And wasn't this the essence of tragedy: to acquire wisdom only when it was too late? Not that her situation was tragic, but it wasn't comic either. It was, in truth, a little sad.

On Friday she geared herself up to leave. The students didn't shower her with cards or gifts, heap words of adulation upon her inspirational head. Although her year twelves did give her a box of Cadbury's Favourites (unwrapped), and much to her surprise, a card from Bobby: *Thanks for teaching me about life and women and stuff.* She couldn't have asked for a better reference. Martha and Lucas were taking her for a drink as well. Which was good of them, she thought; generous; and it would give her some alcoholic closure.

She trundled back to the department, thousands of useless calories in her hands, and found a note waiting on her desk, in large black print. *See Ms Hipkins in her office.* Had she done something wrong? Should she have followed the curriculum more assiduously? Placed more emphasis on literacy? (She'd never done that PowerPoint.) Had there been too much discussion and not enough writing? Too much laughter? No one in her office knew what was up, so Hazel made her nervous way to where she'd never been before. Tried to calm down by imagining the worst that could happen. She could hardly get the sack, could she? Still, you wouldn't want a lousy reference.

The principal had been welcoming, and now she was — what — summoning her?

Hazel was met by a smiling assistant, offered a seat. She looked around, avoided checking her phone for distraction. And now, here she was: Ms Hipkins, in a bright pink lacy shirt and a tiny black leather skirt, chorus-girl high heels. And that hair! Like she'd been to an all-night party and was just waking up.

But she was the principal. She had the power.

'Thanks for coming, Hazel.' The principal offered her a chair, then leaned forward, eyes wide. 'I love your hair,' she said. 'You must have paid a fortune for a cut like that.'

Hazel laughed. 'A friend did it. For free. I don't have a fortune, actually. I'm more or less broke.'

Fuck, Hazel. Pull yourself together.

The principal folded her hands in her lap.

'We'd like you to stay for the rest of the year,' she said.

Hazel tried not to fall off her chair.

'The teacher you're replacing...' The principal went on to discreetly explain about the poor man needing a break. 'You'll be doing the school a great favour, Hazel.'

'But...but I'm only the relief teacher.'

'I've had a number of phone calls from parents, saying you've made their children want to come to school.'

'But Ms Hipkins —'

'Julia, please.'

'Julia. Making them feel happy doesn't get them very far. Does it? I mean...' She petered out. Why was she objecting?

The principal smiled. She looked like a woman comfortable in her skin, although that tight leather skirt could make it difficult.

'Feeling happy is a good start, isn't it?' she said. 'I've seen some of your students coming out of your classes. They look ready.'

'Ready?'

'Keen.' The principal waved a hand. 'I was never the best at English but I'm good at reading faces. And I'd be really pleased to have you on board, you'd really be helping us out. It's only part-time but you'll have to come in every day. And having a year twelve class is extra responsibility. Just getting some of them to graduate, step onto that stage, can be a major achievement. Do you understand?'

Hazel nodded.

'And you'll have to do all the routine things like bus duty and lunch duty, although it's a chance to chat with the students while you're reminding them to put their rubbish in the bin. I'm aiming for a litter-free school by the end of the year, even earlier if possible. Less clutter in the quad, less clutter in their heads.'

Hazel listened. She considered.

'Are you worried about their results, Hazel?'

'Well, they need a lot of help.'

The principal nodded. 'I measure our success not by prizes or exhibitions but by the number of students who achieve their goals. And if that means scraping a pass in English, that's wonderful.'

'Or maybe we can help them find a goal?'

'Exactly.' Ms Hipkins—Julia—cleared her throat. 'If you don't mind me asking, Hazel, are you worried about money?'

'No, not at all. I mean, I've been living on Newstart for a while and, well, I can live very simply.'

Because you could, you most definitely could, if other things mattered more than money.

The principal sat up in her chair, stretched her arms, and the middle button of her bright pink shirt went *pop*, bounced onto the floor.

'Now it goes without saying,' said Ms Hipkins. Which meant that it had to be said. 'You have a curriculum to follow. Proper lessons. Programs. Appraisal.'

'Of course.'

'Which doesn't mean your lessons can't be fun.'

'Of course. I mean, of course not.'

The principal smiled, her job done. She was practised. Approachable. Committed. And, Hazel thought, a decent kind of person doing a valuable job.

'Is there anything you'd like to ask me?' she said.

'I just want to thank you. It means a lot. Your faith in me.'

The principal's face brightened. 'So. Welcome to Cranfield,' she said, then looked down at her feet. 'I've lost a button from my shirt. Did you happen to see where it landed?'

***

Walking back from the office, Hazel had a call from her mother.

'I've compromised,' she said. 'I told your father he can have sex whenever he loses a kilo.'

Hazel tried not to laugh at her down-to-earth mother, who by the usual rule of families ought to have embarrassed her.

'We came to an agreement,' said her mother. 'After we had sex.'

This time Hazel did laugh. Because her parents were happy and she was happy and the rest of the term would be a challenge, and the one after that until the end of the year. Growing. Creating a spark.

'How are you, Hazel?' said her mother. 'We haven't heard from you for a while.'

What could she say? I met a man who broke my heart? Except that he hadn't, not really. He was a good man, a good father, but he hadn't been attracted. What did it really matter, in the end? At least she'd had his respect. Because she *had* tried hard to change some minds and it hadn't been just to impress him. She *was* smart and informed and prepared to work hard, because Hazel always tried to do her best.

'I have a new haircut,' she said. 'It's very very short.'

'Honestly? Why? I mean…your beautiful hair.'

Further confirmation that mother-love was blind.

'I was kind of press-ganged into it, Mum. But I like it. And, well, I have a job, too, a real one. For the rest of the year.'

'Sweetheart, that's terrific. What is it?'

'Teaching.'

Silence.

'It was only relief to start with but they've asked me to stay on. It's a pretty rough but wonderful school.'

'Are you sure?'

'It's kind of funny. I thought I'd left teaching forever but it seems it never left me.'

Her mother invited her to celebrate, said she'd even let Jim have one glass of wine if he chose to stick to the bargain. Because it was important to give people a choice, she said, to let them decide for themselves.

Hazel made a date for a glass of champagne, said goodbye, looked up and across at the oval. She saw boys and girls running and leaping, in training for football or netball, games that gave them the pleasure of using muscles and limbs, their arms flashing, legs pumping. Fifteen-, sixteen-, seventeen-year-old kids: she would have such creatures in her care. It didn't really daunt her now, even though she'd have to dig deep, listen carefully, patiently, to what they were saying, instead of only thinking of herself. Just like she'd tried to do with Jessie when she'd seen him whole and true. Because that's what she'd done without knowing it, and it was good to know it now. Even if she never saw him again, would never know what happened to a trusting little boy. He was destined to be one of those people who leapt into your life and then suddenly disappeared but who left something pure in their wake. Which made her feel happy, and a little empty, before the emptiness went away.

She kept walking towards the office — soon to be her office — to talk to the head of department. Len. She would call him Len and compliment his colourful ties. And then she saw something else as well: that sitting with the principal and considering her offer, she hadn't once thought of Lucas. A guy to have around to admire her, to take her out to dinner and tell her she was ravishing and whatever might follow from that. He simply hadn't featured in her boy-meets-girl soap opera, with those really annoying ad breaks for feminine hygiene products.

What would Beth make of all this newness? Her return to the bad old days? She would laugh, of course, and put her arms around Hazel's waist and tell her she had a long journey ahead of her, with no discount for the fare. And Hazel would say something lame in return, about her very modest journey being more important than the destination. She wouldn't be Jack Kerouac, leaning forward to the next crazy venture beneath the skies, but she would try to do a solid day's work, do a bit of good in the classroom.

She wasn't sure about that part, anyway: *beneath the skies*. It needed some more adjectives: *the next crazy venture beneath the something something skies*. For the rhythm. To evoke that sense of longing.

Maybe she could have been an editor. In another life.

***

Martha drove her to the bar in her rusty, dented Toyota, but Hazel didn't mind the rust or the dents because she was alive with a sense of good fortune. Once she would have told Adam about her brand new job. Once upon a time, before his indifference got in the way. But now it was comforting to be with a lively, unpretentious woman who might well become a friend, and who told her straight away that she didn't want to talk about school on the weekends. Or the break-up from her long-time girlfriend at all. So they talked about how they'd both lived in Perth all their lives, except for the two years Martha-had spent in Sydney, feeling like she'd been locked inside a sauna. She loathed the heat and, like Hazel, disdained the hedonistic worship of the sun. They discovered they were both afraid of sharks.

'It's a very common phobia,' said Hazel.

'Which doesn't mean it's not important.'

Martha could definitely become a friend.

They talked about family as well. Martha's parents had split up when she was a kid, which was why she took the break-up from her lover even harder. And she was a *singleton* too. Such an odd word, Hazel thought. And how was it possible she'd never heard of it before? When it named her: Hazel, who could have had a sister, maybe more, but who had the gift of other sisters in her life: Beth, Chloe, Rikki, and now Felicia. Her mother. The woman sitting beside her. A small army of women to help her through the battles, and to help when they needed it themselves.

Martha gave her a sly kind of glance.

'So, do you have the hots for Lucas?' she said.

Hazel stared through the window, saw the traffic racing past, rows of ugly bunting and vacant shops for lease, then turned back to look at Martha.

'He seems like a really nice guy,' she said. 'He has good politics and a good sense of humour. And he reads good books. So he's, well, he's good, isn't he?'

'That's not what I asked you.'

Hazel laughed. 'Well, I didn't have one of those rushes of emotion,' she said. 'One of those kiss-me-right-now-before-I-die kind of moments.'

'That's what it was like with Abby,' said Martha, keeping her eyes on the road. 'Every time I saw her.' And then she shrugged. 'So much for not talking about it.'

'Talk as much as you like. I'll listen.'

**

The bar was packed with girls in denim and lace, and some good-looking guys in tight jeans and open-necked shirts. The music was pumping loudly and Martha was yelling in her ear, pulling her to an empty table. Hazel caught the glimpse of a guy's sensual mouth; dark brown hair falling onto a forehead; the vulnerable nape of a neck. She felt aroused, in a general kind of way. It was good, the feeling. It meant that her body had righted itself again, just as her mind had cleared itself of craziness. And no one in the bar looked over forty. Martha was nudging her into a seat, one of those retro plastic jobs that after half an hour of sitting made your bum really sore. But people weren't here to be comfortable. They unwound. They flirted. They took someone home and had sex. Would people look at the two of them, two women who'd walked into a bar, sitting close together, knees touching, and see them as a couple? But what did she care about who put what where, as long as the putting was consensual. If you were lucky, pleasurable. And if you were even luckier, when two bodies were entangled or caressing or fucking, you would find the one who was different. The one who would choose to stay.

Then her favourite person in the world walked in: Beth. Because Hazel had asked her to fly from work, celebrate her brand new job. And there was Felicia striding in behind her: two more women walking into a bar, two women who'd bonded over dickhead fathers. She looked radiant, Beth, in a dark pink dress that Hazel hadn't seen before, with her bouncy hair flying about, and Felicia of course looked stunning, turning many heads. Then hurried introductions and Martha staring too, at Felicia's very short silver dress, shiny and bejewelled like a disco globe. Beth took Hazel's hand and started shouting in her ear because they'd pumped up the volume even more and Hazel looked up for a moment and—it was Candace. Candace. Walking into the bar. It was better to pretend she hadn't seen her. It was better to look at Beth instead, who was shouting about the thrill of Hazel's job and how she knew Hazel would be terrific and it was about time she...and something else about some client who deserved a kick in the groin.

'He asked me if I lived alone,' she said, 'and when I told him about us, Haze, how we've shared a flat for years, best friends from school and all that, he snorted, he actually snorted, and said it was so *unhealthy*. And then, get this'—Beth faked a yawn—'he told me I needed a man to sort me out.'

'So what did you tell him?' asked Martha.

'That men like him were the reason women chose to live with women. And do you know what he said next? He said, so, you're one of those women who hates men, are you? So I told him I was a separatist feminist. That is, I believe in separating men's genitalia from the rest of their stupid bodies.'

'Well, good luck with that one, sweetheart.'

They looked up: four women who'd walked into a bar, looking at another woman who'd walked into a bar. Candace. With her eyes like Jessie's, her hair like Jessie's. Was she on her own? Was she waiting for someone? Or, help, no, was she hoping to join them? Couldn't Candace see her fear? Take a not-very-subtle hint? But it seemed the woman wasn't going anywhere, standing like a sentry, arms folded across her chest. And so Hazel did the introductions ... *my friends ... Beth, Felicia, Martha ...* wishing she could shelter behind them.

'This is Candace,' she said.

For whom she had no more words.

'Do you have a moment, Hazel?'

'A moment?'

'Yes.' Staring with intense brown eyes.

Hazel stood up, her friends all staring too, and she found herself trembling as she trailed behind, jostled her way into a quieter place.

'Can I get you a drink, Hazel?'

'No, thank you. But please, go ahead.'

And it struck her again: how your guts could be churning while you kept up the patter. *Please go ahead. Be my guest. After you.*

'I'll wait,' said Candace.

Which made Hazel feel even more jittery.

They sat down and Candace placed her hands on the table. She had long, thin, ring-less fingers; decisive-looking hands.

Hazel frowned. 'Is something wrong with Jessie?' she said.

'No, no, he's roaring on all four cylinders.' Candace drummed her fingers on the table. 'It's Adam who's wrong, he's bloody miserable.' She drummed some more. 'Look, I know it's none of my business, but when I saw you just now, you dear, sweet young thing, I thought hell yes, I'll make it my business to tell you.'

'Tell me what?'

'That Adam's a good man. Too good for his own good most of the time.'

'I don't know what you mean.'

'Then let me keep it simple. Adam's been smitten with you. From the moment he saw you on the train.'

Hazel tried to take this in. 'I see,' she said, slowly.

'No you don't, not really. When I say smitten, I don't mean to make light of his feelings. He tells me everything, you see, and he was — look, he couldn't stop thinking about you and he wanted to tell you how he felt but then every time he saw you he'd feel it was wrong and so he'd back off again. Turn tail and run, the stupid man.'

'But —'

'Just listen, Hazel. That's why he told you he wasn't attracted. Why he pushed you away.'

'Pushed me…away?'

'He didn't mean to be cruel. He's the kindest man in the world, helped me through some very tough times. My two shits for husbands. Drink, fists, I can't tell you. And then one of my sons who — But look, that's not important. I want to find out about you.'

'What do you mean?'

'I want to know how you feel about him.'

Hazel took this question and held it up to some kind of light. What was she feeling now? To know that he'd been smitten. Had forced himself to push her away. She looked across at her friends, the new and the old. At Beth: the safety of a lifetime's friendship.

'I hardly know him, do I?' she said.

'So what have you discovered so far?'

What she'd known from the beginning.

'That he's thoughtful. Kind. Acts on his principles. That

he's lovely with Jessie. I…I well, I guess I admired him.'

'You're speaking in the past tense, Hazel.'

'Because it's past.'

'Are you sure?'

Hazel was lost for words.

'You see, the beginning and the end of it…' Candace pulled a face. 'Adam can't give you children. He's had a vasectomy. You know. The snip.'

Snip. Such a breezy word, and yet Candace made it sound so ugly, so final. And something else was falling into place now, beginning to make a sad kind of sense.

'Are you telling me that Adam…are you saying he gave me up because …'

Candace nodded. 'You see? Too good for his own good. A bloody saint, that man. Especially since Jessie's not his child.'

'Not…his child?'

'Adam's a saint and a fool. He would have given Thea anything she wanted, in the beginning, anyway. Anything. And she didn't want a child. She was adamant. So not long after they were married, she made him have the snip. Twenty-three years old, he was. I ask you.'

As though someone might have an answer.

'The stupid things people do when they're young and madly in love. Present company excepted.'

Was she madly in love? In any kind of love at all?

'So…who is Jessie's father?'

Candace shrugged. 'Thea had an affair. But the father took off like a rocket as soon as he found out she was pregnant. Jessie appears to have been an accident, although with my sister, who knows? It could just as easily have been a plan. Changing her mind when she was heading for forty. I wouldn't have put it past her.'

'And she never told Adam? Whether she'd planned it or not?'

Just saying his name now was difficult.

'I don't know,' said Candace. 'But whatever she was thinking, or not thinking, Adam took the child as his own. That's just who he is, Hazel. Big-hearted. Completely forgiving.'

'But that must have been so hurtful. Knowing he couldn't have a child of his own.'

'Well, he never showed it. He never judged her, never complained.'

He'd held Jessie in his arms and been enchanted. Besotted. Utterly transformed.

'Adam's biggest fear was that the real father'—Candace pursed her lips—'well, the man who put his dick into my thoughtless sister. Adam was afraid he'd come back to claim his son. But it's all sorted now, the legalities, and Adam will tell Jessie the truth when he thinks the time is right. Give him the chance to meet his biological father, if that's what the boy ends up wanting.'

Hazel looked into those dark brown eyes, which might have been like Thea's eyes.

'You didn't much care for your sister, did you?' she said.

Candace shrugged. 'She wasn't a bad person. But she was—oh, we all have our faults, don't we?' Then she laughed. 'It didn't help that she married the man I was in love with, did it?'

Hazel sat up. 'And are you still? In love with him?'

'Of course.' Candace reached out her hand, and Hazel found herself taking it. 'Not that I've ever told him. The closest I came was a joke, telling him he'd married the wrong sister. The dopey things you say when you've had too much to drink.' She squeezed Hazel's hand. 'Adam loves me, of course, but not in a romantic way. Nothing sexual. So don't worry, my dear. I don't plan on trying to steal him from you.'

'But he's not mine to steal.'

'He's yours if you want him. He's in love with you.'

'Did he...I mean, did he actually use that word?'

'And a whole lot of other ones as well. Bewitching. Beguiling. Warm-hearted. Funny. Smart. Sincere. Endearing. Disarming. He's a regular bloody thesaurus, that man. And like a boy in love for the very first time.'

Hazel couldn't speak, couldn't think, about a boy in love for the very first time. How could she have been so blind? To have misread him in this way? To have been so wrapped up in her own indignation that she hadn't listened to his distress. His love. He was in love with her. He was in love with her and had driven her away.

Candace released her hand. 'So what will you do now?' she said. 'With my story. Adam's story.'

She was a magician, this woman, performing a series of tricks and voila! she'd presented a lavish bouquet from behind her generous back.

'You're not saying anything, Hazel.'

'Because I'm still not sure what to think.'

'Maybe you should try not thinking at all.'

'But I have to reflect on what you've just told me. It's—'

'Are you worried about his age?'

'Should I be?'

'Adam's forty-five.'

Which was more or less what she'd figured. She found herself smiling, like a secret.

'I thought I could forget him,' she said. 'But, well—he torments me.'

She hadn't known this until she'd said it.

'Very good,' said Candace. 'Excellent. Because it's been the same for Adam.' Her eyes looked suddenly stern, like a teacher's. 'Now I'd like to say he'll be a walkover but I do have to warn you, Hazel. That man has as many principles as a porcupine has quills, so you'll need to be pretty damned persuasive. And he needs to start thinking of himself for a change instead of trying to do the right thing by everyone else. What *he* thinks is right, anyway.' She laughed. 'He thinks too much as well.'

Hazel laughed with her, even as she felt on the verge of tears. For she'd heard the kindness in Candace's voice. This woman who'd chanced to walk into a bar, who might well be changing the course of another woman's life.

'You have a big heart, too,' she said.

'Not at all. I just want Adam to be happy, and it's a long time since he's been happy. I have a feeling you might be the one.'

'But you don't even know me.'

'Well, Adam's told me so much about you, hasn't he? I've had the full confession. And it's Jessie, too. Adam knows you really like him.' She frowned. 'Not like the woman who tried to wheedle her way into his heart. Kids can see though the bullshit.'

I love this woman, Hazel thought. She's filling in the gaps and saying it straight and I want to cover her wrists with platypus stamps.

Instead she asked Candace if she was waiting for someone.

'Aren't we all?' She looked at her watch. 'This one was meant to be here half an hour ago.'

'The man with the ginormous beard?'

'No, the new one's clean-shaven. But he's still late.' She pointed in the direction of Hazel's friends. 'Who's the young man who keeps looking this way? Is he anyone important?'

Hazel didn't need to look to understand. 'He might have been,' she said.

And because this sounded so dismissive and verging on smug and she didn't want to be smug, ever, because everyone mattered, everyone had worth, she said that Lucas was a really nice guy. Which didn't sound much better.

'But he's not Adam,' she said.

Candace nodded. 'I want you to listen to my very cunning plan,' she said. 'I'll go and pick up Jessie and keep him overnight. Give yourself a couple of hours and then go round to Adam's. But first you need to scurry home and change.'

'Change?'

'That dress you're wearing. You look like a boring school teacher.'

Persuasion

She'd been waiting for an hour with nothing but her phone for company, sitting on Adam's porch on his dilapidated sofa, craning her neck, willing him to arrive. She hadn't seen his car in the driveway but she'd climbed those four steps, knocked on his front door, her breath suspended. No answer. She'd knocked again. No answer. Then she'd walked around to the back door—stomped, really—and banged on the flywire screen. No answer. A No Show. Leaving her sitting on his sofa, tapping her feet, inspecting her nails, and the more she looked at them the stranger they seemed, as though they didn't quite belong to her. Where was the man? Why wasn't he here, and it just wasn't fair, not knowing where he was or how long he'd be gone and maybe he was off seeing someone else even though Candace said he loved her and was mopey and miserable or maybe he'd been smashed up on the freeway and she'd never get the chance to tell him how she felt and it would all be too late. All of it, everything. Too late.

You couldn't live at this pitch of feeling. You would die with the intensity.

She took several deep breaths and made herself listen to the birds, until their cooing and squawking drove her mad.

Fucking nature.

She looked down at her dress: her little black lacy number. Her seductive flourish. She'd said goodbye to her bewildered friends, caught a taxi to Claremont Quarter and tried on the dress and knew it looked just right: both elegant and alluring, at two hundred hard-earned dollars. But now, looking down at this extravagance, this conspicuous symbol of hope, she was feeling silly and cheap, with her bare shoulders and hint of cleavage, trying not to think of what on earth she might say and what she might do with her body. Because the words coming out of her mouth would come out of a person with a heart and hands and legs and hips and breasts and all of her that wanted him. She'd been anxious and afraid and incredulous and brave and now she was stewing with anger. Was this what it meant to be in love?

And then, at last. His shiny blue car slowing down, pulling into the driveway, and all her impatience and vexation and feeling ridiculous flew up into the sky and she was left on the ground feeling nothing in her body but the weight of her desire. His door began to open—why did it take so long to open a door?—and she saw his legs and his chest and finally his handsome, rather sombre face, and he was closing the door and he would soon be with her. He was wearing an oversized T-shirt and baggy shorts, a bright red towel slung over his shoulder. So. He'd been swimming. She saw him brush back his hair and look up at the porch as she stood up to meet him. He stopped. Stopped dead. Stared.

'Hazel?'

He climbed the steps carefully, still looking, always looking, but keeping his distance and mightily unsure.

'I didn't recognise you,' he said. 'Your hair.'

'It's still me.'

'And…your dress…'

She smoothed it over her hips, pushed her breasts forward, just a little.

'Why…I mean…why are you here?' he said.

'Because you live here.'

Still he didn't move towards her.

'I thought we could go dancing,' she said.

The towel slipped off his shoulder but he didn't pick it up.

'Dancing,' he said, blankly.

'Yes. Is that agreeable to you?'

He didn't speak, didn't move.

'I've been talking to Candace,' she said. 'Or rather, she's been talking to me. She walked into a bar and I just happened to be there. Talk about lucky.'

He flushed.

'What she told me was—how can I say this—instructive. Enlightening.'

He was looking anxious and frozen to the spot but she was feeling bold now, and fearless. Because she knew him and she wouldn't let him leave her again, gathering all her strength into her two bare arms, walking towards him, stopping right in front of him.

'I've come for you,' she said.

'Me?'

'Oh yes. Most definitely.'

His hands dropped by his side. 'I can't do this,' he said.

'Can't do what?'

'This. Us.'

'Oh, you told me that once before. When you lied to me.'

He swallowed. 'Because I was afraid.'

She waited. He said nothing.

'What were you afraid of, Adam? Please tell me.'

He lowered his gaze, then looked at her again. 'That you would find someone else.'

'But I'm not your wife.'

'That's not what I mean. I mean...you'll end up wanting someone much younger than me. You won't want to spend the best years of your life looking after an ailing man.' He shook his head. 'Hazel, I'm much too old for you. I'm—'

'Oh, Candace told me how old you are. And I must say, I was pleasantly surprised. I had you pegged at around seventy, sixty-five in a really dim light.'

His face tightened. 'It's not funny,' he said.

'Well, that amazes me, too. You'd led me to believe that my sense of humour was one of my most attractive features.'

'You don't understand what it's like to be me. I don't want to be a—you know—a cliché.'

'Oh, I see.' She felt suddenly stung. 'So what does that make me, then? The answer to your midlife crisis? Your little bit of fluff, just for fun?'

'No, no, I didn't mean that.' He was agitated now, his voice almost pleading. 'I mean that it's impossible. It can't be done. There's Jessie. He's exhausting. He often wakes up in the night.'

'And I often wake up in the night. Easily fixed. I can read him a story and we'll both fall asleep again.'

'But…but…he never stops talking.'

'I have the same problem.'

'He likes to be the centre of attention.'

'Likewise. So we're a perfect match.'

'But you've only spent a few hours in his company. Hazel, you don't know how difficult it can be. I'm afraid—'

'That I'll tire of him? Well, if I do, I'll sit down at the table and put my face in a bowl of custard until I feel ready to play with him again.'

There wasn't the flicker of a smile on his face.

She took a step back. Decided to change tactics.

'I want you to listen to me, Adam,' she said. 'Listen very carefully. I'm a very serious woman, and you're the most serious thing that's ever happened to me. I know you're a good man. You've always puts others before yourself. You wouldn't sleep with me because you didn't want to take advantage of my feelings for you. Although'—could she risk a joke?—'I wouldn't have minded a bit if you'd taken advantage of my feelings.'

No smile there either.

'I know how much you love Jessie. And it doesn't matter to

me that you can't give me a child, not at all. And—'

'But—'

'You have a child who isn't yours, biologically, I mean, because Jessie is yours in every meaningful sense of that word. Because you love him for who he is. Which is about as good as love gets, I would have thought.'

He was listening intently now, his face softer. She knew she was getting closer.

'You see, don't you?' she said. 'That it will be the same for me. I'm not Jessie's mother but I would hope to love him too. Just as I would hope to love you.'

'Hope to love me?'

She knew she almost had him.

'Or would you prefer me to love you right now?' she said. She moved a fraction closer. 'I know that you love me. Or you said you do, anyway.'

'But how can you doubt that?'

'Because you're standing here full of excuses and evasions and you won't let yourself be happy. And I can make you happy, whether you like it or not.'

Was that a smile shadowing his face?

'And how do we know what might happen?' she said. 'In five, ten years time. In a lifetime. You of all people, Adam, should understand that.'

She knew she had to touch him. She would shatter into tiny, useless pieces if she didn't touch him. And so she moved towards him and cupped his face with her hands and at last he was putting his arms around her, drawing her close, and she felt his body trembling. Now his mouth was on her mouth and they were meeting in a kiss, softly, carefully, and she tasted the salt of the waves on his lips and felt her own longing, she had never felt such longing in her life. Then their kisses became more urgent, fierce, hard kisses travelling right through her, until he drew away and searched her face again. As if he still wasn't sure.

'Why didn't you tell me how you felt?' she said. 'We could have talked it through.'

'Because I was afraid you would say yes.'

***

He guided her to his bedroom with a hand in the small of her back. He took her hands and kissed one palm, the other palm, and she felt herself shiver as he took off her inessential dress, her bra, undies, stood back to look at her, caressing her body with his eyes. And she moved towards him again, because she would always be moving towards him, pulling off his T-shirt and running her fingers through the hair on his chest, kissing that chest which wasn't like the chests of the skinny boys she'd known, but solid. Substantial. And he was cradling her breasts, taking her nipples in his mouth, running his hands down her flanks, around her hips, and then it was her turn to lead him, hurrying him to the bed, pulling off his clothes, pulling him down on top of her. But he made her wait again, stroking her hair, kissing her neck, her stomach, her thighs, and at last he thrust inside her and she heard herself cry out as if it was the very first time. And they began to move together, slowly, looking into each other's eyes, needing to see the pleasure they were giving and taking. Hers. His. Wanting to tell each other: you couldn't be anyone else. She felt herself rising and coming and taking him with her and she held him close as he collapsed onto her chest, throbbing inside her, his hair damp with sweat, and curling on his neck. She let him rest in her softness, because she had never felt so tender, so loving. It felt to her like loving, as she began to press the bones of his back, one by one, counting him back into life.

'You weren't supposed to happen,' he said.

'But I did. You did. And it's lovely.'

She knew if she looked into a mirror, she would see a different face.

***

It was a new kind of time, and a different kind of space, lying on his chest, just making out the shadow of his face, featureless and blurry. Or she would move away from him, trace the shape of his nose, brows, cheeks, mouth, wanting to know him through touch. They couldn't stop touching, never moving from the bed. They couldn't stop kissing, greedy kisses and gentle kisses and nibbling kisses and he held her and told her she was beautiful and how sorry he was for treating her so coldly, so cruelly, pretending not to care and yet wanting to know that she cared, telling her—blushing now to recall it—that a part of him had enjoyed knowing she was attracted, which was so cruel of him, so—she put a finger on his mouth. She was done with apologies and guilt and remorse, forever.

'I didn't know what to do with you,' he said. 'And with my feelings.'

'And now you do.'

He began to stroke her hair.

'You look like a street urchin with that haircut,' he said. 'Gamin.'

'Gamine, actually. For the feminine.'

'Of course,' he said, smiling, and then nuzzled into her neck, as he loved to do, as she loved him to do. Already there were patterns, gestures to delight her.

'It is very fetching, your hair,' he said. 'Very arousing.'

She felt light-headed, lighthearted, with joy. 'And you're the most arousing man I've ever had sex with,' she said. 'And I've had seventy-eight lovers, remember?'

He put an arm behind his head, lay back on the pillow. 'So I'm good, then?' he said. 'With the sex thing.'

'Pretty good. Although number seventy-two wasn't bad either.'

He rolled on top of her, asked her to tell him something true.

'I'm ridiculously happy,' she said.

Later they dined on toast and tea and she told him not to get crumbs in the bed because she hated crumbs in a bed and because she somehow knew she could nag and boss and berate him and he would never stop wanting her. And then they made love again, which was more like fucking this time, and she liked this too, the feeling that he could have been a stranger, because she was safe in the arms of the most unique and magnificent man in a universe where gravity had ceased to exist, where everything was flying apart and floating and she had never felt so free.

Later still they talked about Jessie, as she knew they must. Adam told her how his son kept asking when she was coming for lunch again. How she'd made him feel all strong on his birthday. How the gnu was really awesome, his favourite animal of all time because of the horns and beard and everything and why did you have to say the *g* in g-nu? She could hear Jessie's little voice in Adam's story.

'He'll be very pleased about us, Hazel.'

'Are you sure?'

'Well, let me put it this way. He was mad at me because I didn't bring you home anymore. He told me I must have been really horrible to you to make you stay away.'

Hazel laughed. 'Well now you can tell him that you're being nice to me. Very nice.' She traced his mouth with her fingers. 'I'm pleased that both of you like me so much.'

'He's never warmed to anyone as he has with you.'

'I don't know how that happened.'

'Which may well be why it did.'

'You're so wonderful with him, Adam. Not that—I don't mean to patronise you.'

He laughed. 'Feel free,' he said. 'Patronise, lecture, tell me I'm a fool. I don't mind at all.'

He pulled her from the bed and slipped her little black dress over her head, smoothed it down and zipped it up. Then he pulled on his shorts and led her from the room. He put a CD into the player and moved towards her, embraced her, and they began to dance, swaying in time... *I do, I do, I do, I do, I do*. Which made her laugh and tell him she couldn't possibly respect a man who liked Abba. He told her he didn't want her respect, just her sweet mouth and pert breasts and the curve of her hips, the birthmark near her collarbone. And they began to sway again, moving together slowly, dreamily, to the world's most soppy love song.

She moved away, smiled into his eyes. 'I heard you were miserable without me,' she said.

'I was bereft. I ached. And those doorknocking days without you... But it was easier, in a way, a lot easier. I didn't have to keep hiding my erection.'

Then he told her he wanted to be serious.

'But an erection is very serious,' she said, and bit his cheek, softly.

'I longed for you every single day,' he said. 'Everything I did or said or thought, everything. It always came back to you. You've upended me completely and I'm madly in love with you.'

She had released him into extravagance. She intended to keep it that way.

'What did you notice first about me?' she said. Because she was greedy now, for his stories.

'Your eyes. I'd never seen eyes like the grey of the ocean.' He shook his head. 'And then I started talking nonsense, didn't I? Peppering you with stupid questions.'

'I remember. You didn't want to accuse me of being unpatriotic. Because I'd never heard of your Australian novel.'

'It was the first thing that came into my head. You must have thought I was stark raving mad. I'm surprised you didn't find another seat.'

'Just as well the train was crowded, then.'

'And I remember how startled you looked,' he said, 'because I caught you snooping at my book.'

'Snooping? I was taking an interest, Adam.'

'Oh, I know you were. You were really very obvious.'

'And I thought you'd never make a move. Even when I came to your house for that first meeting. That was just plain good luck, being on your training list.'

'You have no idea how thrilled I was, and so nervous too, when I saw your name on that list. I'd met you once and it felt so right but I thought it was so wrong. Wrong for you, I mean. And, to tell you the truth, I didn't want you thinking I was a dirty old man.'

'I wish you were a dirty old man. It would have saved us a whole heap of time.'

'But it was only four weeks, Hazel. Even if it felt like the longest four weeks of my life.'

'Try waiting seven years,' she said, and laughed at his confusion.

***

That night, as Hazel lay in Adam's arms, she felt a blissful calm, and yet triumphant too, soaring on the wings of her persuasion. Because she had claimed him for herself and made him call out her name, she had given him his beauty and he'd offered her such kisses and she had never felt so sure of anyone, anything. This sense of belonging and deep peace and drifting...There was light streaming through a window because her eyes were open and night had somehow turned into day and there was an empty space beside her and the bedside clock glowed eleven am. Eleven am! How could she possibly have—She drew in her breath, heard clattering from another room and sprang from the bed and hurried to find him and there he was, he really was. In the kitchen, standing at the bench, whisking something in a bright green bowl.

He looked up and gave her the widest, most comforting smile, as if he'd known her for years.

'I didn't want to wake you,' he said. 'But then again, I did.'

Rallying

The sun was beating down like a tom-tom on her head and Jessie was beginning to grizzle and she'd told Adam a hundred times that they should have left him home. Was this the thirteenth speaker now, trying to rally and inspire? She was well and truly done with inspiration and all the hanging around in the heat. It will be too much for the child, she'd said: all the talk he wouldn't understand, and then a long hot march into the city. But Adam had been insistent. Jessie had to know, he'd said, he had to understand that all around the world people were gathering to save the planet. Besides, who was going to look after him? Every single person they knew was here. Except for Candace, who would be rallying in Sydney, holidaying with a man Hazel hadn't met: the fourth man since that day of revelations in the bar. Hazel hadn't warmed to the previous three: Grumpy, Dopey and Sleepy, she'd called them in her head. Only four more to go and Candace could be Snow White. But I shouldn't make a joke of it, she thought, because Candace is still looking for love and made everything possible for me.

Adam put an arm around her. 'Shouldn't be long now,' he said.

Long? It was already bloody interminable. After an admittedly joyful welcome to country, they'd had droning politicians, an incomprehensible unionist and a dozen community leaders sprouting clichés and motherhood statements. They'd also been rallied by people of faith, every damned faith in the world. She'd nearly lost it when the archbishop or bishop or one of those men in a frock had looked at the massive crowd and said he thought he'd *died and gone to heaven*. Well, why are you wasting our time here, she thought, we hot and bothered earthlings. Can't we just get on with it and march into the city?

Then she looked at Adam and felt calmer. How she loved that face, especially when she woke in the mornings to see him lying beside her. Sixteen months of mornings. Although sometimes she had to peer over Jessie's sleeping head to see him: this man who gave her such pleasure, her sensitive, passionate lover, who adored her. Who insisted on picking her up from school because he'd already lost her for so many hours and wasn't going to waste another minute. And sometimes, as they sat in the car and she looked at him without speaking and he had to ask her to stop because her looking made him so aroused and he needed to focus on his driving, she would wonder if he'd ever been like this with his wife. Then she would tell herself it didn't matter and put her hand on his thigh and feel the warmth of his presence and know that she was lucky.

They never argued, either. Well, rarely. They did have a difference of opinion about Jessie's teacher. Adam thought she worried too much and Hazel thought he should have worried more. But he needs to understand — it was like a mantra for Adam — Jessie needs to understand that it takes all kinds, he needs to accommodate to different personalities. *Different personalities*! Hazel had tried not to shriek, called the teacher *completely unimaginative and regimental*: making six-year-olds line up outside every morning and after lunch, making them do colouring in. *Colouring in*! But Adam insisted there was no way he was going to make a fuss or send Jessie to a private school like the one he'd been shipped off to. He wanted his son to mix with all kinds of people, for starters, not just the western-suburbs types. And what about those exorbitant fees—you could buy a new BMW every year with that kind of money—when everything he'd read about education said it wasn't worth it. That the most important element in the intellectual development of a child was the encouragement of the family. And right now, his family needed a new roof to replace the leaking tiles, and it was going to cost a mint. Then he'd taken Hazel in his arms and told her that he loved her. Reminded her to be grateful for any kind of roof over their first-world heads.

But they did, in fact, have the money. They had a truckload of money, inherited from Adam's father. Hazel had been shocked when Adam told her. He was testing her, he'd said, *to see whether you want me for my wealth or my astonishing sexual prowess*. But now, having piles of cold, hard cash had become just one more thing to discover: Adam's donations to charity, especially cancer research; an international peace movement for children; helping refugees settle into the community. And money for the Greens, of course, to help finance election campaigns, buy new computers and software, print booklets about renewables. So much effort to clean what Adam called his father's dirty money; and no wonder he'd been able to retire. Money was also why Hazel didn't need to keep working, but she'd wanted to stay on and Adam had encouraged her. Her second year at Cranfield and it was getting better all the time. Her students were becoming real to her: that gradual unfolding of an unknown self that could only come with time. A few of them were here right now, the ones she'd persuaded to join in. It was disobeying the rules, she knew, making political pronouncements, but she didn't give a toss. She saw Magenta and Armina deep in conversation. Magenta was still writing poems—always free verse and often awkwardly confessional—while Armina kept insisting that *the best poems* used regular metre and rhyme because that required discipline. And there was Rita bouncing up to them, dragging a tall, lanky guy behind her. It had to be the boyfriend who, according to Rita, had to just get over the fact that she needed to study hard because she was going to uni next year, wasn't she?

Hazel spotted Mavis and Jamal in the distance. Mavis was training to be a primary school teacher and Jamal was waiting tables while dreaming of becoming a chef. Two graduates from last year, along with the other kids who'd made it: the bright, the dim, the prim and the skanky, the lazy, the aspiring, the bullies and the victims. The ones with such diminished lives who offered their kindness freely. All those kids who'd galloped or shuffled across the stage and were handed a certificate before stepping out into the world of casual work or part-time work or no damned work at all. But it had been their moment, and moments could teach you. Moments could modify. They might even give you the courage to fight for your difficult life.

Jamal's father had come to the school, at her invitation, to tell the staff his story. His hazardous journey from a village in Afghanistan, attacked by the Taliban one too many times. How he'd run through the mountains, been hidden in a series of trucks and ended up in Pakistan, made two failed attempts in a leaky boat setting off from Indonesia before finally reaching Australia. He'd told them, too, tears running down his face, about the six years of waiting for the family he'd had to leave behind: his wife and five children, and his mother. But now they were all together, except for his mother, which grieved him still, would always grieve him, because he wanted her to come to this brand new country he was learning so much to love. A land where people were *so good, always helping*. Where his children, including his small daughters, could go to school and never have to see a gun. He'd spoken in the stumbling English of a man from a different culture, a world of violence and terror and the arduous journey back to hope, but Hazel had felt the power of his words. Because sometimes, she knew, simplicity was eloquent and deeply, ethically, necessary. Then she'd looked across at the staff and seen the tight face of Lecherous Paws. The *big fat arse* man. Well, at least he'd heard the story. At least he'd seen the tears. And maybe one night he would wake up from a terrible dream of dangerous mountains and merciless guns, of leaking boats and mothers left behind, and understand the suffering of a single family, of hundreds of thousands of families, of the millions of people all over the world who were desperate and powerless and lost. Or maybe he wouldn't.

But some of the teachers had been visibly shaken. A few of them had cried.

Hazel saw her mother bend down to adjust Jessie's hat, keep the sun from his eyes. She had embraced him, she and Hazel's father (looking much trimmer these days, as well as shamelessly glowing). They'd welcomed Jessie, just as she had, as if he was their own flesh and blood. It made her feel rich and expansive and content when they all sat down to dinner and Jessie would chatter away, and then later her mother would put him on her lap and read him stories and her father would show him how to carve animals out of wood, setting him up on his workbench, teaching him how to handle the tools. Sometimes her parents would simply stare at Jessie in amazement, as though he'd had just landed in a rocket ship and said *Take me to your leader*. And of course they loved Jessie's father. How could they not? The man who loved their daughter, had given them a grandchild and worked assiduously for the Greens. The trifecta.

Now baby Jasmine was starting to howl and Dora was starting to fuss. Again. She was the world's biggest fusser and cooer, and Jazz was of course the most gifted baby ever to have emerged from the womb. Jessie adored her, too, pulling faces to amuse her, kissing her plump arms, stroking her tiny fingers. Todd was coming round as well but waiting for Jazz to talk, because babies, he'd whispered to Hazel, still didn't really do it for him. They still didn't do it for Hazel, who sometimes looked into the chubby, dribbling face of speechless Jazz and wait for that baby spark that never seemed to ignite. And what did it matter, when she already had a child, one she loved with such tenderness and ferocity that she hardly recognised the woman she'd become. So when Jessie had spent months pestering for a sister, she'd had to bend down and look him in the eye—because he was still a little boy you needed to bend to, to comfort or explain or sometimes chastise—and told him she could be his big sister if he liked. *But you could be my mum*, he'd said, his face lit up. So she'd reminded him of the woman who'd made a home for him in her body, kept him safe and warm until he was ready for the world. *So just call me Hazel,* she'd said. *You know, like a nut.*

He was tugging at her dress now and asking for water, his green-painted face looking up at her. Her funny little leprechaun, who still woke up in the night sometimes so that she and Adam had grown used to fucking quickly, sometimes sneaking sex in the shower while Jessie was asleep, their bodies slippery with water and desire. Hazel smiled to herself, remembering how Adam had hoisted her up last night and they'd nearly toppled over, crashed onto the tiles, but he'd hoisted her up again and they'd tried again and it was very quick, strong, coming together and gasping for breath and she'd murmured into his ear *tell me something special*, and he'd whispered *that having sex in the shower is an environmentally sound use of water.*

Another speaker. Hazel sighed, tried hard to listen. A firefighter this time, giving them more facts. Deadly facts: fires were becoming more frequent, more dangerous... *just bloody awful... devastating*. And then his voice went a bit quivery, as if he were remembering the charred bodies, the ruined homes, the ruined lives. Until he pulled himself up, pumped his fist, and shouted: *The government keeps saying we've always been a country of fire, but don't believe their lies … there's no climate sceptic on the end of a fire hose.*

A wave of applause, shouts and cheers: the momentum rising, like a tide.

'Preaching to the converted,' said Chloe.

Simon glared at her. 'Well, you should have gone to the pub and hung around with all the other dummies,' he said.

Then he flushed, smothered Chloe with apologies. His friends suspected he was smothering her with kisses as well. No one was really sure. But he and Felicia had faded, as young love often did, Hazel thought. Not like her love for Adam, which was strong and true and made to last. Unshakeable.

Was she becoming smug? Beth thought so. Beth had expressly told her. So, yes. Smug. Very.

Beth was *ensconced* in Felicia's apartment and overjoyed with her latest plan: her own travel agency—oops, consultancy — with Felicia handling the books, her father having agreed to finance the venture because according to Felicia, he was *pity in my hands.* They'd become staunch friends: madcap Beth and resolute Felicia, who must never be called Flick. Hazel wasn't sure if they were lovers, had been lovers, would one day become lovers, and kept waiting for Beth to confess her desire. But it seemed she was a work-in-progress; her garrulous, slaphappy friend whose silence spoke of something serious. Maybe in time she would tell her, when and if she discovered the shape of herself. All that Hazel could be sure of, with a blazing, steadfast clarity, was that she, Hazel West, twenty-six, going on twenty-seven and happily, usefully employed, would never become one of those women who ditched their female friends when Mr Right/the Chivalrous Knight rode up on his trusty horse and swept her…well, onto his horse. Hazel disapproved of such women. It was a crucial weakness in their character. They met every week, she and Beth, over coffee or wine, when they would laugh and gossip and ponder the state of their work or their friends, the world at large or small. And no, Hazel had once replied, she and Adam had never once discussed marriage. In any case, it wasn't going to happen until Australia dragged itself out of the dark ages and legalised marriage equality. *Although you'd make the perfect bridesmaid, Beth*, Hazel had teased her. At which point, the thought of Beth in a frothy pink dress, her bouncy red curls all sprayed and stiff, had made both of them fall about laughing.

Now Simon was beginning to shout above the noise of the crowd…pleased that people had come out en masse…anyone could go online and press a button to protest…how it took physical effort to…and they were off, debating the pros and cons of social media versus taking to the streets, as Hazel took a long drink, patted water on her face and neck. Water in bottles, water from the tap, *water water everywhere nor any drop to drink*. She remembered that from a uni quiz night, the line from 'The Ancient Mariner'. Most people thought it was not a drop to drink, but did it really matter? A single, misplaced word? Although words remained a passion in her teaching, and when she could find some time for her own private reading. She was currently immersed in *The Man Who Loved Children* because after years of reading Shakespeare and stories from many other lands, it was time to focus on Australia. Adam had never finished the book, though, because as soon as Hazel moved in with him, Molly had insisted on having it back. She'd been hoping for something in return, he'd said, having thrust the book upon him. Hazel had given him a very dark look, told him that trying to make her jealous was unworthy, and so he'd rushed in to say that he'd only been teasing and she'd rushed back that she didn't want him teasing about such things. Ever. She'd made that very clear. Then he'd taken her to bed and done a lot of thrusting and she'd felt a whole lot better.

He was keen on her new reading glasses too. Big red frames that made her look even more appealing, he said. Jessie thought she just looked weird.

She looked down to see the child leaning against his father's legs. The good father, the one who had chosen to stay. She had asked him once, in the early days, if he'd ever resented his wife pushing him to have a vasectomy, but he'd insisted that people always had a choice. But didn't you feel cheated, she'd said, pushing him herself, wanting him to show her his wounds. Didn't you feel angry and deeply hurt when you learned she was carrying a child? When you couldn't have one of your own? Adam had spoken calmly, told her that of course he'd felt hurt, how could he not? But then he'd made another choice: to release himself from bitterness and all that might have been, because bitterness was a waste of a life and what mattered most was the child. So Hazel let her questions go, just as she'd learned not to pry and prod about Thea. Adam would give her only fragments: a wife who'd been *generous...smart...a florist with a knack for pleasing arrangements...she could be difficult sometimes.* For while Hazel longed to know Adam's feelings more fully, she had come to learn this, too, about the nature of abiding love: that it must accept the limits of intimacy, honour the separateness of the loved one, in his difficult, unique opacity.

Adam had come to her school to talk to the staff in the middle of a busy day. To give them the shameful story he had once given her, the tale of a leaking boat all but erased from history. But this time he'd offered something else as well, something uplifting and essential: the story of the *SIEV X* Memorial, built in the nation's capital in the face of strenuous government opposition. It hadn't been easy to find, he'd said; there were no glossy brochures or conspicuous tourist signposts. He'd taken a bus past a marina crowded with sleek white boats, then past a sports club for BMWs and the banality of a kiosk selling Coca Cola, until he'd finally seen the memorial laid out before him. Hundreds of white poles curving up a grassy incline, stretching out like a wave in the ocean on the shores of Lake Burley Griffin. Three hundred and fifty-three poles, he knew, one for each of the dead. He'd stepped out of the bus and begun to walk, studying the poles carefully; each one bore an Arabic name, in stark black print. Immediate, insistent. Then Adam's voice had faltered as he remembered, relived, walking up the hill and seeing how the dead, known by those who loved them, had become simply, and terribly: A Father. A Mother. A Husband. A Wife. A Child.

Then, as he'd looked around the staffroom, at teachers being attentive or wolfing down their lunch, he'd told them what had sustained him on that long and difficult walk: a painting on each pole, created by children from all around Australia. Images of suns and moons and stars, rainbows, birds, flowers, neat little houses, bicycles and kites, dolphins, trees and oceans. Each painting saying that while we mourn your loss of a joyful life, we believe that love is stronger than fear. That compassion is stronger than hate.

He'd promised to take his own family to see the memorial. Because everyone must see it, he'd said.

The crowd in the park began to shuffle about, preparing to march into the city.

Beth turned around to Hazel. 'How many people do you reckon?' she said. 'A few thousand?'

'Five,' said Felicia, decisively.

Chloe laughed. 'Any more than fifty people is great turnout for Perth.'

Hazel looked around at all the thousands in the park: three or five, maybe even more, who'd come from the sprawling suburbs and from distant country towns. There were members of staff, Martha and Lucas among them, her precious sources of support. There was Elsa and Max, Abdul and Nahiri: Adam's friends, fast becoming her friends, her world expanding with her love. And all around her so many couples and families, elderly people and middle-aged people, jiggling children and whining children, a little girl doing a handstand against her father's legs. There were people from different races and cultures. Defiantly happy gays. People wheeling bikes. Hippie dresses and neatly ironed shirts, painted faces, weathered faces, baby faces. She looked across at Adam again; he was wearing a green T-shirt, like her, to symbolise the ecosystem. Some of their friends were wearing red, in support of people already damaged by the effects of climate change. Hazel's parents were in orange, to celebrate jobs that helped the environment, while her students in the distance were decked out in blue for the future generations. Jessie was in his yellow T-shirt, for people inspired by creative solutions. Yellow: the colour of ducks. Jessie had told her, in his piping voice, about the ducks watching the train as it went choofing past. He'd put his hands on his hips and sized her up and decided that he liked her.

He was looking so tired, poor lamb. She bent to talk to him.

'Would you like me to carry you?' she said.

He nodded.

'You've been very patient, Jessie. How about a piggy-back?'

She lifted him up, hoisted him onto her back. God, he was getting heavy. Adam shot her a guilty look and she told him they could take it in turns. Because Jessie belonged to both of them, she knew; he belonged to the whole wide world. And when he looked back, maybe decades later, if he wasn't slowly withering in a desert or drowning in the ocean or burning in a raging fire, raging like the panic in people's hearts, he would be able to say, quietly, proudly: I was there. I was there with Adam and Hazel, and the thousands of people who marched in the streets, determined to save the planet.

He needs to know. He needs to understand. Adam had been right to insist. He ruffled Jessie's mop of hair.

'Don't do that,' snapped the boy, whose legs were growing longer by the month.

'Sorry, buddy.'

'I don't want you to call me buddy anymore,' he said. 'I'm Jessie.'

'Indeed you are,' said Adam.

He raised a Greens flag, watched it flutter in the breeze: Take Action Now among all the other flags and placards and banners.

'Can I have an ice-cream, Dad?' said Jessie, in his best-manners voice. 'Hazel said I've been real patient.'

Hazel was poised with a maxim, something about patience being its own reward. Or was it goodness?

'We've all been very patient,' said Adam. 'So I deserve an ice-cream too. Mango, I think. Or maybe strawberry.'

'I'm going to have a triple decker,' said Hazel. 'Chocolate, toffee and blueberry.'

Adam gave Jessie the nod. 'Hazel's very greedy,' he said.

'Like a pig?'

'Absolutely, my son. But I'm one too. A pig contented.'

'That's Aristotle,' said Hazel.

'Socrates, actually.'

'Are you sure?'

'One hundred percent.' Adam flashed her his charming smile. 'You're not the only one who knows about ancient Greece.'

She poked out her tongue, to prove her adult credentials.

As they began to follow the crowds, Hazel thought about tomorrow, when the family would take the train to Cottesloe Beach and she would have to endure the biting sun and the spectacle of bodies frying to a crisp, turning over like glistening chooks on a rotisserie. But she needed to be there, because Adam was teaching Jessie how to swim in the sea. She could already picture it: she would dabble in the shallows of the Indian Ocean or sit waiting on the shore, as Adam taught Jessie how to negotiate the waves, holding onto him, showing him not to be afraid. Then he'd hoist him onto his shoulders and throw him into the air and the boy would scream with hysterical delight and plunge into the water and come up laughing and screaming for more while Hazel's chest would tighten as she waited for that sudden shadow, a swift and deadly creature with a hideous cavernous mouth and rows of vicious teeth that could tear off a limb and leave the victim screaming and bleeding, maimed for life. Or dead. She would watch and watch like a hawk, like a mother, until Jessie came running ashore and she would laugh and chatter as she rubbed him with a towel. They would build a castle, too, and Jessie would press the shells into the walls, drape seaweed on the turrets, squeal when the water rushed into the moat, and she wouldn't say a word about the fear that had risen inside her. Because her child was safe and Adam was safe and she could breathe in her love and be grateful.

'Hazel.'

Jessie's squeaky voice behind her back. A pair of clammy hands around her neck.

'It's your turn to read me a story at bedtime.'

'Most definitely.'

'If you read me two, I'll try real hard to sleep through the night.'

She smiled to herself.

'Or maybe three,' he said.

Acknowledgements

I wish to thank Fremantle Press for their faith in my first novel, and for including me in their fine history of local story-telling. Special thanks to Georgia Richter for her astute and meticulous editing, for her patience and good humour. Thanks, too, are due to Amanda Curtin, Linda Martin, Josephine Taylor and Terri-ann White, for feedback on a much earlier version of the novel. And thank you to Nada Backovic for her elegant, lovely cover. Thank you to Michelle de Kretser and Ryan O'Neill, two writers I greatly admire, for their generous endorsements. As always, I am indebted to Dan Midalia, for earning the money, conquering technology and cooking the dinners. Most of all, I thank him for his love.

Thank you to Fremantle Press for permission to quote from Dorothy Hewett's poem 'Wanderlust' from *Wheatlands* (edited by Dorothy Hewett and John Kinsella, Fremantle Arts Centre Press, 2000). Thank you to Rosemary Sayer for permission to use the story of an asylum seeker recounted in her wonderful book *More to the Story: Conversations with Refugees* (Margaret River Press, 2015). And of course, special thanks to the asylum seeker in question.

Finally, thank you to the Uniting Church, Steve Biddulph, three hundred community groups and children from across Australia, all of whom were instrumental in creating the deeply affecting *SIEV X* Memorial in Canberra.

also available

'… a ravishing achievement, a dazzling work of art in its own right.' *Dominic Smith*

'Goldbloom's is a work of imaginative intensity but it is spun from an armature of facts … Her re-creations of London and Paris at the turn of the century are as compelling as the louche sexuality of the narrative. The reader can smell the chill, sooty London air, be mesmerised by the shrill choruses of spring in the French countryside and smell the turpentine and wax in their threadbare, unheated Paris lodgings.' *The Australian*

at www.fremantlepress.com.au

First published 2018 by
FREMANTLE PRESS
25 Quarry Street, Fremantle WA 6160
(PO Box 158, North Fremantle WA 6159)
www.fremantlepress.com.au

Cover image: Elena Miloslavskaya

National Library of Australia
Cataloguing-in-Publication entry:
Midalia Susan, author
The Art of Persuasion / Susan Midalia
ISBN 9781925591033 (paperback)

Midalia, Susan, author.
The art of persuasion / Susan Midalia.
ISBN: 9781925591033 (paperback)
Romance fiction. Australian fiction

GOVERNMENT OF
WESTERN AUSTRALIA

Fremantle Press is supported by the Western Australian State Government through the Department of Cultural Industries, Tourism and Sport.

Publication of this title was assisted by the Commonwealth Government through the Australia Council, its arts funding and advisory body.

www.ingramcontent.com/pod-product-compliance
Lightning Source LLC
Chambersburg PA
CBHW031944010726
47493CB00007B/2067

9 7 8 1 9 2 5 5 9 1 0 3 3